PAINTED

KIRSTEN MCKENZIE

This edition published 2023 by Squabbling Sparrows Press

ISBN 978 0 4733984 39 (paperback)
ISBN 978 0 4733984 60 (ebook)

Cover designer: **Robert Rajszczak**

I sobbed great ugly tears when you left.
You were, and remain, a spectacular friend.
This book is for you **Emma Oakey**.
Stay away from the sun, the snakes, and the spiders. Everything in
Australia is trying to kill you.
(There's probably a horror novel in that...)

Why does the eye see a thing more clearly in dreams than the imagination when awake?

— LEONARDO DA VINCI

CHAPTER 1

"He can go whistle himself into his own grave, because I'm not driving there again. I wasted hours last time driving there and back, so he can damn well courier the paperwork. You get hold of him and tell him," Alan Gates dismissed his secretary with the flick of a wrist, muttering to himself about the self-entitled elderly who refused to embrace technology. As if he had time to drive out to the coast to amend the last will and testament of a rambling idiot. The letter had been splattered with paint and addressed to his father, who'd been dead and buried three months now, hardly a professional approach at all.

Now he was running the family law firm, things would change. No more pandering to the poor and indulging the elderly, this business needed a firm hand and profitable clients. The mess his father had left behind never ceased to amaze him. Fortunately he'd died when he did, while there was something still salvageable in the firm.

Alma Montgomery sniffed her dissatisfaction as she closed Alan's office door. His father would be turning in his grave if he knew how his clients were being treated by his son.

Clutched in her gnarled hand was the letter Alan found so offensive. A handwritten letter from one of the firm's oldest clients, Leo Kubin. She'd never met him in the thirty years she'd been answering phones and typing legal documents for Alan's father, and now for Alan himself, but she'd recognised the letter as soon as it had arrived. The faint scent of mineral turpentine clung to the paper and a kaleidoscope of paint droplets smeared the corners and along the edges of the thick paper.

Despite the assumption that he was an untidy man as she knew bachelors usually were, his thoughts were clearly expressed in the letter—terminally unwell, he wanted to finalise his affairs. He'd included a sheaf of annotated notes, less paint marked than the letter, but unmistakably from the same hand. His writing slender, the product from a school system long since consigned to the scrap heap. Page after page detailed how to dispose of Kubin's extensive art collection after his death.

It wasn't unusual for passionate collectors to leave instructions on how their belongings were to be managed, but, as Alma leafed through the papers, Kubin's instructions seemed bizarre even to her. Each portrait must be crated as soon as it was removed from the wall and not be left leaning against a wall, laying on a table, or boxed with other items. Every portrait *must* be packaged individually and shipped to the National Portrait Gallery. Of the other pieces in his collection, they were to be sold and the funds distributed to the needy. Given the dubious accounting practices of Alan Gates Junior, she wouldn't be at all surprised if Alan counted himself among the 'needy' referenced in Kubin's instructions.

Alma removed that final page, the reference to the 'needy'.

Nothing good ever came of shredding legal paperwork, but Alan had been insistent they buy a shredder to better dispose of old paperwork. With a wry smile, she fed that one page through the shredder. All of Mr Kubin's art could be donated to the gallery. They were best equipped to decide what to do with it. In these times of fiscal cutbacks, every public art institute could be considered a charitable cause. And, after all, how many pieces of art could one man have in his house?

A tiny obituary appeared in the local newspaper recording the death of Leonard Kubin, Artist, aged eighty. *No known family.*

Alan Gates Junior closed the paper he only bothered reading in case it mentioned any of their clients. Divesting the firm of the dead and unworthy was an enjoyable hobby and the menial task of shredding their files a highlight. Thus Mr Kubin's file could also be disposed of shortly, once the sale of his house and estate was finalised.

Calling Alma to bring him Kubin's file, he pondered how much of a fee the firm could expect from the sale of the estate. He had some vague recollection of a vast art collection. He'd not paid that much attention at the time, but those reclusive types were more than likely to have squirrelled away a Matisse, or half a dozen long lost Monet oil paintings. His eyes were shining more than the handmade Italian brogues he wore on his feet. It could be a good payday for the firm, yes indeed. Not everything needed to be donated. The man had been old, his mind failing him. Better to sell everything of value and donate the dregs. The potential to slip one or two of the nicer pieces into his own collection also existed.

After instructing the old biddy about what he wanted

arranged for Mr Kubin's estate, he rubbed his hands together. As a golf lover, he'd calculated that soon he'd be able to upgrade to the better club on the other side of town. Membership was at least five figures more than he currently paid, but that wouldn't be an issue soon. He deserved to be mixing with a higher class of person than his father had, that's where the monied clients came from, fresh from the manicured lawns at the Bolton Hills Golf Club, and he could not wait.

Against her better judgment, Alma Montgomery typed the letter to the Nickleby's Trusts, Estates and Valuation Service, requesting their services to catalogue and sell Mr Kubin's estate and left it on Alan's otherwise empty desk for his signature. Clipped to the back were Kubin's comprehensive instructions detailing how his portraits were to be treated. She rubbed her chest, unsure which hurt more, her arthritic hands or her chest. It'd been bothering her for days. Time to retire. There was no joy working for Alan Junior. She'd known him since he was a boy, a boy fond of cruel jokes, snide asides and everything money could buy. No, life was too short, he wouldn't miss her if she left. He'd prefer a malleable young thing in short skirts and heels, flouncing around the office. Not her in her orthotic soles and sensible slacks. She'd tell him tomorrow she'd decided to retire.

Locking the office, Alma paused to catch her breath. Pressing her hand to her chest, she came over all clammy. The feeling passed and she pushed off, shuffling to the bus stop, not realising she'd never step foot into the office again.

CHAPTER 2

If Alan Gates Junior had any emotion about the sudden death of his secretary, no one could tell. He stood to the side of the burial plot, jiggling from one foot to the other, eager to be away. He didn't interact with Alma's adult children, whose own emotional offspring were clinging to their legs. *Couldn't they have been left at home* he thought as one of them tugged on his trousers. If anything, it annoyed him that she'd chosen now to die. Here he was, busy trying to grow the practice and clear out the dead wood and Alma, with her encyclopaedic memory of their clients, had left him in the lurch. How was he supposed to remember who they all were, or if they were worth keeping?

It never crossed his mind to attend the wake, given that he had to employ another secretary and he had a business to run. *Let these little people carry on with their little lives* he thought as he scurried away from the knot of mourners and slipped into his red sports car without any concerns about proprietary or respect for the deceased. Music blaring from his stereo as he peeled away from the cemetery, Alma was already struck from his mind.

❄

The office had been in turmoil since she'd died with unopened mail piling up in the doorway and the red message light on the phone system blinking constantly, querying where Alma was and why she wasn't clearing the messages. He'd unplugged the thing since he had no idea how to clear the messages anyway, that'd been Alma's job. If people needed him they could email. Alan scooped up the mail and dumped it on his desk. What a mess she'd left him in, bloody ungrateful woman. And what a waste of his time, listening to that dullard pastor droning on and on about the charitable work she'd done. If she'd had enough time for all of that, she hadn't been working hard enough for him. Someone new in the office would be an improvement.

Sitting at his desk, clicking his engraved ball point pen, he came across the paperwork Alma had left for him to sign and send to Nickleby's. He read the letter, eyes popping out of his head when he saw the itemised instructions Alma had stapled to the back. There was no need for those to be passed on to Nickleby's. They'd think him stark raving mad if he included them. Who in their right mind would dictate that once each painting had been removed from the wall they were to be boxed immediately. That wasn't the way any sane art appraiser worked. Each piece would need to be examined, photographed, then packed in the most cost effective manner by the experts. The dregs siphoned off to the National Portrait Gallery, and Nickleby's would sell everything else, with his firm taking an appropriate cut of the proceeds of course.

Alan had been to Kubin's house once, when he first took over the business and on that visit he'd formed the irrefutable opinion that the man was crazy. Alan could've sworn he'd overheard the man talking to the portraits on the walls as he fumbled about the old house. Anyone who spoke with such familiarity to pieces of art should be consigned to the lunatic asylum. He couldn't be bothered wasting any more of his time driving out to the crumbling old house on the coast until it was time to review the value of the art. Undoubtedly a developer would buy it and knock it down. That's what he'd do.

And so it was that Alma's letter, minus Mr Kubin's detailed instructions arrived at Nickleby's and landed on the desk of junior appraiser Anita Cassatt.

An arts student at a mid-range university, Anita had graduated with honours, those honours landing her a dream job with the Art Valuation Department at Nickleby's. Her days were filled with cataloguing art from some of the finest homes and minor works by moderately well known artists passed through her hands every day. The better art was handled by the senior associates. The job a perfect grounding for a new graduate, but there were only so many watercolours by Edwin Fields and John Varley that she could stomach, and she was tiring of landscapes decorated with horses and watermills.

Like a gift from the gods, a note had been stapled to the letter by her manager, instructing her to appraise and catalogue the collection of portraits detailed in the lawyer's letter.

Excitement tickled. An on-location job, out of the office, an obscure collection of portraits with no mention of landscapes or gauche hunting scenes. Anita entered the address into her computer and a house standing on its own materialised on her screen. Grey stone walls competing with rocky outcrops, fallow fields falling away beyond the house and an angry ocean attacking the cliffs below. The exterior of the house void of the decor common to most luxury coastal estates.

The printer whirred into life as she printed out the directions, her excitement dampening any concerns about the remote location of the estate. According to the lawyer's letter, the sheer scale of the estate would require her to stay several nights and arrangements had been made for her to be accommodated at the house for the duration. Bliss, a mini vacation.

A one sided telephone conversation with the uppity lawyer finalised her plans. He'd been less than helpful, his snippy anecdotes about the deceased owner completely inappropriate. The poor man was being done a disservice by his chosen legal representative and she'd felt dirty after the conversation, wiping her hands on her skirt after hanging up.

Despite her unsatisfactory conversation with the lawyer, her enthusiasm for the task bubbled to the surface. The artist had been a rising star in the fifties, exhibiting his portraits in New York to some acclaim, but even the Internet couldn't tell her what had happened to him after that. He wasn't an artist she was overly familiar with and he'd disappeared from the art circuit in the late fifties. Whenever one of his dark portraits came on the market, they'd been purchased anonymously, never to reappear. Nickleby's themselves had only auctioned two in the past fifty years. The images in their old catalogues more haunting given the black and white photography of the day.

Few images existed online and she printed out what she could find for comparison with what she might find onsite. You never knew what sort of wifi access would be available somewhere that remote, and Mr Kubin wasn't deemed important enough to be included in any of the reference books she'd stuffed into her briefcase.

"You all set, Anita?" asked Warren Taylor, her manager, as he approached her desk. A good man, great at his job, knowledgeable and affable. An unheard of confluence of attributes in a manager. Anita knew she was fortunate.

"I'll be okay, honestly."

"You're sure you're okay being there on your own for a few days? There's just no one else available to join you till Wednesday at the earliest. I did try the other departments, but…"

"I'm all good," Anita jumped in. Taking in the concern on his face she added, "I'm a big girl. It's okay really. I'll be fine there. It's just art, what could go wrong?"

Warren laughed. "Yes, yes of course, well I was just thinking of, well you know what… and you being on your own. Wanted to make sure you felt okay about it, about being there on your own. Anyway, we'll join you either Wednesday afternoon, or Thursday morning at the latest to help finish it off. Frankly, I was amazed at the quantity of art in the house, if the notes from the lawyer are accurate. Can't wait to see the place myself. Make sure you leave something for us to do, don't try and get it all done on your own. Nothing good ever comes from hurrying a job." And off he went.

Hopefully this collection would be her lucky one. She tried not to dwell on Warren's concerns, nothing good would come from worrying. She would be fine on her own.

CHAPTER 3

Following a three-hour car ride with the stereo blaring out the year's greatest hits, Anita struggled through the last hour on a gravel road, with only plumes of dust to show the road behind and nothing inviting ahead. A far too close an encounter with an antique tractor on a corner had left her shaken and she'd arrived at Leo Kubin's gothic revival home with her heart still racing, a sheen of sweat on her brow.

Perched on the barren windswept eastern coast, the house had no neighbours, bar the wildlife hopping through the fallow fields. Taking a gulp of the bracing coastal air Anita unloaded her car. Her overstuffed briefcase in one hand, balanced out her overnight bag in the other, she started the ascent to the heavy oak door.

Alan Gates opened the door, his dour face lightening as he took in her age and condition, although it did little to improve his manners, "Miss Cassatt, I had expected you somewhat earlier. Sadly I have a prior engagement I must attend, so there's no time to show you around, but I'm sure you can work it out. One of the bedrooms upstairs has been prepared for you and there are provisions in the kitchen. I shall be in touch tomorrow to check on your progress." Nudging a rusty chain tied to the railings, he smiled, "There was a dog, but it hasn't been seen since the old man died. You probably won't see it, but, you know, best to keep an eye out… now you'll have to excuse me as I really am running quite late for my game." With an obvious leer and without Anita uttering a single word, he struggled into his coat and stepped from the doorway to the driveway and into the only other car there, a high-end low-slung red sports car; the type favoured by men of a certain age the world over. It too looked like it had fought a losing battle on the gravel roads, with a large stone chip on the windscreen.

Anita watched the pompous lawyer manoeuvre his beast down the drive until it vanished from sight, nerves crowding in on her. Just as unpleasant in person as he had been on the telephone. She turned and entered the house, stepping in front of an audience.

An audience of eyes, immortalised in portraits clustered on every wall. Oil paintings, sketches, watercolours, every permutation of portraiture hung on the walls of the foyer. Hung haphazardly, no rhyme nor reason to the display, no cohesion or system.

Anita allowed the solid door to shut behind her, her breath trapped in her lungs. She turned as if on a carousel, overwhelmed by the task ahead and by the hundreds of pairs of eyes following her every move.

Shaking off nudges of apprehension settling on her shoulders, and leaving her bags in the entrance, she set off to explore the house, and, more importantly to find a toilet. Every wall she passed was papered with portraits. Some exceptional, most ordinary, a small number childlike in their simplicity. Anita peered at the signatures as she explored the house, pausing at one which she knew was a *Thomas Fairland*. She'd get round to it eventually, but made a mental note to make it one of the first she catalogued.

Thankfully the one room devoid of portraits was the old fashioned toilet, her relief immeasurable. She didn't fancy sitting there with a dozen pairs of eyes judging her.

That bit of business taken care of, she started to unwind, her level of concentration improving now she could genuinely focus on the art surrounding her. Dust motes swam drunkenly on weak shafts of sunlight marking the way she'd come. Back in the entrance hall, she checked her phone, she needed to ring her mother to tell her she'd arrived safely. Her mother hadn't wanted her to come all this way on her own, *"I hope they're making this worth your while"* had been her exact words. *No service.* Hardly surprising being this remote, but still she felt a prick of panic. Not being able to use her phone would be a reality check but her mother would never forgive her. They had an unwritten rule she'd ring her mother whenever she arrived somewhere. She frowned as she considered the state her mother would be in now. The lawyer had disappeared before she could ask if there was any phone service at all, or wifi. She'd figure it out and then she'd have to work out a way to placate her mother.

Deciding that getting settled in before nightfall would be a better use of her time, she picked up her bags and made her way up the ornate staircase, the light layer of dust on the wooden riders the only indication that the house was empty. It had yet to acquire that peculiar smell of decay which envelops an empty home, as if the carpets were composed of stagnant mould and the curtains a haven for desiccated moth carcasses. It would come to this house soon, as soon as the hot water was switched off and the power cut. The winter storms would buffet the slate roof tiles, and broken tiles would welcome in the winter snow and any animal seeking refuge.

Shaking those thoughts from her head she made for the only open door in the hallway, her bags weightier with every step. It was clear it was hers, with towels laid out on the bed and a note addressed to her on the Victorian dressing table. Dropping her bags in the middle of the floor, she cast her eye over the room.

The visible patches of wallpaper were old and faded, the corners peeling back from the crumbling plaster. The rest of the wall was hung with art. Not all portraits; it would have made it impossible to sleep if it were. Here in this room at least the majority of pieces were stormy seascapes, with vicious waves plucking hapless ships from the crests of waves, drawing them down into the murky depths to an unknown fate. Not uplifting, but not the stuff of nightmares.

The note as succinct as the lawyer, not even a greeting, just straight into an itemised list of things she could and couldn't do, the parts of the house which were off limits and arrangements for the packers and movers. Most of it she'd ignore, she was here to do a job.

Her eyes slid to the only portraits in the room, a series of four, they'd been hung in a semblance of age order and framed in identical gilt frames. Each showed a child; different children but of the same stock, with bright blue eyes and wheat coloured hair, with the youngest girl slightly different, her eyes a dark brown, her hair less blonde, but a face still cut from the same cloth. Such unusual subjects for portraiture, not the usual sullen faced men in starched suits or military dress. Almost modern in appearance, frames older than the paintings, their faces looked as though smiles were as rare as winter sun and as fleeting. The sadness in their eyes had been exquisitely captured by the artist, although Anita wished they hadn't been quite so skilled. She preferred children to be happy, to have a childhood such as she had, with loving parents and buckets of joy.

Turning her back on the portraits, she unpacked her toiletries and sleepwear. Sleep beckoned and the drive had sapped all her energy but she needed to finish her circuit of the house to get an overall feel of the task at hand. It wasn't just the art that needed to be catalogued but the contents of the house as well — the furniture and decorative pieces, although the rest of the team would be here to help with those later.

The temperature had dived south since she'd arrived as the winter sun set quickly here. She shrugged into a cardigan before investigating the rest of the house. The dust motes had gone, settling into hidden nooks and crannies, gathering their strength for tomorrow.

In the half light, the hall appeared longer, the doors more foreboding, reminiscent of back alley entrances to places of ill repute. Anita squared her shoulders, brushing off such foolish notions and grasped the chilled brass handle of the next door, surprised when it turned easily, swinging open, revealing another bedroom. The same pastel pink wallpaper obscured by a conglomeration of portraits mixed with landscapes, and yes, even some hunting scenes. Wild eyed hounds racing across an open field, a fox shown in the distance, his terror palpable. Beautifully rendered but too terrifying for most, it would undoubtedly sell well in London.

Another made up bed, in preparation for her colleagues she presumed. She didn't envy whoever got to sleep in here. Instead of children on the walls, there were a variety of men. Each portrait capturing a different time; a Victorian stiff upper lip, a Regency era toff, a labourer in the fields, glaring at the artist and daring him to paint his portrait. Their eyes the brightest part of every portrait, capturing the essence of their humanity, more than any public speech could portray, indeed more than the subjects thought they would ever reveal to anyone. Anita shivered. It was a rare skill to capture someone's essence in a portrait, yet at first glance these portraits had been done years apart, centuries even. Tomorrow, tomorrow she'd examine them, no point jumping to just yet.

Easing her way along the hallway opening door after door, each room a cookie-cutter version of the previous one, only the artwork differentiating the rooms from each other. The portraits growing darker in tone and subject. The furniture too changing to heavier pieces, more manly in appearance. Gone were the feminine dressing tables with elegantly turned feet, replaced with functional pieces designed for use, not aesthetics.

The last door opened not to a bedroom but to a staircase leading up to the turret room she'd spied from the impressive driveway. She expected it would deliver spectacular views of the coast and the countryside surrounding the desolate house. She paused, her hand hovering above the polished bannister. She pulled away and examined her hand, odd that the dust hadn't made it this far. Anita laughed, *of course*, the lawyer would've been here keeping an eye out for her. Why wouldn't you sit somewhere with a view? That's where she would have waited instead of in one of the formal rooms downstairs, with hundreds of pairs of eyes watching her every move. Her stomach rumbled. Turning her back on the staircase she closed the door. Tomorrow she'd have her coffee there and that would give her something to look forward to, to keep her mind occupied during the long night in this old house. "Stop it," she said aloud, chastising herself. "Let's get something to eat." And she marched off to hunt out the kitchen to see what the smarmy lawyer had provided for her, expectations weren't high.

Humming to herself in the kitchen, she neither saw nor heard the turret staircase door open. There was nothing to be seen, not from the bottom of the stairs.

CHAPTER 4

After a quick supper, Anita fell into bed exhausted from the long drive and the realisation of the enormity of the task ahead of her. As she slept, darkness dominated the room and the shadows crowded in on Anita, watching but not disturbing. Morning came as quickly as the night had fallen the day before, so, with the sun cresting, the shadows slunk back to their corners and the frigid air dissipated as the first rays of the sun hit the thin glass.

Anita had burrowed deep under the covers, the chilled air caressing her exposed skin, her dreams punctuated with shadows and half seen faces, turning, just as she reached them.

The dawn delivered a chorus of birdsong and Anita woke with the sun, knuckling the sleep from her eyes, stretching, her muscles sore from the long drive and an uncomfortable night. She hadn't slept well; the house creaking and moaning through the night, every crack sounding like an intruder on the stairs, before creeping heavy-footed along the hallway, pausing outside her room. Still, she must have dozed off, the last vestiges of her dreams slipping velvet-like from her subconscious.

From the warmth of her feather quilt, Anita's eyes drifted to the children on her walls. Two boys and two girls, the girls younger. The… wait, *the youngest child, the girl in the short-sleeved white dress. Had the tilt of her head moved? Her eyes. Now they were looking at her?* Anita shook her head, she was imagining things. *What an idiot.* Today she'd concentrate on these paintings or she'd never sleep tonight.

Throwing back the covers, she shivered in the morning air, purposely avoiding the frank stares from the children on the wall, she gathered together her toiletries and clothes for the day ahead, the children behind her silently judgmental. Despite them being rendered in oil, she felt uncomfortable disrobing in front of their frozen gazes, so, slinging on a dressing gown, she padded down the hall, her night terrors fading as her adult sensibilities took over.

The bathroom was as dated as the rest of the estate, the bathtub a coffin for moths and midges, their pale grey bodies decaying in the aged porcelain. Of a shower head, there was no sign. Anita rolled her eyes, in this day and age you'd expect every house to have a shower, no one wanted to wallow in their own filth in a bathtub. Unlike the toilet, the bathroom had pictures on its walls. She took each of them down putting them out in the hall. Regardless of the potential damage to the art from water and steam, having portraits in a bathroom was peculiar and she wasn't going to get naked in front of a gaggle of strangers.

Turning the taps rewarded her with a far away gurgle of functional pipes. If hot water failed to materialise, she wouldn't stay here, she couldn't stand feeling dirty. Anita considered herself as average as the next person, but she couldn't abide being dirty. Even as a child, she'd driven her mother mad with her insistence that any dirt on her hands be washed off immediately. If tomato sauce dripped down her front, it rendered her clothes only suitable for the washing machine. As she'd aged, she'd tempered her phobias but unfettered access to hot water was still non-negotiable.

Hanging her clothes on the generous hooks, she tried not to check on the water temperature, her skin already crawling at the thought of working with the filth of the previous day still on her skin. To her immense relief, steam filled the old room, fogging the mirror and the clanging of the old pipes changing to the soothing sound of running water.

Shrugging off her robe, her skin prickled at the sudden cold, before testing the water with her toe. Satisfied she slid into the rising water, sloshing it over her goose-pimpled skin. As the temperature of her skin began to match that of the bath she reviewed her feet wiggling at the end of the porcelain tub. Void of polish, her toes were a pretty accurate representation of her life — basic, sensible, boring. No point in applying polish when there was no one to appreciate the effort. She kept the hair on her legs, and elsewhere, tamed, an ingrained personal hygiene habit borne from teasing she'd endured during school swimming sports, for the dark hair protruding from places society dictated it shouldn't. She'd sobbed on her mother's shoulder that night, blood running freely where she'd nicked herself half a dozen times trying to wield a razor to rid herself of her hair. The memory of the blood swirling down the drain as her mother gently washed it away had stayed with her. It wasn't the only time in her life she'd watched blood running from her body, rinsed away by the cleansing water.

Her toes sank under the steaming water and she turned the tap off. The sudden quiet punctuated by the occasional groan of the old water pipes, their job done for the moment. Steam rose from the still water, swirling on unseen draughts, into corners long forgotten by whomever did the cleaning.

Anita closed her eyes, this job could be the making of her career. Cataloguing art was more than listing the title and the artist, every sentence she wrote needed to be as nuanced as the art itself. She had to capture the essence of the art in her words, as accurately as the artist had depicted his or her subject. Rarely did she see work by female artists, probably because their efforts were deemed more hobbyist than professional. She'd written her thesis on just this subject, but she still obsessed about it. Where were all the women artists? She tried to attend solo exhibitions by female artists but they were few and far between. She sank under the water, immersing herself under the silent waves. Eyes closed, safe, she didn't see the condensation on the brass door handle disappear as if someone had just grasped the handle.

CHAPTER 5

Bathed and dressed, Anita made her way downstairs to the generous kitchen. She'd been surprised the night before at the quantity of food the lawyer left for her. The eggs, fruit and fresh bread a welcome surprise. The ancient refrigerator held salami, a quart of milk and a small block of cheese, enough to last the week as long as the rest of her team brought more provisions with them.

She wrestled the stovetop into life through trial and error to fry some eggs. She was more a microwave and takeout girl, but the scent of eggs frying always sent her tastebuds into overdrive. Her mother had never bothered teaching her how to cook and she'd never had the need so didn't miss it. You couldn't butcher the frying of eggs. Get-togethers with girlfriends were usually over a Thai takeaway; dinners with potential partners were at restaurants — she hadn't wanted to scare anyone with her nonexistent culinary skills, not that anyone hung around long enough for it to matter. Dinner at her parents was always a Sunday roast which her father insisted he cook. Fried eggs were an acceptable breakfast, lunch and dinner dish. Add some sliced salami, a hunk of cheese and voila, a gourmet meal.

While the eggs were frying she checked her phone again — a habit. Still showing no service, she put it back in her pocket. There'd be somewhere she'd pick up a signal, there always was.

Hunger sated, she looked for the dishwasher. No dishwasher. Ah well, there had to be a downside to the perfect job. Piling the dishes in the sink, she washed her hands in the sudsy water mingling with the egg smears from the heavy chinaware. She'd do the dishes later, after lunch, or to be honest, after dinner. There was no point doing more washing than she needed.

Hands clean and dry she wandered around the cavernous halls taking in the art clustered on the walls. There was a hell of a lot more than she'd appreciated last night. Around every corner an occasional table threatened to clip her ankles and rickety plant stands adorned random alcoves, the planters filled with half dead fairy ferns and a botanist's dream collection of rare orchids. Most beyond salvation now but some looked like they could pull through given some water. Anita had foresworn caring for any living creature after the prolonged death of her cat and she avoided house plants for the same reason. She didn't want the responsibility. A foreign sense of guilt stole upon her as she passed plant after plant, the guilt sent her scurrying back to the kitchen to fill a jug. She'd water the ones which looked salvageable. She couldn't imagine the lawyer running round the house doing this. Maybe the estate was paying for a housekeeper to keep things running until the sale was completed?

Pouring a little water here and a dash of water there, she fancied she could hear the grateful sighs of the ferns, akin to the joyous sounds of a marooned sailor at the first splattering of rain, as he caught raindrops on his swollen tongue. She imagined those sounds following her around the house as she refilled the jug several times over, her satisfaction at this menial task magnified by the idea of saving lives.

Catching herself cooing over a receptive lily, she laughed, her joy echoing down the hall. Tipping the last of the water into the soil of a long deceased orchid, she left the jug at the bottom of the stairs. Enough of this foolishness, she had work to do, but at the top of the stairs, something caught her eye. A shadow? No, there was nothing there. She remembered she'd promised herself coffee upstairs in the turret room, which would have to wait till later. If the rest of her team were arriving soon she'd need to get on. Mooning over a view she could never afford would not help her career goals. But thinking of the view made her eager for a quick look outside. Clouds the colour of burnt toast hung on the horizon, bringing with them rain or snow, so this might be her only chance to have a look outside.

Using an old-fashioned iron to prop open the heavy front door, Anita could smell the metal tang of rain in the air, just a short walk then. She zipped up her jacket and stepping down onto the gravel drive she chose a direction at random, following a path round to the right. Barren flower beds waited under the windows and the woody remnants of lavender bushes were a faint echo of what was once there. The path petered out at the corner of the house where nature took over — long grass sprinkled with vegetation running riot without the razor sharp blades of the lawnmower to tame it. Skeletal immature trees pushed their way through paving stones and blackberry vines threatened to snag anyone foolish enough to try harvesting the berries hanging tantalisingly close to the overgrown pathway. She salivated at the thought of the juicy tartness of the blackberries but stopped when she realised they were well past their edible prime. They had withered on their thorny vines, ignored, even by the blackbirds.

The lawns gave way to gardens now an ode to nature, overgrown hedging spreading like wildfire, where it looked like the gardener had upended a mixed bag of seeds, leaving them to take root wherever they fell, regardless of position or suitability.

Further back, Anita spied a roof, a gardener's cottage or the housekeeper's cottage? This path seemed more worn so Anita felt confident following it. She imagined an older couple keeping the place for the elderly owner, the three of them becoming less and less capable. The garden taking over; the large house and grounds getting away from them all.

Pushing past a lush weeping maple whose branches fell like a veil, she reached the building she'd glimpsed through the foliage. It wasn't a house and her romantic notions were trampled into the pebble-dash pavers once she realised it was the roof of a small mausoleum.

Anita would have turned on her heels and hightailed it back to the house if at that moment the heavy clouds above hadn't opened. Torrential rain raced across the land, pummelling tree tops and flattening the daisy heads decorating the edges of the fallow fields beyond the overgrown gardens.

Anita dashed pellmell under the portico of the mausoleum where there was space to shelter from the worst of the stinging rain, pressing herself into the doorway as the wind whipped the rain into an angrier assault.

Crash

The wooden door disintegrated, plunging Anita

backwards into the stone mausoleum, landing on the tiled floor in a cloud of dust. For a moment she sat motionless, before leaping up, aghast at the damage she'd caused and mortified at her location inside a tomb. Stumbling over an assortment of old fashioned gardening tools stored in the crypt she fled into the rain. A little rain hurt no one, but sheltering inside with dead people was all kinds of wrong.

She tripped, falling flat on the sodden dirt, her shin flaring in pain. Yowling, she sat up grabbing her leg which wasn't bleeding but would soon go a spectacular shade of purple. Pushing her hair from her eyes she tried to figure out what she'd tripped on, there, a concrete slab... a gravestone. Not everyone made it into the mausoleum then. There were a dozen or more gravestones dotted around, well weathered, hidden in the forest which sprouted from the forgotten earth.

This one leaned drunkenly to the side, pushed over by the roots of the maple tree. Scuttling closer to see the inscription, she couldn't help feeling sad reading the names and ages of three children who'd passed away on the same day. Who had *'Died tragically'*. An appalling thing to happen to any family. The gravestone didn't elaborate what tragedy had befallen them but there was nothing worse than losing a child. Not that she had any to worry about.

Pushing thoughts of grief from her mind she stood up, testing her leg. Not broken, bruised, her ego more so than her shin. Thankful there'd been no witnesses to her tumble, although she'd have to tell the lawyer about the door of the mausoleum, it was tempting to say she'd found it like that and lay the blame at the feet of an itinerant traveler.

Limping back to the house, drenched through, she put aside a dreadful sense of unease pummelling her like the rain from the sky.

❄

Cleaned up and dried off, warmed through by another hot bath and an even hotter coffee, she focused on her work. It hadn't taken long to pick a workroom, the dining room well suited to her task. A mahogany table dominated the space, large enough to accommodate the most fertile of families, complete with two dozen chairs standing ready to seat their guests. A quilted drop-cloth covering the table, disguising its true charm, would protect it as she worked on its expansive surface. If only every job had workbenches this size her life would be so much easier.

Retrieving her laptop, she searched for a power point. Although charged, she knew from experience that losing a days worth of work, for want of power was a mistake she didn't want to repeat. The walls were unmarred by electrical outlets of any sort, the bakelite switch the only nod to electricity. Flicking the switch the room lit up with refracted light from a crystal chandelier hanging from the ceiling. That would have to be catalogued unless it was being sold as a fixture of the house, but usually chandeliers were sold separately. Then the future owners of the estate invariably went round purchasing back the original fixtures and fittings, the very ones they could have paid for in the beginning. A merry-go-round of antiquities lining the pockets of everyone involved.

Opening the curtains showed the inhospitable coast outside, worthy of its own oil painting. Gulls launched themselves from rocky outcrops, oblivious to the wind whipping the breakers far below. Their cries carried above the sounds of the waves pummelling an unseen shore and seeped into the house through sash windows which had never sealed properly, bringing a briny scent into a room overpopulated with heavy woods and an enviable collection of religious portraiture. But still no power point.

If she was going to base herself in this room, then she'd start here, followed by the unnerving children in her bedroom. She could no more stand their staring, than she could the pious eyes from the subjects in the dining room.

Powering up her laptop, she counselled herself to keep an eye on the battery icon at the top of the screen and then allowed her mind to consider the family who'd eaten at this table. Were their images the ones on the walls? What on earth had possessed them to hang these devout prophet-like devotionals in a room she presumed was for joyous occasions; Christmas feasts, birthday celebrations, marriages even. She doubted she could have sat through a meal here without falling on her knees and confessing her sins. From what she'd seen in the gardens, there had been little joy here, not after losing three children.

Ever practical she thrust those thoughts away and turned on her camera. She worked her way around shooting photographs of the paintings. Point, shoot, check, take again, or move on. Point, shoot, check. The settings on the camera could be silent, but the old fashioned sound when she pressed the button was innately satisfying. The solid click signified achievement, job done. She lost track of how many photographs she took. She had to drag one of the chairs with her, kicking off her shoes to step on the worn leather seat, to shoot the smaller pictures hanging above the larger pieces. Every available space utilised.

Being higher than normal gave a unique perspective. The legs of the sideboard matched those of the table. Reflections from the lustres of the chandelier bounced off the age-foxed mirrors of the ornate overmantel. The ceiling rose a tangled wreath of ivy with no beginning nor end. Once covered with paint, faint touches of green now peeped through, giving the plasterwork a touch of verdigris.

The memory card full, Anita tried calculating how many pieces she'd photographed. Giving that up, she counted instead the number left, seventeen. Scrolling through the images she'd taken, she deleted the double ups, the blurred shots. She should do one of those adult learning courses at the local high school in the evenings to get the best out of the camera, she hadn't even uploaded any of them onto her computer and the day was half done.

The quick passing of time came as a surprise. Outside gulls were still stalking imaginary prey, trying to emulate their cousin the hawk. The sky filled with bulging grey swirls threatening the possibility of snow to follow the rain which had tapered off. Unseen waves continued their relentless onslaught on the rocky cliffs, punishing them for standing in the way. Only seventeen more photos, then she could have a break.

Snapping off sixteen photos, she paused before taking the last shot. This portrait was different. Gone was the formulaic religious iconography, applied to each painting like a paint-by-numbers effort foisted upon art students at college. This one a study of a man in quiet prayer or contemplation, his face in profile, head bowed, posed on a chair his hands clasped in front of him, a third of the picture in shadow. Had the painter run out of time to complete it or had he meant for the man to appear in supplication to the darkness surrounding him? Would taking a photograph disturb him?

Don't be daft she told herself, raising the camera to her eye, ignoring the sensation of being watched by the man. An elegant man with fearful eyes seated beside an ornate overmantel, the edge of a doorway just visible in the far corner. Peering through her lens and adjusting the focus, finger poised to take the picture, when her breath caught.

She lowered the camera, recognising the familiarity of the angle of the overmantel to the doorframe. They were the same. This had been painted here, he'd been in this room.

She made every effort to ignore the unease creeping up her spine. It made sense for a man who collected portraits to have some painted inside in his own home. He could've hosted artist retreats as a source of income, standard fare for owners of ancient buildings, an accepted means to pay for roof repairs and old electrics.

Click

The last photo taken, she let the camera swing idle around her neck, freeing her hands to lift the painting off the wall. Awkwardly she stepped off the chair, cradling the heavy frame.

Laying it on the end of table closest to the window, the weak light cast no further clues on what the artist had intended. It only plunged parts of the portrait further into darkness. A trick of the layers of paint applied with the precision of a master craftsman. Unnoticed by Anita, the recumbent man tracked her with his eyes as she searched for the artist's signature.

Inserting the camera's memory card into the external drive, she waited for the program to start transferring the photographs. After another glance outside she stood up, hunger nibbling at her, coffee long gone. Leaving everything on the table she wandered off to the kitchen, oblivious to the fresh shoots from the derelict plants she'd watered hours earlier. Once brown fronds now exhibiting delicate new growth.

She didn't have the energy to wrestle the ancient stove into life so settled for slices of salami on thick slabs of bread, the sort she hadn't eaten since her mother had stopped making her lunch once she had left primary school. A large glass of milk completed the meal.

Ivy snaked around the kitchen window, whipping against the panes as a gust of wind tore round the corner of the house. Anita jumped in fright, mistaking the tapping for human knocking. The electric scent of rain forced its way under the door. No point in trying to go for another walk, not until the weather cleared, being struck by lightning an hour from any paved road wasn't her idea of fun. If only she could reignite the same level of motivation she'd had straight after breakfast. That's it, coffee was the answer, a quiet coffee in the turret room to assuage her curiosity, with the added entertainment of watching a mammoth storm over a churning ocean.

Decision made, she coaxed the gas into life, putting the kettle on the stovetop. Wrapping her arms around herself she waited for the water to boil. The temperature had dropped even further and although used to winter snow at home; she didn't know if it snowed this close to the ocean. She watched the leafless trees bow low in the wind's embrace. Trees shaped like hunched old ladies, resigned to the onslaught, their growth deformed by decades of strong winds. The kettle whistled its merry tune, a sound so reminiscent of her grandmother's house Anita turned to speak to her long dead grandmother, before she caught herself and hurried to turn the gas off, worried that the piercing whistle might crack the windows already straining under the dual attack of wind and the ivy flinging itself against the window.

The aroma of fragrant coffee permeated the kitchen and the stirring of a teaspoon restored an air of normality. Pouring creamy milk into the tiny whirlpool, the ever-decreasing swirls mesmerising, she took a sip and felt the caffeine hitting her bloodstream and then the delicious punch as it hit her brain.

Hands cupped around the mug, she walked upstairs and

down the hall. Concentrating on her drink, she reached the open door to the turret stairs and pulled up short. The memory of shutting it behind her last night was sharp. The wind? Yes, of course, it made old houses do curious things. She pushed it all the way open. With the inherent trepidation women the world over have, she placed a foot on the bottom step and, heart in her mouth, she climbed the circular staircase to the turret.

CHAPTER 6

Daylight in a coastal storm is mottled, more a half light as if it can't decide whether it wants to be darkness or sunlight, good or evil. The light-flecked rain flung itself at the windows encircling the turret and redundant drapes billowed at the edges allowing glimpses of the most magnificent views.

Unfettered ocean for miles, unobstructed and unmarred by man, roiling as far as she could see. You couldn't fail being drawn in by the magnetising power of the waves. It was sacrilegious to turn away, but the other windows provided their own vistas, a different majesty. Undulating fields left fallow now, trees naked in their defiance of the weather thrown at them. She spied a picturesque pond with a summerhouse in the middle, but too far away for her to be sure if it was even part of the estate.

Cushioned bench seats encircled the turret room and an unfinished painting sat on a wooden easel with an artist's palette on a paint smattered stool. A set of brushes lay ready for the artist's return. Anita stood in front of the canvas, assessing the work. The rough outline of a girl had been done before the artist abandoned the piece, or before he died? No signature. At least she didn't need to do any cataloguing in here.

Anita wondered what it would be like to live surrounded by art and nature, unbothered by commute times or clock watching. She imagined herself standing in front of the easel, staring out at the ocean, then painting —one stroke at a time - the only limitations on her the abundance of daylight.

Ripping herself from the views, she traipsed downstairs pulling the door shut behind her. The thud as the latch fell into its cavity as satisfying as the coffee. There was work to do and given that the house's ancient lighting wasn't up to specialist evaluation, daylight hours were all she had.

With the photos uploaded, she set about creating an entry for each of the paintings. She gave them each a unique identifier, followed by a title, the artist and description. Often the title was missing, not all art has a convenient gold plaque, bottom centre, naming a piece in perpetuity. As for the artist's name, she expected more gaps than completed entries. The phrase *Artist Unknown* fills auction catalogues and rarely did those pieces make money. The stock-in-trade of high street bric-à-brac shops catering to prop buyers and ladies playing at interior designer. They are the least exciting articles an auctioneer sells. Old dental implements far more exciting than unsigned art. This was her job, it paid the bills and grew her client base, one middle class housewife at a time.

Starting with the piece on the table was a mistake, it was unsigned. Turning it over to check for any distinguishing marks, she found the name *Abraham*, written in red ink on the bottom left-hand corner. Not an easily searchable moniker, she made a notation identifying the piece as

Abraham. Lifting it off the table, she leaned it against the wall. She didn't want to look at his eyes, he looked scared, pleading almost.

The rest of the art took another hour and she'd found signatures on four of them, although they required more investigation. One had its name notated on its reverse and the balance had no identity other than what she assigned them - *Boy With Halo*; *Woman On Knees*; *Woman In Red Dress Praying*. Another portrait, an older man, sat posed with the city of Jerusalem behind him. His gnarled hands holding a pine cone in his lap. An unusual composition, he was dressed in a green jacket and appeared disinterested, his eyes looking past the artist. She labelled him *Man With Pine Cone*. As the least religious piece in the room, she chatted to him as she propped him up against the others.

"I wish I knew what you were thinking. How did you come to be here?"

As night crept upon her, Anita felt as if she wasn't alone. Surrounded by portraits, it's natural to feel watched by the souls depicted in pigment, isn't it? She'd appraised dozens of pictures, which she'd stacked in a corner of the dining room, and with the light fading and her stomach rumbling, Anita powered off her laptop and returned to the kitchen. At lunchtime she'd spied a pie on the bottom shelf of the fridge she'd missed the night before. Cutting a large chunk, she heated it through. The oven was an ancient piece of equipment and it was an exercise in patience waiting for it to warm up giving her ample time to explore the cupboards in the kitchen. She poured herself a glass of wine from a bottle she'd found in the pantry, whether it was for her or not, she wasn't sure, but given how the lawyer had treated her she didn't care.

She carried her dinner through into the sitting room and devoured the steak and kidney pie. The strong drink a perfect accompaniment, cosseting her senses from a room adorned with portraits and mixed with hunting scenes too gruesome for anyone but a hardcore fanatic. Anita tried not to look at them as she forked the great hunks of steak into her mouth, she would not be dissuaded from finishing her meal.

She'd been more than relieved when the ancient television had proven itself as reliable as the oven. Her viewing choices a home renovation show or an old Tom Hanks film. Settling for the movie, she poured a second wine.

Curled on the couch, the outdated television mumbling in the background and two glasses of wine under her belt, she dozed off.

A man in one of the catalogued portraits, his face in shadow, shimmered momentarily as if he'd been caught in candlelight. He eased himself out of his frame, stretching, released from his slumber. He leaned over Anita, his intentions unclear, observing her sleep, before tucking her hair behind her ear. Fingers to his lips, he touched her forehead before turning on his heel and leaving the room.

Anita woke in the early hours of the morning, the television an avalanche of static snow. Confused, she bolted up, heart racing. Rubbing sleep from her eyes, she stumbled her way upstairs to bed, leaving the still lit chandelier swaying ever so slightly, the empty frame unnoticed in the corner.

In the turret, a lone artist stood in front of his easel cleaning his brushes with turpentine, before wiping the soft sable bristles on a cloth. Dipping the tip of the brush into the smear of paint on his palette he began applying a blush to the face on the canvas.

CHAPTER 7

It was clear when Anita woke that the storm hadn't blown itself out yet. Catching the mournful gaze of the children on her bedroom walls was the catalyst for flinging herself out of bed, regardless of chill in the air. She'd tried not to look at the creepy little poppets, annoyed at herself for not taking them down the day before, grateful she'd had the two large glasses of wine with dinner or she would never have slept.

A breakfast of farm fresh eggs and lean bacon strips followed by a mug of strong coffee flushed the remnants of the wine from Anita's system and pushed her gritty eyes open. Now she needed to work, the portraits wouldn't catalogue themselves. She had a couple of days left to complete the mammoth task ahead of her before the packers turned up, and one more night before the rest of her team arrived, if the weather didn't close in. There was lots left to do, so leaving the dishes in the sink she headed off to retrieve her computer and camera.

She paused beside one of the half-dead ferns she'd watered the afternoon before. Its new growth and healthy foliage a far cry from the shrivelled desiccated plant she'd tipped water into the day before. She wasn't a botanist but the quick recovery struck her as unusual. Mind you, the lily in her mother's kitchen always looked half-dead, but a cup of water revived it in minutes and it would remain pert and healthy for another couple of weeks.

Unconsciously she twisted the tiny diamond studs in her ears, a nervous tic she had when she was thinking, checking to see they were still there in her lobes.

Ignoring the paintings she'd dealt with, she ticked the dining room off her to-do list as she climbed the staircase back to her bedroom. Each tread that tiniest bit wider than the standard stair tread in modern homes. Her calves would feel it after a week of running up and down. She wouldn't be making any gym sessions this week so she'd take what exercise she could get.

The paintings of the children were so artistically distinct from the rest of the paintings in the house, but whether they were done by a different hand she couldn't tell, not yet. Putting her camera up to her eye for the first shot, she pressed the button and, nothing, a flat battery. In vain Anita searched her room for a power outlet for the charger.

"Blast it". Grabbing her camera and charger she went downstairs in search of a power point. She already knew the dining room didn't have any. There was one for the television in the sitting room, hidden behind an ugly seventies entertainment unit — the only 'improvement' she could see anywhere in the house, and bar taking a crowbar to it, there was no access. There was no way she could get to the plug for the fridge when it seemed like the kitchen had been purpose built around the old fashioned behemoth. The fridge was wedged so tightly into an alcove, that it probably wouldn't come out until the house was being demolished and some burly workman manhandled it out with the help of a couple of equally burly friends. Whoever the original electrician had been back in the day, he hadn't thought through the placement, and quantity, of power points. Of course no one could have predicted exactly how many electrical appliances and gadgets people used these days. If there was a power point she could access, it would be in the study, so she ventured there first.

She had only glanced through the doorway on her initial walk through the property and now felt dwarfed. A giant roll top desk dominated the study, stuffed to the gunnels with generations of paperwork. Floor to ceiling bookcases filled three of the walls, with not an inch of space spare. Leather-bound books, first editions, religious tracts. A rare book dealers paradise. She wasn't an expert but at first glance the books far exceeded in value most of the portraits she had seen.

Focusing on the desk, she spied an old-fashioned green hued bankers lamp. That must lead to a power outlet. *Bingo.* Bending, she struggled to force her modern plug into the bakelite socket. A cold breeze nuzzled her neck. She whipped around, draughty old house. Turning back to the bothersome plug, she froze.

Her heartbeat slower than a glacier's ponderous path, she turned and backed into the bulging bookcase, willing the shelves to embrace her, to offer her their protection.

A brass valet stand, complete with suit jacket, scarf and hat, tucked behind the door. She'd caught sight of it from the corner of her eye and thought someone was in there with her. Her worst nightmare and one which had once come true, a long time ago now, but it still gave her the jitters. So many nights she'd climbed out of bed to double check the windows and doors; the inside of wardrobes and under the beds, before she felt safe enough to sleep.

Her phone rang. Jumping, she fumbled in her pocket, pulling out the impatient phone, the display showing the number of Alan Gates, the lawyer. He said he'd ring and despite her feelings about the lawyer, the normality of speaking to another person was a relief.

"Hello?... Yes, I'm making good progress, two rooms done so far—"

Interrupting her, the lawyer impressed upon her the need to finish before the packers arrived. Anita undertook to reassure him she'd finish well before then, with the help of her colleagues, but he'd rung off already. She looked at the silent phone in her hand, odd that it was working now when she hadn't been able to get any signal anywhere else in the house. Dialling the number for her mother, conscious of needing to check in, the call failed, no signal. Trying a second time, moving about the room, holding the phone further away, up higher, the way you do even though you know it's futile, but nothing. A frown fled across her face, weird, she'd try again later - she had to.

The camera on charge, she poked about the room. Where there weren't books on the shelves, they were full of knickknacks. Doulton pottery, old wind-up tin toys, shoe boxes piled atop of other boxes, filled with postcards, first day covers, cigarette cards. Meticulously labelled in sloping script. A gentleman's hat box, with more than a lifetime's collection of stamps. Mostly used, there were others still hinged to their neighbours. To the right person, a hatbox filled with stamps was manna from heaven. To the auctioneers, unless a *Penny Black*, or a *Tyrian Plum* turned up, they weren't interested. It's not that stamps didn't sell, it was more that a collection this big never recouped the time spent sorting the wheat from the chaff, so they didn't bother.

The study hadn't avoided the proliferation of portraits. Despite the lack of wall space a number of small pictures hung from nails hammered into the cross supports of the bookcases. These were more in the style of realist painter Gustave Courbet, where the subjects stared out wide-eyed with desperation on their faces. With a limited palette, the artist had captured their fears with his brush. Where the rest of the pictures in the house were life size renderings, these were more the size of the miniatures common in the 17th and early 18th centuries.

This job was turning out to be bigger than the Vatican Museum's collection. Every surface held something of value, rooms full of antiques of varying ages and condition. She hadn't looked everywhere yet and now she wasn't sure she wanted to. The decision to send her on her own was the wrong one. This task needed a dedicated team working on it. In fact, holding the auction on site might have been the best play. Auction at a desolate country estate, cash and carry, imagine the media mileage they'd get out of it.

A watched charger doesn't charge any faster. Given the others would be here soon, and although they would concentrate on the furniture and collectibles, she should continue with her side of things.

With her focus restored, and her nerves resettled, she removed the miniatures from their hooks, stacking them in a wood basket next to the empty hearth. She gave no thought to the lack of dust or silky cobwebs linking the artworks. Carrying the basket into the dining room, where the light was better, she laid them on the table. They'd photograph fine here given their size and she could start describing them while waiting for the battery to recharge. She'd do the portraits in her room next. There was no way she would spend another night sleeping with those children overseeing her every breath. Drinking a whole distillery of rum still wouldn't let her sleep with them watching.

The miniature paintings filled the table, leaving enough space for the laptop and a plate of fruit for lunch. Nibbling on apples and apricots, she carefully created an entry for every portrait.

TITLE: GILBERTO (INSCRIBED ON REAR). OIL. GILT FRAME. SIGNED "GLK"

TITLE: JAMES BENHAM (INSCRIBED ON REAR). OIL. OAK FRAME. SIGNED "GLK"

TITLE: HOPPER (INSCRIBED ON REAR). OIL. GILT FRAME (DAMAGED). SIGNED "GLK"

TITLE: MARY C. (INSCRIBED ON REAR). OIL. STERLING SILVER FRAME. UNSIGNED

TITLE: UNTITLED. WOMAN IN WHITE DRESS. WATERCOLOUR. PINE FRAME. UNSIGNED

She got into a groove, working her way along each row, before starting the next. Before she knew it, she'd come to the end of the miniatures. She counted them, double checking she had the corresponding number of entries in her spreadsheet. Excellent, it worked. Now she needed to take the photographs, upload them and that'd be two rooms done.

She checked her phone, still no signal. She wasn't too concerned, if anyone tried ringing and left a message, she'd be able to pick it up next time she went into the study. At least there was one room in the house where there was a signal, sometimes.

One more coffee then she'd photograph this lot, then straight to her room to photograph those children, before she took them on a one way trip downstairs. She'd have to figure out how to store them after she'd catalogued them. Somewhere convenient for when the transport company arrived. The last thing they needed was for some buffoon to run a chair leg through a priceless painting. Not that she'd found one yet. Give her time, Anita thought to herself. She needed to prove to Warren and to his managers above him, that she was an exceptional appraiser, to get her own territory to manage, to grow. Her goals weren't as lofty as others. She wanted to handle the best pieces of art out there. To meet up and coming artists. Going to galleries, museums and art shows gave her a reason to live, even during her darkest times. She couldn't paint to save her soul although you didn't need to know how to paint to appreciate art. All types of art, not just art acceptable to closeted housewives or oil barons, or to the docents of mid-level galleries, who were in a world of their own. Their interpretation of art and artists akin to an octopus injecting itself with heroin and being let loose in an art gallery with a set of crayons. Their opinions scaring people away from art in droves.

The view from the kitchen window as gloomy as that from the dining room. Rain pummelled the sea and the shore, clouds obliterating any view of the farmland or ocean. The house could well be floating on a carpet of cloud and she'd be none the wiser. Surprisingly it had proven itself watertight, a miracle. She'd taken from the paperwork that the former owner was a bachelor, with no family. So either he'd died suddenly and had looked after the place till then or the lawyer had someone overseeing the house. If he did, why hadn't she met them yet?

Pondering this over her coffee, she wandered back to the staircase.

Finding the stairs as a form of enforced exercise, she began the ascent. She'd dispense with those children now, she couldn't help but feel creeped out.

Hands wrapped around her mug, she walked into her bedroom. It wasn't as messy as her room at home, but given she'd only been here two nights, it was heading the same way. The bed unmade, pyjamas in a heap at the end, dirty clothes lay on the floor jumbled together with castoff shoes unworn since she arrived.

The huge Narnia-esque wardrobe stood shut against the far wall. Curious, she pulled on the turned knob and the door swung open revealing a row of white cotton dresses of various sizes. Pristine on their hangers, they mirrored the outfits the girls wore in the paintings.

She dropped her mug. It smashed, coffee splashing onto the hems of the longer dresses and over the clothes on the floor.

Anita wrestled her crazy thoughts into something sensible. These children lived here, this had been their home. Most people left stuff at their childhood home. Boxes of her own adolescent memories remained stacked in her parent's garage, things her mother begged her to dispose of. She slammed the wardrobe door shut, too creepy whatever the circumstances.

Hesitant, as if removing them from the walls was a sacrilege, she lifted the first portrait from the wall. The one of the older girl, perched on an upturned sailboat, a china faced doll resting by her feet. Anita tilted the frame to read the name of the boat, "*Tabitha*," she mumbled reading it, and before she could save it, the painting slipped from her hands and plummeted to the floor. The frame disintegrating on impact, a tiny silver heart-shaped locket skittered beneath the bed and Anita screamed.

The portrait landed facedown, broken picture wire hanging from the eyelets. Lifting the painting from the wall had pushed the wire past its limit, and the weight of the frame had finally snapped the wire — nothing otherworldly about it, but not the best look for an appraiser to damage the art before cataloguing it.

Tabitha had been a name on the gravestone, meaning two of the other children were the owners of the other names. Heart racing, she shivered. The clothing left in a wardrobe? The lack of heirs? If one child survived, what had become of them?

The sooner these pictures were catalogued, the earlier her heart could return to normal. She thought she'd be fine here by herself, but paranoia filled the isolation. They were paintings on a wall, nothing more. The coincidence of their names on the gravestone no different to a portrait of George Washington, or Queen Victoria and their graves, no different.

She gave up examining them in her room and her skin prickled with irrational fear as she removed the remaining three from the wall and carried them downstairs. She dumped them onto the dining room table before feeling guilty and laying them out in a more dignified way.

There was nothing she could do about the broken frame. They'd sell better as a set at auction, like subjects with like, so she should go looking for tools to repair the frame with but, to be honest she didn't want to handle these children more than what was necessary.

A sense of unease was palpable. They were paintings of children long dead, who'd have been long dead even if they hadn't died tragically. Ignoring the dread lurking in her subconscious, she entered the descriptive details;

Title: *Tabitha (inscribed on rear). Young girl on rowboat. Oil. Gilt frame (damaged). Signed "GLK".*

Fingers poised above her keyboard. *"GLK"*? The portraits in the study had the same signature, but their ages were so different it couldn't be the same artist. Drawing her magnifier from her bag, she flicked on the light before settling it on her head. She almost looked like she was wearing a virtual reality headset and she'd learnt to ignore the sniggers when those outside of the industry saw her wearing it. The headset provided complete freedom for her hands and cast daylight into dark corners.

Through the magnified lenses, the tiny initials in the corner loomed large; "GLK". Each letter done with one smooth red stroke. No sign of a second stroke on any of the characters, showing utter mastery with a brush. She stroked the letters with the tip of her finger. She couldn't achieve that with a ballpoint pen, let alone with tricky oil paints.

Staring at the screen she settled for making no statement about the possible connection between the artists. She'd revisit it later. Sometimes a collection itself was enough of a tie. The artists might be related, but the auctioneer's commission would say whether they needed to prove it.

Moving *Tabitha* to one side, she focused on the boys. There was no mistaking them for brothers, twins? Haunting blue eyes and matching clefts in their chins, they looked awkwardly out from their frames, each holding a small *Meccano* model. Hard to tell what the models were — boats, or a bridge, it didn't matter, they seemed to reach towards each other, as if they'd been standing together but the artist had painted them apart.

Turning the frames over, neat labels were handwritten on the back; *Cole* and *Saul*, the other names on the gravestone. Simple names compared to the exotic sounding *Tabitha*.

Apart from entering their names, all she needed to do was some judicious copying and pasting. She could add the dates of the children's deaths, although that didn't help date the portraits.

She'd left the youngest girl till last, the surviving child, unless there was another gravestone inscribed with her name on. Hers was the painting which disturbed Anita the most. She knew the little girl hadn't moved or changed where she looked, but Anita swore that the girl had not been looking out of the frame, that she'd been looking off towards her brothers and sister hanging on the wall next to her. Anita persuaded herself it was a trick of the light, exacerbated because of her tiredness from the drive and coupled with hunger and the unease of being here alone. This was the longest time she'd spent alone in years, she used to enjoy living on her own, the solitude and the lack of anyone else's negative vibes, but then that changed.

Two years ago Anita moved into a small flat, cheap due to its proximity to the train line. Trains didn't bother her, for as long as she could remember she'd had a love affair with large locomotives, choosing them over flying whenever possible. Their clackety clack over the tracks more soothing than the constant wash of waves upon the seashore. As a child her parents indulged her with vintage Hornby train sets, now packed away in the attic at home.

Her new flat had been perfect — perfect size, perfect location, safe until the night it wasn't.

Anita remembered going to bed, the humidity too high for sheets, the fan on high, windows open. She never made that mistake again.

She remembered waking with a start, a man standing in her bedroom doorway, she first asked if there was a fire, was that why he was in her room? Then as he'd sidled up to her bed, reality dawned and before she could scream he was on her, hands reeking of oil covered her mouth, the fumes making her dizzy. His knee between her thighs, his other hand… she tried not to think about it.

The train going past her flat had disguised any sound of him clambering in through her window. Of everything that happened that night, the ruination of her love of trains the hardest to accept, their sound now a horrific trigger to unsettling flashbacks.

She moved home to the safety of her parent's house and

her second floor bedroom. Her windows never open, even at the height of summer.

Her parents had never wanted her to move out. They'd even refused to pay for her to attend a better college because it would have meant her moving away, so her degree was from a lower tier college nearer to home.

Relieved to have her back under their roof, despite the circumstances, she not only suffered debilitating nightmares, but the unspoken *I told you so's* from her mother, who'd warned her about moving out and cosseted her like a broken doll. Through counselling she'd been able to sleep through the night and get on with life. Apart from going to work, she sheltered at home never far from her mother's reach. She hadn't realised how stifling it was until stepping out of the car upon arriving here.

Shaking those thoughts from her head, she went back to the art, a tangible solid combination of pigments on canvas, not an unknown stranger reeking of oil. It was just art.

Anita adjusted her headset and examined the fourth painting — the youngest of the four children, she was five or six in the portrait, maybe a year either side of that. Painted wearing her hair loose, in a white cotton dress identical to her sister's. A child-sized artist's palette held in one hand and a paintbrush in the other. The cleft in her chin more than marked her as a sibling despite the contrasting eye colour. She didn't have the same anxious expression as the others though. Hers was more of a smirk, as if she knew something they didn't and that bothered Anita the most.

She turned the frame over, looking for a name. *My Ruth.*

CHAPTER 8

Ruth. A biblical name for an innocent child. Anita added her details into the spreadsheet, the child's eyes following her as she did. She would not achieve much with her on the table. Stacking *Ruth* on top of the other portraits, she piled them on the floor by the empty hearth, well away from where she was sitting. She fancied Ruth's eyes were on her, pure fantasy, but not having Ruth in her line of sight was better and now she could concentrate on the calming landscapes.

The first proved to be anything but soothing, the long frame held a hunting scene featuring red-coated riders on sweat-slicked horses tearing after their hounds and on the far edge of the painting, a hound had caught the hapless fox and was ripping into it, blood oozing from its powerful jaws. The other hounds appeared poised to join in, to finish the unfortunate beast. Anita wondered who in their right mind would have such a bloodthirsty scene hanging on their wall?

The words *The Hunt* were engraved on a plate screwed to the frame. More likely *The Massacre* Anita thought. The picture lacked any signature and was only memorable for its subject and its style would only appeal to a narrow segment of the art market.

She stacked it to the side and moved on to the next one. Lush hills, misty moorland in the foreground, a pleasing palette, no dismembered animal carcasses anywhere in sight. Signed in the bottom right-hand corner, the unmistakable left-slanting signature of *Ivan Shishkin*, a Russian landscape artist. What a coup. There'd been a recent boom in Russian art, with the sales of Russian masters in the millions of dollars every year. The commission on this piece alone would feed her for a year if it sold. She worked with a great team, but it wasn't always straightforward who'd get the lion's share of the finder's fee in the commission structure. The exquisite realism of *Shishkin's* work was so sublime, that finding words to describe it was easy. In the back of her mind she couldn't help but think that if there was one, there might be another.

Bright eyed and bushy tailed, she slipped into a fugue. She hadn't found another *Shishkin*, but located two pieces by *John Absolon*, from his Switzerland series. The mountains had aspects of the majestic Swiss Alps to them. The rest were of a lesser quality, something you'd buy from a community art collective, done by ladies in twinsets who painted together then drowned their elderly sorrows in tea and scones. Unsigned, they'd decorate spare rooms and bathrooms around the world.

Hours flew by in a blur and engrossed in her work, it was only her empty stomach which forced her to the kitchen. She wandered down the hall, swinging her arms like a champion shot-putter prepping for competition. Her windmilling arms slowed to a halt as she paused in front of one of the woebegone houseplants she'd watered earlier. Except they weren't so sorrowful, they were glorious. Lush green fronds cascaded over the rim of the copper planter, the plant hummed with vitality. Weird. She carried on to the kitchen puzzling over its resurrection.

The kitchen provided the perfect distraction. Rummaging through the fridge, she tried to find something other than pie, she couldn't face another night of congealing meat. She discovered a packet of bacon which passed the sniff test and paired that with more of the eggs from breakfast. If she kept eating this way she'd be able to call herself Paleo in no time. Her poor maligned body was more used to regular infusions of fast food and leftovers and couldn't recall ever being this healthy before . The psychological pull of unrequited sugar cravings was relentless, but there was nothing here to sate them, although there was sugar in wine.

Pouring herself a glass from the bottle she'd found the night before, she sipped it at the formica table and in the short time it took for the bacon to fry, the sky had blackened, colouring everything beyond the windows an inky black. She gazed at her reflection in the window and saw average, which suited her, as long as her work wasn't average.

Anita slipped into bed, grateful for the naked rectangles adorning the wallpaper where the paintings had previously hung and abandoned hooks reached out for their stolen wards. Turning her back on them, her eyes were drawn to the windows where she'd left the curtains open, secure in her second-floor room. Clouds struggled against the racing wind, the moon probing its way through clouds flushed with rain. It was a lulling battle to watch, moon and stars darting in and out of sight, like Christmas lights blinking on and off around harried shoppers flooding through the festive season.

She was drifting off, lulled by the wind, when the baying of hounds filtered in through the poorly fitted windows.

Somewhere, a pack of dogs howled at the disguised moon. Anita shuddered, pulling the covers up higher. She pitied whatever creature had caught their attention and tried not to imagine what was happening, drifting off to an uneasy sleep with visions of rabid animals tearing at the flesh of a hapless hare filling her mind.

She slept, her brow furrowed as her dreams took her to places she never went in her waking hours. Flashbacks of what had happened years ago blended with visions of running through barren fields, the dogs hunting her, baying for her blood, before morphing into a gang of faceless men chasing her through the dark.

Click

The handle of Anita's bedroom door turned with a languid calmness, in direct contrast to the woman thrashing about in bed. The door opened silently on its ancient hinges and a shadow filled the doorway, two shadows. The little girl looked up at the man standing beside her, her small hand in his. Looking down, he smiled. Dropping the girl's hand he stepped into the room, moving closer to the bed. The woman looked so different from the night before, where she'd slept well, face calm, her breath gentle against the soft pillow. He'd watched her then, taking in every detail. Tonight she was different. Her face showed anguish, deep lines marring her complexion. Which woman was she, the calm, self assured one or the one he saw before him now?

Somewhere in the house a door slammed and the girl turned towards the noise, he hesitated. The woman's breathing changed, the slamming door wrenching her from her nightmares. He only had seconds, he vanished.

Anita screamed, a heart-rending, ear splitting scream of absolute terror few experience. On the cusp of sleep and awake, her consciousness lost to her night terrors, she was in that indefinable place where you're not awake, yet not asleep.

That moment where reality is unattainable, she flung her arms up, as if warding off someone or something. And then the sobbing began.

Whimpering, her throat sore, she hadn't had a nightmare that vivid for months. Waking with the vision of a man leering above her, the man from her nightmares who still roamed free. As in her earlier nightmares she would have sworn that he was standing over her and, like the other times, the nightmare fading like a Polaroid photograph in reverse. She was shaking, the after-effects of the adrenaline coursing through her veins and the only thing which would counter it was to fill a mug of tea with a pound of sugar.

Swinging her legs out of bed, Anita stood unsteady on her feet. As she reached for her dressing gown, her hand froze mid air as she spied the open door. Paralysed with fear, she looked like a plaster devotional statue beseeching Christ for salvation. The door she'd shut was open.

She lowered her arm, unsure of what to do now. Her throat ached and a band of pain had snaked its way further around her head, gripping it vice-like. The pain throbbing in tandem with her heart rate. She repeated the mantras she'd learnt from her counsellor. "This too will pass," she whispered, shrugging on her robe. "I'm stronger than I know. Breathe," she muttered, tying the cord around her waist, eyes on the doorway, lips barely moving.

Shoulders hunched, she argued with herself for and against going downstairs for tea. She was in the house alone and it had only been a nightmare. It was an old house, it made sense that the doors wouldn't stay shut, it was fine. Eyes darting like a thief in the night, she peered into the empty hallway, the blackness complete. She retreated into her room and picked up her cellphone, the torch function a lifesaver for someone suffering from a fear of the dark. With the illumination from her phone, she braved the corridor.

Shadows cast by the potted plants spidery fingers inching towards her on the walls, another reason not to bother with house plants. It was easy to ignore the known, it was the unknown which made her mouth dry and her pulse race.

The kitchen filled with light at the flick of a switch and the appliances calmed her with the stovetop flame chasing away the last of the nightmare. The kettle whistled, bringing reality crashing into the room. Anita busied herself with opening cupboards and drawers, pulling out a mug, a tea bag, teaspoon, milk and sugar; uniting them was as soothing a mother's quiet words. She tried ignoring the mounting pile of dishes as she sipped the scalding hot drink. Doing dishes was preferable to going back to bed, but later, after her tea. Rearranging the crocheted cushions, she curled up on a chair and pondered the family who'd once lived here. The outcome of the artist's death might have been different if those children hadn't died, if they were related to him. It was conceivable he was no relation to them at all. And what had happened to Ruth? No, she would not think about the children.

Swallowing the dregs of her tea she got up, the sugar hitting her bloodstream. She threw the dishes into the cavernous sink and filled it with hot soapy water. The routine of doing the mundane exactly what she needed. Immersed in clanging crockery she had no idea what was happening in the turret high above her.

CHAPTER 9

He stood over the unfinished portrait on the easel. It had been an ill-defined outline of a woman's face, the eyes still empty. Just the almond outline and eyebrows done, waiting for the artist to capture the hardest part of any woman. He pondered the direction he should take, sleeping or awake? The calmness of sleep or the terror he'd seen swathing her face. This was the point of no return, he could always paint over if his viewpoint changed but he wanted to record her essence, if he could define what that was. He needed more time.

His shadow watched him prepare his brushes, her tiny feet curled underneath her as she perched on the window seat, the howling storm framing her young face.

His sable brush danced over the canvas, creating cheeks flushed with youth, lips open. Wisps of hair appearing like magic, blown by an unseen wind. Strand after strand appeared on the stretched canvas, his brush mixing an auburn hint in the hair as it peaked on her brow.

Selecting a finer brush he dabbed it into a darker hue — an indescribable grey and worked on the neck, before defining the shoulders. With a damp cloth he smudged the oil — giving the illusion of the subject being caught mid turn, casting a glance backwards. The smudged paint ethereal in the twilight of the room.

The little girl reached out and swirled one of her fingers through the mass on the palette. With her finger she smeared the paint across the canvas, the colours in stark contrast to the grey tones of the artist's deft strokes.

Together they admired their efforts.

"Not long, two nights," he said, stroking her hair. Loosed from its white ribbon it spilled past her shoulders like the fairy ferns in the hallway, vibrant and alive. His own smile fading as a familiar pain pulsed in his knuckles.

Her smile played around her mouth, never quite making it to her mirthless eyes. Her gaze returned to the painting. Two nights were two nights too long and she didn't want to wait.

CHAPTER 10

It was Anita's third morning and still the rain fell. She would need an ark if this continued. After her disrupted sleep it felt as if grit filled her eyes and her mouth was an arid desert.

Despite her normal fastidiousness, she needed sustenance more than a bath. She didn't bother dressing; she threw her robe on, her feet encased in old bed socks. At some stage in her life, her mother had given her a pair of woven purple socks, thicker than her heaviest winter jumper, they'd seen her through a dozen winters and negated the need for slippers.

Her throat ached from her nightmare and she wandered downstairs absorbed in the half-remembered fears from the night.

"Good morning."

Anita screamed, slipping on the edge of the stairs before coming to a crumpled halt at the foot of the staircase.

The lawyer looked on, raking her tangled legs with his piggy eyes.

"Thought I'd pop in to see how you're going. Wondered if the old pile could withstand this weather."

Struggling to understand what was happening, Anita couldn't respond. The sneer on his face enough to turn the stomach of a butcher.

"How did you get in?" she whispered, her throat still raw. Standing up, her legs jittery like a newborn foal. She tried to compose herself, fully aware of her state of undress. The last thing she'd expected today was company. She didn't want to remember the last time she'd been this vulnerable.

Gates checked his ostentatious watch with faux seriousness.

"Sorry to get you out of bed at such an early hour. Ten o'clock is early isn't it?" he mocked.

"Ten o'clock?"

Anita didn't wear a watch, her cellphone the only timepiece she ever referred to. She hadn't checked it when she woke. No point since there was no coverage anywhere other than in the study. She wasn't even sure it was still charged.

Gates waved his arm over the paper carry bags.

"I brought morning tea with me, thought you'd relish the company, being alone… in this house. I also assumed you'd be hard at work, but… then again?" head tilted, he raised his eyebrows.

Before Anita could rebut his ridiculous query, he said, "Have you already done these paintings? Odd they're still on the wall then."

Anita had had enough, his appraising gaze as unnerving as the house last night. She recognised his sort, a misogynistic, small town mentality, where women were possessions and a woman with brains was dangerous, worthy only of being given a good beating behind closed doors.

"Can you take the bags to the kitchen and I'll…"

"What? Get changed into something a little more comfortable?" Gates laughed.

Anita clenched her jaw as she limped upstairs, she wasn't sure what was more bruised, her ego or tailbone. She felt irrationally uncomfortable that the lawyer was here. It wasn't so much that she was undressed, it was more that his presence disturbed the whole atmosphere in the house. She fancied she could sense a subtle change in the surrounding air. Mad she knew, but it was virtually palpable and it niggled at her.

Ducking into her room, she slumped against the door, her eyes drawn to the wall where the children's portraits had hung only the afternoon before. The children wouldn't have liked the lawyer, young people had an innate ability to judge those around them far better than adults.

Dressing in sensible jeans and shirt she made her way downstairs.

"How is a man meant to get a coffee round here? Where's the bloody kettle?" Gates ranted as Anita fronted in the kitchen. Pastry crumbs adorned the florid man's face making him even less attractive than when he'd ogled her at the bottom of the stairs.

"By boiling the water on the stove," Anita said, bustling businesslike in the dated kitchen, lighting the gas stove with a practised hand.

"Jesus, the old guy was living in the past wasn't he. So, found any Picasso's yet?" Alan's eyes shimmered with greed.

It gave Anita no end of pleasure to dash his dreams of a payday paved with gold. "Sorry to disappoint you, but I've not found anything out of the ordinary. A few pieces by some well known artists, which will do okay at auction, but most are by an artist I don't recognise. It'll need more research when I have internet access, although the furniture should compensate for the lack of performance by the art. There are several rooms I've yet to catalogue, so you never know. But I have had a quick look around and nothing spectacular caught my eye apart from a *Shishkin* which should be impressive at auction but that's all."

Gates looked lost at *Shishkin's* name. Aware that he didn't have the foggiest clue whether she was referring to a painting or a piece of furniture, Anita refrained from educating him.

"I'd expected more from this old pile, gold hidden in the cellar, that sort of thing. Was also expecting you to know a little more about the art you're meant to be cataloguing. Still, the rest of your team will be here soon and they'll have a better idea of the true worth of the stuff, given their experience," Alan laughed, slapping his thigh with the hilarity of his statement.

Anita busied herself with the kettle, her mouth a thin line.

"Its good of them to give you this experience. It's not every employer who'd let someone so inexperienced do such a big job."

Anita clenched the edge of the stove, knuckles taut, and turned towards the lawyer to respond to his outdated viewpoint when a hammering reverberated through the house. Already on edge, Anita jumped, knocking the kettle, which spewed boiling water across the tired linoleum, and the lawyer.

Alan leapt from his chair, the boiling water soaking his trousers, his face a twisted caricature of the amiable face he'd presented earlier.

"Stupid woman," he said, tugging the fabric away from his legs, trying to escape the scalding heat.

The hammering continued.

Anita dashed around the kitchen, filling a jug with water from the ancient tap.

"Here, let me pour cold water over it, to cool it down."

"Are you crazy? You stupid girl, give it here. I'll not have you throw more water on me. These are expensive shoes and you'll ruin them if you get any more water on them."

Yanking the jug from Anita, he trickled water over his leg, trying to avoid splashing water on his hideous suede loafers. He looked like a toddler showing how a toad might hop from one spot to another.

The hammering registered in Anita's flustered mind, the front door. Leaving Alan to his theatrics she hurried to the door, wrenching it open before whomever was on the other side broke it down.

The door opened to an apocalyptic scene, sheets of rain pounded the gravel driveway and the ocean blended with the smoke-coloured sky, the horizon invisible to all but God. And in front of her stood a man, his face as angry as the storm. His age indecipherable, he was wearing a heavy oilskin with boots gripping his calves.

The verandah provided little protection from the weather and Anita shrank from the stinging rain. The tang of salt was all pervading and the shouts of the waves drowned out the stranger's words, for he was talking to her.

"Sorry I can't hear you, please come in," she said, taking a step backwards, the sanctuary of the entrance hall preferable to the frigid air outside.

"I'll not set foot inside thank you. I need a word with the driver of that car," came the raspy response. The stranger motioned towards the sports car in the driveway, behind which idled an ancient tractor, its age somewhere near that of the man at the door.

At an impasse, Anita tried again, the rain slicking the tiled floor. "Please, it's pouring, there's no point us both getting wet, come in."

He mumbled under his breath but wiped his boots on the soaked doormat and shuffled inside, eyes downcast. Anita tried to close the door behind him but the wild wind caught it and slammed it shut, the echo reverberating around the cavernous house. The stranger stood motionless in the hall, his eyes fixed on the geometric patterns of the tiles, hands thrust deep into his pockets.

"Is he here then? The owner of that car?"

"He's in the kitchen. Come through and have a coffee?"

"I'll wait here."

Anita shrugged. Her mind imagining no reason he'd need to speak with the lawyer but it wasn't anything to do with her she reasoned and walked down the long hall to the kitchen leaving a salty trail of water in her wake.

The kitchen was a scene straight out of an American sitcom. Alan had downed his trousers and was fussing over his scalded legs, the skin pinker than the rest of his body although hardly worthy of the performance he was making in her kitchen. Her kitchen? She felt an affiliation with the house and the last thing she needed was this buffoon ruining that sense of safety.

"There's a man here who wants to speak with you."

"Huh?" Alan looked up from his ineffectual dowsing of his leg. Anita tried concealing her distaste at the scene. She'd had little to do with men in any state of undress since her assault. She worked with men and lived with one, her father, but she saw none of them in their underwear. This was unacceptable. Her heart rate rising, the familiar tingle of adrenaline flinging itself around her body. There was no risk, but the fight-or-flight response was strong, she would not let him make her panic.

"A man is at the door who wants a word about your car.

Please pull your trousers up and speak with him." Anita said, moving as far away from him as practical while remaining in the same room. Shaking, she leaned into the doorframe to steady herself.

"Are you mad? You're the one who threw boiling water over me. How am I meant to walk with these burns? First degree burns I've got. Tell him to come see me here. I can't even walk. Damn near pulled my skin off when I took my trousers off. Got to it just in time."

Anita tried to hold back her tears, clenching her eyes shut, willing the man to put his trousers on. The image of his thick hairy thighs crawled through her, hammering against memories she'd fought hard to repress. Naked thighs pinning her onto the bed, scratching against her skin, bruising her.

"Second thoughts, tell him to come back tomorrow. He wants to talk cars, in this weather? *Muppet.* Anyway, tell him it's not for sale. What is he some country bumpkin? Got all excited about seeing a city car?"

"Might be a country bumpkin but at least I don't make girls cower in the corner. Stand up and pull on your pants," said the farmer, dripping in the kitchen doorway and glaring at Alan, who sat open-mouthed at the temerity of his words.

Anita's panic subsided and her body relaxed. The farmer was more a stranger than the lawyer yet he exuded the aura of a man of reliability. Unlike Alan, who was a worm and a bully.

Alan couldn't bluster his way out of this, not with his trousers round his ankles. Pulling them up, the belt buckle flapping around like a dying fish, Alan opened and closed his mouth like a fish, the power of speech lost.

"I don't intend being here more than the minute it will take me to tell you this. I know you. You're Alan Gate's little boy, so you sit there shtum and listen. You near killed me this morning. Forcing me off the road, screaming round the corners as if you were a rally driver, and in this weather. That tractor's my livelihood and I'll be billing you for the damage. You shame your father. If either of you knew what was good for you, you'd not stay here. Place isn't right. Never has been."

Alan tried interrupting, but the farmer wasn't having it.

"I've warned you and now I'll be sending my bill."

"Now hang on a minute you nutter," Alan said, his cheeks reddening, but the old man had left the kitchen.

Anita barrelled after him, almost colliding with him as he stopped to peer at the now luscious ferns adorning the hall.

"He's a bad apple that one. And this house. You watch the house. Sent Leo mad," he said, turning to look at her. Shuffling to the door he pulled it open with ease. Anita's last view of him was him making the sign of the cross before he bent into the sleet obscuring him.

CHAPTER 11

Anita busied herself with the art but with Alan looking over her shoulder it was a slow process. He fired a hundred questions at her as she worked and the incessant clicking of his pen more annoying than the inane questions he asked. The atmosphere in the house was heavy with an expected eruption, she felt her heart rate increasing with every moronic question, sapping her will to live.

"Why don't you know who that artist is? His signature is obvious, even an idiot could read it."

"Reading a signature doesn't mean the artist ever became famous or even well known," Anita said through gritted teeth. She had good manners and although the lawyer was a moron she tried to maintain the facade of civility. He was for all intents and purposes her employer, who'd engaged Nickleby's and could disengage them. A common bully capable of petty retaliation if ever confronted.

"Do you know the names of the artists in these local circles? Farmer Bumpkin and his band of merry pumpkin farmers or whatever they farm here. Nuts for a start," he said, laughing at his own joke, oblivious that Anita hadn't joined him in his mirth.

Breathing deeply she tried to explain the art scene, how painters evolved and why their social standing more often than not influenced their style. How every small town had its own amateur watercolour group or oil painting club, older residents who encouraged and championed each other regardless of talent. They churned out dozens or even hundreds of pieces of mediocre art, spawning annual art shows in church halls and community centres the world over. Add in talented high school students, art graduates, and stay at home mothers who dabbled in their spare time and you have a market flooded, in an apocalyptic sense, with art. Valuable only to those acquainted with the artist, the name behind the signature. Occasionally someone with a rare skill; an indefinable something, emerged onto the scene backed by a mentor from the art world who had been at the right exhibition at the right time to take the genius under their moneyed wing. You could call it fate, timing or luck. Even Botticelli would have faded into obscurity if it weren't for the Medici family.

"If I'd wanted an art history lecture I'd have gone back to college. So are you saying you don't know who these artists are because they're local hacks or because you're inept and shouldn't be here in the first place?" he sneered, leg resting on another chair as if he were an invalid and the chair an orthotic stool and not an antique of exquisite age. "Which is it?"

Alan sat there clicking his pen.

Could she swallow her pride and allow him to treat her this way? Was any career worth being belittled?

"I have my suspicions about who the artist is. But until I'm sure, I have to follow Nickleby's guidelines-"

"Which are?"

Anita smiled her own spiteful smile, "Company policy is that until we're certain or until we're sure we don't know, we mustn't release the artist's name. It's best to keep these things quiet. The art world is far more cutthroat than you'd be aware. Art theft is a profitable black market so I'm sure you, as a lawyer, understand the need for discretion."

Anita tucked her chin into her jersey, its woollen collar hiding the smile she couldn't wipe from her face. The lawyer was silent. Score one for her. It felt so good and her mood lifted to dizzying new heights. It didn't last.

A few clicks of his pen later and he dropped a bombshell. "I think I should stay the night."

"What?" Anita dropped the battery she was trying to insert into her camera. It bounced on the hearth tiles. Her good spirit evaporated. "Why?"

Alan shifted melodramatically in his chair, "It's my legs, the burn from the boiling water you spilt. It throbs so much, it'd be unsafe for me to drive in this state. The pain would be a distraction. Better safe than sorry, you understand that?" He turned a pair of puppy eyes on her as false as a Louis Vuitton bag on sale in a Balinese market.

Anita bit back what she wanted to say, choosing her words carefully. "It's a big house, rooms are already made up. Up to you." She retrieved the battery from the glazed tiles. Instead of the usual floral or geometric patterns, these tiles were pairs of ravens confined in a repeating diamond design, looking conspiratorially at each other. She sat on her haunches examining them. They were the distinctive blue used by Minton at the end of the 1800s, expensive and rare. There were similar ones in the British Museum but this was a whole hearth decorated with the creepy birds.

She straightened, ignoring the probing eyes she knew were ogling her. The disturbing gazes of the children on her bedroom wall preferable to the salacious looks from the lawyer.

"I need another battery, this one's damaged," she said and scooted past Alan's chair to the safety of the foyer and the staircase.

"Can you make me a coffee while you're at it?" Alan called behind her.

Her skin bristled at the effrontery of the man. Moronic sexist prick she thought and stomped up the stairs. A childlike response but well suited to the situation. Reaching her room she shivered in the cold, the central heating clearly wasn't on and it felt like worse weather was coming. Wiping condensation from the window confirmed her theory. Snow, billowing, brilliant snow. She'd been so engrossed in her work and her physical dislike of the lawyer, she hadn't noticed the absence of the soothing cadence of the rain, which had been replaced by the eerie silence of snow.

Anita rested her forehead against the glass, her breath fogging around her face. A small respite from the stress downstairs. Sighing, she retrieved the spare battery she'd come for and left the room, closing the door to trap a small measure of heat in the chilly room.

Behind her, an unseen hand wiped clean the misty fog Anita's breath left on the window. Tiny lines left by tiny fingers marred the otherwise clean window.

CHAPTER 12

Alan looked flushed, with a guilty aura surrounding him when she returned to the living room with her battery.

"All okay?" she asked.

"Yes, yes, it's my legs. I tried stretching them and, well, the pain was horrendous. Attempted to ring my office to let them know I won't be back in for a couple of days but I couldn't get a signal anywhere," he whined.

Ignoring his words, she seized upon the only thing she could answer without strangling him, "You can get a signal in the study or you could try the landline there. I haven't tried the phone because I assumed you had the services cancelled after the owner died?"

"Cancelled?"

"Yes, cancelled, so the estate doesn't pay out more than it has to. That's the usual way of things. Phone, power and water. Internet, gas, newspapers."

Alan laughed, "My office girl handles that drudgery. I focus on the more important aspects of estate management like building relationships and managing investments. Utility companies aren't my remit."

Alan had no one to ring back in the office. He hadn't replaced Alma but he needed to tell his golf buddy he might not make it to their game tomorrow. It was galling but keeping an eye on this inept, but pretty girl, was more pressing.

"And it's snowing," Anita added, pulling aside the curtains to look out the window. Fat snowflakes caressed the overgrown garden beyond the lounge window. "That'll affect the signal no matter where you try ringing from."

Alan sniffed. Snow was an unfortunate byproduct of the location and the time of year. The call could wait. He'd sit here and allow the little thing to wait on him while she worked and milk the sympathy. It was a fine thing having a woman wait on you. "Did you put the coffee on?"

Gritting her teeth, Anita didn't reply. She lowered her camera and stomped out of the room. The second time in the space of twenty minutes she'd reverted to toddler-like behaviour.

The rest of the day was arduous. She'd fashioned an acceptable meal once she lost the light she needed to examine the pieces she'd removed from the walls. The front foyer now resembled an art gallery waiting to hang a new exhibition. Small pictures jostled for space with larger frames. Gilt edging vied for attention amid glossy polished oak frames. Hand worked plaster frames adorned with cherubs and roses were out on their own. A large stack of art, yet only a fraction of what was still hanging on the walls.

Following on from an uncomfortable dinner where Alan spoke and she didn't, she made her excuses and escaped to her room. The unadorned walls and frigid temperatures more inviting than sharing space with the man she'd had to help climb the stairs.

The touch of his skin against hers was as appalling as the sight of his hairy thighs earlier in the day. She'd bitten her lip so hard helping him, she'd drawn blood. The smear of red across the back of her hand and the taste brought back its own terrifying memories and she was a wreck by the time she closed her door behind her. She fumbled for a key, leaving a bloody smear. Nothing. She sank to the floor, tears threading their way down her cheeks. She tried to tell herself he was no threat and unlikely to open her bedroom door in the middle of the night, smothering her screams with his pasty white hands. For sure his injury wasn't as serious as he made out but that didn't make him a rapist. Even thinking the word rapist set off another round of tears which threatened to freeze on her face if she continued sitting on the floor.

Logic struggled with fear but the battle was won when she dragged a wooden chair from the corner and thrust it under the door handle. Only then could she relax. Crawling into bed fully dressed, she pulled the covers over her. The marks of her tears still visible, tiny hiccups emanating from under the blankets until sleep stole her.

And on the door, her blood dried. Seeping into the old paint. It wasn't the first time bloody handprints had decorated the door, and it wouldn't be the last.

And upstairs the artist stood by the easel, his dark eyes clouded with something undefinable. Was it anger? Or concern? His slender fingers held his paintbrush above the canvas as he considered his next stroke. On the window seat, the little girl slid her gaze from the tumbling snowflakes to the man behind the easel. She knew that look and it didn't make her happy. Unfolding herself she cast her eye over the painting.

"There," she said, pointing to the unfinished eyes.

"Yes, you're right."

With the careful stroke of his sable brush, he pulled them downwards. Removing all trace of happiness he'd applied the night before.

CHAPTER 13

A morning disguised with papery snow, the horizon wiped from sight with the ocean no more visible than the Tooth Fairy. Crystallised snowflakes blanketed the earth, their geometric shapes merging with their neighbours. White clumps turned trees into shapeless blobs on the landscape. Every windowsill half obscured by snowdrifts trying to force their way inside.

Walking downstairs was like stepping into Narnia through the wardrobe. Anita's breath hung in the air and she fancied ice crumpled under her feet as she made her way down the hall. In contrast, the kitchen was warm — retaining a measure of heat from the night before and it didn't take long to get the kettle going.

She sat at the table and nursed her temples, a headache threatening. An Alan Gates sized headache. She had to push past it. Gods willing, her team would be here tomorrow and she still had most of the upstairs to do.

The kettle wailed, its strident scream reminiscent of a child's scream. Lifting it off the stovetop did nothing to lessen the wailing. Confused, Anita turned back to the oven.

She had turned it off so why could she still hear a panicked scream? She peered out the windows trying to locate the source, the wailing louder now.

Alan appeared in the doorway and the screaming stopped. As if a closing door cut it off, the way a bullet strikes down a raging bull.

"Did you hear that?" Anita asked.

"Hear what? Is that coffee you're making? Excellent, I had an appalling sleep, legs kept me awake the whole night. It could be an infection. I should really see a doctor."

"The screaming? You didn't hear it when you walked in the room?"

"I only heard the sound of that ancient kettle. Bloody thing, I'd finally dozed off and that antique woke me, though I'm more than happy to have a cup of coffee and eggs with a couple of strips of bacon if you don't mind."

Alan settled himself into a chair, groaning as he lifted his legs. It was then she noticed he was wearing a pair of gaudy Bermuda shorts, more at home on a geriatric cruise out of Florida than in the middle of winter. His shorts revealed legs covered in thick black hair, his thighs showing angry red welts from the scalding he'd received. Perhaps the theatrics were genuine. His thighs weren't as disturbing as the screams had been and Anita felt her anxiety rising. For once it wasn't caused by a man.

With much clashing of plates and grinding of teeth, Anita made the man his breakfast, studiously ignoring him as he mopped up his eggs with his toast, shuddering at his open-mouthed chewing. She escaped from the kitchen as soon as she'd eaten her own breakfast.

Back at work in the dining room, she couldn't help

glancing over her shoulder. What she expected to see, she couldn't have told anyone. She tried to rationalise the feeling something was awry; she was thrown off kilter being so near to a man. Following the deep breathing techniques her counsellor had taught her and mixed with the soothing repetitiveness of her work, her headache tapered off. It came crashing back when Alan stormed into the room, his injured legs all but forgotten.

"What the hell are you playing at?"

"Excuse me?"

"You were here to catalogue the art, not to paint it. You fancy yourself an artist, huh? God knows what sort of damage you've done mucking about upstairs. What if that was an unfinished Matisse or Picasso? It's not as if you'd know, you incompetent girl."

"I... what are you going on about? I've got no idea-"

"You enjoyed playing lady of the manor before I got here didn't you? It's just as well I checked on you. Should I check your car to see if you've spirited away anything valuable which you haven't catalogued, hmm?"

Anita stood up to battle the dinosaur in the room.

"What you are talking about? I'm just doing my job," she said, the words sticking in her throat.

"Oh, all high and mighty now are we? Trying to gloss over a serious breach of protocol, it won't wash with me missy. You city girls think you can get away with everything. Throw peroxide through your hair and slap on some war paint and bluff your way through? Not on my watch."

Anita shook her head. He was a lunatic or maybe he was high on drugs? Nothing he said made sense. Calming exercises forgotten, her breathing quickened, threatening a panic attack. Her eyes widened, hands fluttering like a sparrow trapped inside, struggling to escape. She sought the closest exit but before she could force herself to move Alan grabbed her arm and he pulled her from the dining room out to the foyer and up the hollow stairs.

Shocked, screams filled her head but never made it past her lips, such was her total paralysis. She shut down, a form of self preservation. She stumbled behind Alan upstairs, along the corridor to the door at the end of the hall. And up another staircase, the winding wooden turret stairwell. She bounced off the metal handrail, Alan too ensnared in his indignant righteousness to worry about her well being. Her logical self had never really considered him a threat; he was just a bully and hadn't shown signs of being violent. But now there was a strength hidden behind his pudgy belligerent self. And it terrified her.

No one would cheat Alan Gates Junior out of what was his. And certainly not this painted harlot. He'd get an apology from her and an admission. He'd not have it said anyone pulled one over on him. She was nothing but a pretty face. Everyone knew you could buy degrees on the internet. She'd probably used that worthless bit of paper to wheedle her way into Nickleby's. A ploy to steal from the collections she was handling during her work.

Undoubtedly she had valuable antiques and artwork stashed away in a storage locker. But this, what she'd done here, was inexcusable. Probably planned to palm it off to someone less knowledgeable than him as a priceless piece of art. She hadn't counted on his turning up. Hah, but now he had her.

Alan thrust Anita towards the easel. Hands on her shoulders, he held her in front of the canvas.

"There," he said, his pronouncement all encompassing, brooking no further discussion.

Anita slipped into a safe place in her mind. She was looking at the painting but couldn't see anything. Inside she was still screaming, flashbacks of the rape flashed in her brain, each image building on top of the preceding one, a shaky tower of the worst kind, where demons scrambled over each other, tormenting her again and again. The face on the canvas never registered with her and she crumpled to the floor.

CHAPTER 14

"Shit, shit, shit," Alan attempted to lift the unconscious Anita from the floor. He hauled her onto the window seat. Typical female, weak, taking the easy way out of the conflict.

The fragile cold against Anita's face forced her eyes to open and the scream she'd been holding in escaped. She skittered backwards, fleeing from the threat posed by the man shrouded in the shadows of the snow. Had he come back to rape her again?

Alan couldn't understand why she was screaming. It was irrational.

"For the love of all things you'll wake the dead with that noise. I'm asking you about the bloody painting."

Anita curled into a ball, hands clasped over her mouth stifling the scream which had torn at her throat. Her eyes flickered between the lawyer and the art. She couldn't focus and thoughts slipped wraith-like through her brain. The lawyer's words tried to force their way through to her traumatised mind, but nothing made sense. Her arms ached from where Alan had manhandled her, his naked legs standing over her. She retreated to a safe place in her mind.

Her eyes flicked back to the art on the easel and comprehension settled. Someone had mucked around with the unfinished portrait. Mucked around wasn't fair, the changes were beautiful; eyes mournful yet sharp. Eyes capable of seeing through subterfuge or any effort to doctor the truth. The brow was high, hair lightly sketched in around the woman's crown. There'd been an attempt on a jawline, but the artist had abandoned their efforts, leaving the face half formed. She tried gathering her thoughts. To consider the feasibility that the lawyer was an artist of some talent.

"What did you do to the portrait?" Anita asked, fear tempered by curiosity.

"What did I do? It's you missy who ruined this piece of art. You're not the next Van Gogh are you? This could have been worth thousands and now you've ruined it. A child can paint better than what you've slapped on this paper."

"Canvas."

"I beg your pardon?"

"It's not paper, it's canvas." Anita mumbled. Art she knew and focusing on it calmed her. The adrenaline which held her captive, ebbed away.

"I don't care if it's the Turin Shroud. You shouldn't have taken it into your little head to daub it with your own incompetent efforts."

"I didn't," Anita replied. "You must-"

Their conversation interrupted by the sound of screaming thrust through the windows by hurling winds, stopping Alan Gates in his tracks.

"What was that?"

Anita shook her head, too afraid to take her eyes off of him to look. The screams sounded childlike, like those she'd heard from the kitchen, but had put out of her mind.

Alan prowled around the turret, cleaning the foggy

windows with his sleeve, peering through the snowy curtain. His bare legs incongruous in the cold.

"An old bit of pipe loose rubbing against something in the wind I'd say," Alan decided.

"But what if it's a child? Maybe it's a farmer's child?" Anita countered.

"A child? Out there? Don't be daft. Look at the snow, how am I meant to drive home in this?"

Anita took her chance and ran from the room. No way was the screaming from a loose pipe. It was the scream of a child. She had no children herself, but a primal urge forced her downstairs to save a stranger's child.

Running to her room, she grabbed her coat, struggling into it as she flew downstairs. The screaming more muffled here, but intensifying as she ran towards the kitchen.

She had no gloves and her shoes weren't designed for snow, but she didn't hesitate. Zipping up her jacket and tightening the hood over her head, Anita wrenched open the back door and plunged into the icy wind. It grabbed at her, pummelling her from all directions, relentless. The high pitched wailing continued. She had no trouble following the sound. Apart from the crunching of snow underfoot and the blowing wind, the screaming was the only other sound.

There was no sign of the cattle she'd seen when she first arrived. Any half decent farmer would have moved them to shelter after hearing the weather report or smelling the snow. She'd once read about a farmer who swore he could smell snow and how this skill had saved his herd many times.

Anita stumbled, her city shoes no match for powdery snow disguising every root and raised garden bed. White virginal traps for the unwary. She glimpsed the summer house. The child must have taken shelter there.

"Hey it's okay, I'm coming," Anita yelled through numb lips and chattering teeth. She buried her hands deep under her armpits keeping them as warm as she could. She stumbled. The ground sloped and she reached out too late to grab a handful of shrub to stop her falling, landing heavily. She carried on, having trouble gripping the sheer surface, but pushed forward by the sound of sobbing. With renewed determination, she struck out faster, breaking into a run.

The cracking of glass filled the air. It was the cracking of the thin layer of ice covering the pond she was flailing across. Anita was oblivious to the risk, not realising the snow disguised a pond. A thinly iced over pond. Her only thought was of the child. To save the child.

And then the ice gave way.

CHAPTER 15

The cold was all-encompassing driving every thought from her mind other than self preservation. The cold even stole away her ability to scream.

Her jeans pulled her downwards; jacket morphing into an unwieldy straitjacket, obstructing every effort to move her arms.

She panicked, using all her energy to claw her way out. She was a competent swimmer but nothing could have prepared her for this. She kicked off her shoes which joined the flotsam and jetsam at the bottom of the pond — old-rimmed reading glasses, a serving spoon, and three pairs of old-fashioned leather shoes decaying on the silty bottom; their soles barely worn, the craftsmanship identical. One broken strap flapped from the disturbance above. A tiny wave.

The cold filled Anita's lungs. Snowflakes bounced against her face, as if they were enjoying her struggle, viewing it as a winter game.

She tried calling out for help, her voice losing the stridency it had had only moments before. She needed to take her coat off before its waterlogged fabric pulled her under but she couldn't get her fingers to grasp the zipper. Not that she was sure she knew how to work a zip now. Maybe she'd slip off her jeans instead.

Anita's head slipped under the water as she tried to undo the button on her jeans. It was quieter underneath the water, warmer too. Her jeans were fine, she didn't need them off, she'd float here a while.

She sank, her long hair marking her passage. Peace settled on her shoulders like a fur cape. Then her world exploded.

Hands like pincers ripped her from her watery cocoon, flinging her onto the snowy shore. Voices wavered over her, like terriers fighting over the newspaper. Angry yaps extolling her to wake up and snap out of it. Then she was flying, arms dangling behind her. Her snow covered world fading to black.

The muffled muttering of men's voices woke Anita. She tried to move but her arms felt pinned to her damp chest. She panicked. Clawing at the heavy blanket around her as she realised someone had removed her jeans.

No, no, no.

Who was in the room with her? What was going on? Too afraid to look and too terrified not to.

"She's awake."

"Course she is. Pulled that stunt because she got caught defacing valuable art," whined Alan.

"You be quiet. You've no idea what you're talking about. As I told the young lady, you'd both be better out of this house. Now she's awake, I'll be going. Keep her warm and get a mug of hot tea into her. This weather won't ease off for a day or two, so you're stuck here till then."

Anita watched the exchange, her memory coming back. They must have pulled her from the water, but someone had taken off her jeans and jacket. The thought that the men had undressed her filled her mouth with bile and her veins with adrenaline. Fear froze her.

"What happened?" she asked.

The other man in the room stomped over, leaning above her. His face a map of weathered lines and worried creases. It was the farmer whose tractor Alan had run off the road.

"Are you okay?"

Anita nodded, pulling the woollen blanket tighter around her shivering body, the scratchy fibres rasping at her goose prickled skin. Her fingers strayed to her ears, checking her studs were still there.

"You rescued me?"

"Yep, was out doing a final roundup of my stock, saw the lawyer dancing about like a headless chook. Didn't need to be a genius to figure something was up. You're not the first person to go into that pond, but not so many come out. Lucky someone saw you go in."

"Thank you. But the child, did you rescue them too? From the summer house?"

"What child?"

"There was! I heard her screaming." Anita sat up, "You've to go back out there."

"There's no child. I've told you that. They should have drained that pond years ago. There's no way anyone can get across to that place without a boat. No bridge, hasn't been for years. Forget it."

Anita sank back against the cushions, defeated by the tone in the farmer's voice. She knew she'd heard screaming, but she had no energy to go back herself. The farmer wasn't going to, and Alan was too chicken to risk his own neck. Tears filled her eyes. There was a child who needed help and no one cared. Maybe a runaway had taken shelter in the summer house?

She barely knew the farmer had been talking to her until he mentioned the other people who'd died in the pond.

"Who drowned?" Anita asked.

"Long time ago now. My parents used to tell us stories about it, to scare us kids from going anywhere near that place. Should have only been a foot deep but they dug too far down. Even a grown man can't touch the bottom-"

Alan interrupted, "Well it doesn't matter now does it? The new owners will fill it in, or put in a proper swimming pool since the hard work of digging has been done for them. Now I'd kill for a cup of coffee. God, I miss my espresso machine. Can't abide instant coffee, but it's the only thing here. May as well live in the dark ages, not even a damn electric kettle."

His grumbling continued long after he'd left the room. They exchanged a look conveying the same thought, moron. Anita wanted to ask again who'd died in the pond, but the farmer had moved on.

"His father was a good man, my lawyer too. Changed to a different firm after he died. More interested in appearances that one." The farmer shook his shaggy head. He paced around the living room, taking in the empty picture hooks and the barren dust rings on the shelves. "You've packed things up?"

"I'm only here for the portraits, the rest isn't my area of expertise, someone else is coming to do that," she said.

The farmer wiped a finger through a dust ring on the mantelpiece and through its twin on the other side. "Someone's been packing things up," he said, holding his finger out for Anita to see.

Anita swung her legs round till she was sitting up, the scratchy blanket tight under her arms.

"I have touched none of the chinaware, or anything other than the art," she said, challenging the farmer to believe her.

"Hmm," he said.

"I guess I should get changed, so…"

"… had to get you out of your wet clothes. You'd have caught your death if I'd left you in those. Didn't let Junior near you. Sent him to make a hot drink, worst coffee I've ever had," he chuckled.

Anita tried smiling. The mutual dislike of the lawyer a positive start, even though this man had seen more of her than her mother had in the past decade. It was a peculiar situation she found herself in.

"I'll go upstairs then…" Anita shuffled out of the room, the heavy blanket held tight against her skin. She'd started up the stairs when the farmer called out as he opened the front door.

"I'll be off. It's not the lawyer you need worry about in this house."

He'd ducked out and had shut the door before she could interpret his words. It wasn't the swirling snowflakes settling on the tiled floor making her shiver.

CHAPTER 16

A change of clothes had done little to dispel the chill which wormed itself around Anita's heart. The farmer's words leaving an imprint which worried at her as she pulled a sweatshirt on over her t-shirt. What had he meant?

Even her trusty bed socks wouldn't do much to warm her, so she rifled through the drawers in the bedroom. The dark mahogany chest of drawers were a goldmine of well-made clothes. Musty with age but still serviceable. She pushed through piles of cotton singlets and starched handkerchiefs yellowing with time. The next drawer delivered sensible skirts in various muted shades, with such tiny waists no modern woman could hope to fit them. In the bottom drawer she found hefty knit jerseys and lighter weight cashmere sweaters. Rolled up in one corner were pairs of thick woollen socks. Picking a pair at random, she pulled them free and noticed a tiny embroidered coin purse tucked into the corner. The catch rusty with age, she forced it open, tipping out its contents. A motley collection of costume jewellery, brooches and rings, missing one or two stones. She had a cursory poke through the things, nothing of any value.

Then her hand hovered over a shiny star-shaped brooch. She stroked its sharp corners, her chilly feet forgotten for the moment. It was a striking piece, most of the good paste pieces were. They'd been an essential part of every woman's jewellery box until fashions changed, leaving them gathering dust in drawers. Just like this one.

She returned it to the pile, her numb toes reminding her why she was here. She pulled on the socks, the itchy discomfort only bearable because of the instantaneous warmth they imparted. In her chunky socks, she padded downstairs, the pile of jewellery left for later.

She found Alan prowling the dining room. Her eyebrows disappeared into her hairline as his limp reappeared as soon as he noticed her in the doorway.

"Miserable weather. It's those jet streams from those foreign airlines which cause it you know," he said.

Anita refused to even consider responding to such a ludicrous assertion. How he'd ever passed the bar exam was beyond her. That he believed in poisonous jet streams showed severe failings in the school curriculum. A smile teased at the corners of her mouth as she tried to predict his next barmy statement. She couldn't decide between alien abduction or that fluoride in the water was the government's attempt to brainwash the population. He surprised her with his next comment.

"It could've been a ghost you heard, like a siren, luring sailors to their deaths on long sea voyages?"

Dumbfounded, Anita gawped at the lawyer.

"The farmer was right, it was the wind, blowing through old pipes, or forgotten machinery. I was an idiot, running outside in this weather. But it wasn't some ethereal being trying to lure me to my death. Where did you get your qualifications again?"

"Didn't sound like wind. Wouldn't surprise me if it was a

ghost. Anyway, why does it matter where I went to school? What matters is that I did. Don't try changing the subject, we still haven't finished our conversation from upstairs. Did you think playing that *poor little me* game would work? That old farmer may have bought your story, but you still need to explain why you defaced property which wasn't yours to touch. That piece of art in the turret could've been valuable. Who knows what damage you've done now." Alan dropped into the old carver chair at the head of the table, dramatically lifting his burnt leg onto the chair Anita had been using.

"I told you, I haven't touched the portrait. Whoever altered it has real skill." She faltered, "But maybe it was like that the whole time. To be honest, I hadn't looked that carefully. It was too cold up there, so I never got round to admiring the view. That's what drew my eye, more than the unfinished portrait."

"Before you got here, I'd had a good look at everything. Did my own stock take, wanted to make sure nothing went walkabout, if you know what I mean? You can gussy it up all you like, but the fact remains that someone has taken it upon themselves to finish it. And ruined it."

"Regardless of who did it, you can't say it's ruined," Anita retorted, her cheeks flushing. She took a deep breath. Confrontation was something she avoided. Her family were masters of brushing delicate topics under the carpet. She offered Gates an olive branch.

"Unless it's an unfinished Rembrandt, it will not be worth anything. So can we leave it? Both of us remember different things which is why we're confused about how much was painted. With so many pictures in one house, it's not surprising. The snow will keep us both here a little longer. And I presume the others won't get here until tomorrow, or even the day after, so shall we have a coffee?"

Gates nodded, mollified by her conciliatory tone.

"Coffee would be fantastic and with some biscuits too."

Anita disappeared to the kitchen. If this is what it would take to survive the next day, or heaven help her, the next two days, she'd play tea lady. She had to keep her anxiety under control. She needed to persuade herself that her unease was unnecessary. Why did she feel the need to keep checking over her shoulder? The screaming she'd heard did not sound like wind wailing through a pipe, but that was the only explanation. She shuddered. Closing her eyes, she waited for the kettle to boil. There's nothing here which can hurt you. There's no one here who can hurt you. You are safe. She repeated the mantra as the kettle boiled.

With the coffee delivered with slabs of fruit cake she'd found in the pantry, the atmosphere settled into something she could work with. Ignoring the lawyer's humming as he leafed through a stack of old National Geographic magazines, she carried on cataloguing the art.

"Did you know sharks only eat once every six weeks?" Alan announced.

"No."

The pages rustled, accompanied by soft exclamations and the occasional click of his silver pen, which was never far from his hand. Now and then he'd underline a passage in the magazine he was reading or circle a word.

"And did you know there's a place in England where people volunteer to dig up old Romans?"

"You mean archaeologists?"

"Lazy unemployed people on welfare, enjoying themselves thanks to generous handouts from the government. Though why you'd want to dig up Romans is beyond me. What did they ever give us? The Pope?"

She could explain underfloor heating and aqueducts but the man was an imbecile and she'd be wasting her breath. Instead she shook her head which Alan interpreted as she expected.

"See, they gave us nothing. Do they still print this stuff?" he asked, turning the magazine over to check the publication date. "This is from the Seventies. Who keeps magazines that long?"

"I guess the information is still factual," Anita said.

Alan grunted and stretched as if he'd been pouring over artwork with an eye loupe trying to discern the artist's signature and composition of each piece. He limped to where Anita was working, his body odour pushing forward despite the chill in the air.

"Who's that one by then?" he asked, peering at the art laying on the table, gesturing with his pen to a morose gentleman dressed in black, hunched over, his mouth a thin humourless slit.

"It's by the same artist who did the miniature portraits in the study. A lot of his art is in the house. He must have lived here or was a regular guest because most of the paintings are of people in these rooms. Although I haven't figured out which room this one was done in yet," Anita said.

The black clothed man was standing next to a fireplace. Which narrowed it down, but there were half a dozen fireplaces and Anita couldn't remember which was where. Not that it mattered for the auction catalogue, but it was an interesting observation. It would help with the provenance of each piece, which prudent buyers of art insisted upon. The prevalence of forgeries on the international art market was growing at an alarming rate. If a vendor couldn't prove provenance, the price plunged on downwards.

A ubiquitous Gingerbread Ansonia clock and a pair of white Parian Ware statues adorned the mantel. The statues were two halves of a whole; one, a naked Adonis poised with a sword, hate carved into his features. The other, a Medusa-like woman cowering beneath the threat of the sword. Hardly a relaxing shepherdess or a pair of loving suitors trading glances for eternity across the polished mantel. This pairing would give even the most sadistic of people uncomfortable dreams.

"He looks miserable," Alan commented.

"I suppose so, but he had to stand there for hours over several days until it was completed. These portraits weren't painted from a photograph like they are today," Anita said, tilting her head examining the expression of the man in the portrait. There was a tie pin stuck in his black silk cravat. Using her loupe she peered closer at the picture. Sometimes tying in a piece of family jewellery was enough to provide provenance and track the artist. Auction houses did it all the time. Easier with paintings featuring substantial articles of jewellery though, not just a tie pin.

The pin had a black enamelled border, the lettering too tiny for Anita to read but which appeared to be in Latin. A family motto? The enamel bordered a delicate swirl of hair, distinguishing it as mourning jewellery. Anita's mind flicked back to the children's gravestone. The death of any child would make a man look miserable, but the death of three would scar your face with a loss no artist could disguise.

Making a note on her computer, Anita heaved the portrait from the table, carrying him into the foyer. With the continual falling of snow, she was losing light and wouldn't be able to achieve any more today. She leaned him against the stack, the mournful face pleading with her to end his misery. Anita was about to walk away but couldn't leave him facing outwards, the pain in his eyes was too much. She turned him inwards, fitting it against the others waiting to be boxed up.

"I'm sorry," she whispered as she stroked the top of the frame.

Straightening, she turned to talk to Alan, who she assumed had joined her in the hallway, only to find no one there. Odd, she'd have sworn she'd heard him coming out. Anita turned around, her socks sliding across the polished tiles. A full circle, but nothing. She could now hear Alan mumbling to himself in the other room. But she could've sworn she'd heard someone else moving about. Old houses, she told herself, but that didn't stop her skin prickling despite the woolly socks and sweater.

She took a few steps back towards the dining room before a flicker up the staircase caught her eye. Nothing there, shadows. Shaking her head, she hurried back to the dining room. Alan's company better than the irrational fear she was experiencing.

Alan was studying one of the paintings and Anita froze in the doorway when she saw what he held in his hands. It had been the portrait of Abraham. Had been, because now the portrait was empty. The man painted sitting in a chair, head bowed with dark eyes looking towards the artist, had gone. The frame devoid of any sign of him. It was as if someone had taken an eraser to the canvas and removed any trace of the man.

CHAPTER 17

Bile rose in Anita's throat and she swivelled her head as if the errant Abraham was lounging in the room somewhere. She must be dreaming. There were no words to describe what she was seeing. Utter disbelief coursed through her.

Walking over to the canvas, her fingers stroked the old paint. The ridges familiar territory and the scent of linseed oil clung to the canvas. There was no sign this painting had been anything other than a sparse architectural composition.

"I don't... I don't understand," she said.

"What? Oh this piece, unusual isn't it? A picture of the corner of this room," Alan said, pointing to the fireplace.

"There was a man in the painting, sitting on the chair," Anita whispered.

"What? Sorry, didn't hear you. This one certainly stands out, far less creepy than the others on the walls. I like it."

"But there's nobody in it," Anita said, pointing at the empty painting.

Alan looked at her oddly before leaning the painting

against the wall. Limping back to his chair, he sighed as he sat, as if in pain.

"It'll be the shock of falling into the pond I expect. Dinner and a drop of wine should fix it," he said, clicking his pen.

Anita's face was a picture of agony, she couldn't drag her eyes away from the empty frame. It would have been better if the canvas itself had disappeared. There had been a man, she'd described him and she'd taken photos. The photos!

Tapping at the keyboard until it powered up, she scrolled through the hundreds of photos of the art she'd catalogued. She didn't notice the battery icon was red, the percentage slipping past critical. Scrolling quickly, her eyes scanning every photograph as they sped past. There! She scrolled back up, and the laptop powered off.

"What?"

Confused, she pressed the power button. No response. Her hand followed the power cable until she reached the plug she'd never plugged in.

"Oh no!" she said, running her fingers through her hair looking at the black screen, praying the computer would power on.

"Should've charged it," the lawyer said. "Good time to prepare dinner then I'd say. How about you find a place to charge it, then we can eat?"

"But the painting…" Anita's voice trembled. She knew what had been in the painting and the photos confirmed it. She just had no idea how it had happened.

"Try the study. Off you go," Alan interrupted.

Anita fled.

Once she'd gone, Alan tried to make himself comfortable. Alan had no time for foolish girls and their fanciful imaginations.

The more he saw of this girl, the more he considered her unsuited to the task, and he was hungry. No golf, no club dinner. It was turning into a dire week stuck in this chilly old pile. Still, maybe she'd surprise him and make a decent meal. Wine would make it better. Wine made everything better.

He wasn't exaggerating the pain, his legs bloody hurt. After that obnoxious farmer had yelled at him, he'd put on a pair of trousers and the fabric was rubbing uncomfortably. At this rate he'd need more than a bottle of wine to get to sleep tonight. He'd be compensated for his discomfort and pain, that was for sure.

Gingerly he lifted his legs onto the other chair, every movement made the cheap cotton fibres scrape away at the raw skin. He closed his eyes, grimacing, so never saw the shadowy figure in the doorway watching him. Dark eyes calculating.

A foreign hand reached towards the bakelite switch.

Flick

The room plunged into darkness. The elegant chandelier snuffed out.

"Hey what's going on Anita?" Alan called out. "Has the power gone off?"

Alan got to his feet and lumbered around until he found the wall where he ran his meaty hands along the flocked wallpaper until he hit the light switch. Flicking it up and down elicited no response from the chandelier which remained in darkness. Alan didn't know if it was a power failure, or a blown bulb.

"Anita?"

No reply, the kitchen too far away for her to have heard. He'd have expected her to come back to the dining room if the power had failed.

He edged out into the dark foyer. The sun had set, so

what little light the snow had let through during the day was gone. The foyer was in complete darkness.

"Anita, are you there?" Alan's voice wavered. He'd never liked the dark. It was his biggest fear; that and being poor. Not that he could imagine that, only stupid people were poor, but anyone could be afraid of the dark.

Bumping into the furniture in the dining room set his legs on fire and excruciating pain ran through his thighs as he crept along the wall. He'd forgotten about the stacks of paintings.

He stumbled into the first stack, sending portraits scattering like a pack of playing cards in the wind. Disoriented in the dark by the crashing of the frames, instead of heading towards the kitchen, Alan inched his way along the opposite corridor, calling to Anita. Panting, one hand groping the wall, the other probing the darkness in front of him, rounding a corner, he careered into a dark mahogany plant stand. The planter jettisoned off the top, smashing into a hundred jagged edged shards. The desiccated remains of the fern joined the broken pottery.

"ANITA," Alan yelled, his eyes wide, the whites the only spark of light in the hallway, his anxiety rising.

Behind him walked a shadowy form, a masculine figure, an older soul. One who hadn't expected to be walking these corridors again. In the gloom he stretched, his black suit showing no signs of ageing, uneaten by moths or time. Adjusting his cravat, he straightened the tiepin which had moved as he'd climbed out of his frame.

CHAPTER 18

Anita plugged the laptop into the one power point. She wanted to wait till the laptop had powered up, but a sense of guilt over Alan's legs and her own rumbling stomach sent her to the kitchen. She puzzled over the portrait, worrying at it like a dog with a bone, she forgot what she was doing until she found herself standing in the kitchen with a wooden spoon. She couldn't shake the crazy thoughts crowding her mind, they were too fantastical. She tortured her brain for a logical explanation, perhaps there were two paintings and the lawyer had found the second one — an early draft of the completed portrait. Maybe the original painting was in the foyer with the others? That was the only explanation. If true, why hadn't Alan said anything? Trust him to get joy out of playing mind games.

Still, a seed of doubt niggled at her, whispering there was only one painting. She would have remembered if there'd been a partial study of the portrait somewhere else in the house. She pushed the problem away, ignoring it for her own sanity. Satisfied she'd figured out a solution, as convoluted as it was, she resumed her efforts in making a dinner for them both. She also persuaded herself that purposely burning the lawyer's meal would be childish.

An ancient radio lurked behind a letter rack and a salt-glazed pot, filled with coins, milk tokens and orphaned buttons. If she'd tipped out the pot, she would have found a gold cufflink inlaid with the same enamelling on the tiepin in the painting she'd catalogued.

The batteries had enough life left to power the radio and she spun the dial until she found a station playing static-free music. Turning the volume up, she set to preparing a meal with the diminishing supplies in the fridge and pantry. At this rate they'd have to experiment with the cans hidden at the back of the pantry whose labels had become adrift. She didn't fancy encountering a can of cat food twenty years past its use-by date. She sent a silent prayer to the weather gods that the snow reinforcements would arrive soon. The concert performance disguised the crashing of the wooden frames and drowned out the house's creaks and groans. Anita carried on cooking, serving the meal normally reserved for the end of the pay week, leftovers.

Anita finished one glass of wine while cooking; a hearty red which knocked the edge off the unease swirling around her, leaving only a dash more than a glass in the bottle.

Pouring it into her glass she left it on the kitchen counter for later, putting the empty bottle by the back door for recycling. She'd tell Alan that there was none left and given it was unlikely he'd wander into the kitchen tonight, she'd be able to enjoy it in solace as she did the dishes. Anita laughed at the thought of the pudgy lawyer offering to help. No, the glass of wine would be safe for her to drink at her leisure later. She'd be able to curl up on the chair with a book and the wine, safe from the lawyer's glances and obnoxious comments.

The radio reminded her of her mother's kitchen

radio; permanently tuned to a talkback station. Anita despised talkback, but it gave her mother a measure of comfort on her long days at home. She'd rather listen to Polish folk music than talkback.

There'd be something on the study shelves she could read. The kitchen more homely though, less intimidating. Anita shrugged. She had to charge her computer and needed to be somewhere where the lawyer wasn't. Work-wise she wouldn't achieve anything until tomorrow. The study then, straight after dinner, stuff the dishes.

Oblivious to the lawyer's frantic cries, she laid out the plates on a butlers tray she'd found next to the refrigerator. Brushing the dust off showed half a dozen different inlaid woods arranged in a floral pattern in the centre. All native timbers from the region, but more unusually, intact. No pieces of the marquetry were missing, which given its art nouveau riches and its probable age, was a miracle. Swapping out her glass of wine for two tumblers of water, she picked up the tray. Conscious she was still only wearing socks, she manoeuvred her way through the door and down the hall.

Leaving the warmth of the kitchen, there was no light in the hall. She hadn't turned the lights on, on her way to the kitchen, and she had no hands free to now. Bugger. She didn't want to carry the heavy tray back. She knew the way to the dining room off by heart so the lack of lighting wasn't an issue, but as she made her way down the hall, a weird feeling settled on her, making the tray even heavier.

Her elbow hit one of the taller plant stands, slopping water over the dinner.

"Shit," Anita mumbled, changing to a more centred course.

"Alan, open the door?" she called out as she emerged into the foyer. Idiot must have shut the door because there was no light to guide her.

"Can you please open the door," Anita tried again.

Acting subservient to live and work in peace was not worth it. She wasn't sure if she'd be able to cope much longer if the lawyer was staying, although giving up went against her nature. She'd worked so hard to get to where she was, to overcome her fear of strangers and of being somewhere alone. This job was her new leaf, a fresh start without fear holding her back.

"Alan?"

Grinding her teeth, she bumped her hip against the door and overbalanced. It wasn't shut at all and Anita tumbled into the void, the dinner flew through the air. Anita screamed before landing atop a mash of watery bacon and wilted greens.

"Alan, turn on the bloody light."

The light flicked on.

Alan wasn't there but Anita didn't notice, she was on her knees trying to scoop up the ruined meal. She decided if she faced the lawyer she'd say something which would be career suicide. Prudence over pain won out.

One plate and both glasses broke, with Murphy's Law dictating that the broken pieces travelled further than physics allowed. Her hackles rose as she fumbled with the broken crockery. She was about to stand up, her tray heaped with glass and congealing food, when she spied something wedged under the table.

She wiggled the tiny piece of metal until it sprung free from its prison under the brass claw foot of the table. A gold shirt stud, edged with black enamel. It had a sense of familiarity. Not at all valuable without the rest of the set but if it was gold there would be a residual value. She added it to the tray and stood up, ready to face the lawyer. But he wasn't there.

"Idiot," Anita muttered, walking out of the dining room, the tray held tight against her stomach.

In the foyer she stood aghast. The darkness had disguised the mess but the light from the dining room showed frames strewn across the entire foyer. At least one looked like a foot had gone through the face of the portrait, a gaping hole in the centre. She couldn't hold back the tears.

She lowered the tray to the ground, the shirt stud forgotten. Turning the lights on revealed the carnage inflicted by Alan's flailing about. She couldn't help the murderous rage which thudded through her veins. If he even dared to show his face she'd kill him.

She moved the damaged paintings to one side, their gilt frames crumbling under her hands despite her careful efforts. Most of the paintings had fallen face down, saving them from further damage. The recycled sarking on their backs protecting them, for an eternity or until someone deconstructed them for something else. It happened all the time. Fashions changed. Families fell out. Various subjects considered immoral after a change in church or leader, so they'd remove the picture and have something else framed in its place, or stapled over the top. Art restorers the world over stumbled across masterpieces hidden for decades, or centuries, under more modern pieces.

Anita pushed the first stack against the wall, satisfied these weren't damaged. She bent to grab a smaller frame which had half slipped under an occasional table.

She picked it up to check for damage, and screamed.

CHAPTER 19

Anita dropped the frame, scuttling backwards until she hit the wall. The painting crashed onto the marble tiles; the sound echoing throughout the house.

"Alan? Alan, where are you?"

Anita's hands were shaking. She pressed them against the wall. The empty frame stared back at her. This she wasn't imagining. It was the frame which contained the portrait of the little girl. And now it was empty. Oh, for sure it still contained a piece of canvas, with the likeness of a small dinghy at the forefront. But it was as if the little girl had stepped away from the boat, dashing away from the artist to join her brothers and sister. It was impossible.

"ALAN?" Anita cried out, never once taking her eyes off the empty portrait. There was no response.

Anita inched her way towards the front door, the breeze from outside nudging her ankles through the bottom of the door. Wrenching the door open, she searched for Alan from the relative warmth of the doorway. The front porch blanketed with unmarked snow, the driveway showing two misshapen lumps — her car and Alan's, with no sign of the pudgy lawyer. He was still inside then, somewhere, playing games with her.

She slammed the door shut, turning back to the foyer, heart thudding in her chest. There at the top of the stairs, a flash of white and running footsteps.

Anita cursed and ran to the staircase. Bugger her career, this guy was an idiot and she'd had enough.

In her socks, she flew up the stairs in time to hear the turret door slam shut. The foyer light didn't penetrate that far, but sound carried and now she knew where he was.

Right then, let's have it out.

Without thinking about last time, Anita made her way along the hall. The light from her bedroom stretched far enough for her to reach the turret door without hitting the plant stands dotted along the walls.

She ran up the stairs, rage fuelling her speed until she reached the top, where in the middle of the turret room stood the stool and the easel, and nothing else.

Anita spun round. He'd come up here, she'd seen him at the top of the stairs. Heard him running. There was nowhere for him to hide.

"Alan?"

The anger from moments earlier replaced with the fear she'd felt downstairs. She couldn't pinpoint what was going on, but someone was playing games with her, and the joke wasn't funny.

There was no light switch in the turret room, only moonlight diffused though the falling snow. The portrait on the easel a smudge in the night, featureless and unfinished, and Anita was grateful it was too dark to see it.

She sat on the window seat, pulling her knees up to her chest, clasping them with her arms and watched the door.

Two could play at this game. The storm outside no distraction to the fear which was her constant companion. Confident that sooner or later Alan would tire of playing the cat to her mouse and hunt her out, she'd wait.

Anita woke with a start, her body cramping on the horsehair seat. She rubbed her face, waiting for daylight to break. Darkness greeted her as her eyes adjusted.

She stretched out her legs and massaged the back of her neck. She'd fallen asleep waiting for Alan to tire of his childish games and with no phone she didn't know how long she'd been out. Her uninterrupted view of the quarter moon and a galaxy of stars proved that the snow had stopped. She stood up, legs protesting at the sudden stretching of muscles. Anita's stomach rumbled. Memories of the ruined dinner and the damaged art swept in. Damn him. She'd wake him and give him something to jump at, serve him right for playing with her as if she were a marionette doll.

She slipped downstairs in the moonlight, her empty stomach and the wish for revenge more pressing than the unfinished portrait standing sentinel. A painting now sporting flowing locks of dark brown hair peppered with hints of fiery auburn. Hair very much like Anita's own.

Anita shuffled along the hallway, the pins and needles in her legs taking their own sweet time to work their way out. The hall was lit by the light coming from her bedroom doorway. Alan's door shut tight.

"Wanker," whispered Anita as she stood outside.

Tempted to hammer on his door like an angry landlord, she found her hand lifting as if by magic, poised to strike. And again, her upbringing stopped her and she lowered her arm, eyes downcast. Keep the peace, make peace, do nothing to upset the apple cart. God she hated herself sometimes. Where was her backbone? Somewhere in the 1800s she suspected. Women hadn't come as far as she thought. Still subservient, playing second fiddle.

She turned away, making her way back to the kitchen. She was hungry and there'd be no more sleeping for her tonight until she'd had something to eat.

At the bottom of the staircase, she skirted the paintings in the foyer. She didn't know how Alan had pulled it off, but the state of the art in the foyer made her skin crawl. She didn't believe in ghosts but apprehension settled on her shoulders, chilling her, which was nothing to do with the cold upstairs.

In the sanctuary of the kitchen, with its familiar appliances, and with the radio tuned to a concert programme, she felt safer than she had upstairs, or in the foyer. Humming along with the music she opened the fridge. She took the cheese, ham, and pickle back to the bench where the last of bread was in the wooden bread bin. This would be a fantastic sandwich and she experienced a moment of peace. She'd never spent much time in her mother's kitchen — it had been at the other end of the house, but kitchens always seemed safe. It's easy to be happy when you're surrounded by the sensual smells of food.

Sandwich made, she found a plate. She needed to do the dishes now she was running out of clean crockery. She remembered the glass of wine she'd poured. Wine and a sandwich, the perfect partnership.

Turning to where she'd left the glass earlier in the night, her hand hovered. It wasn't there. She looked around the sink, the bench, the scrubbed pine table. Gone. Her hands clenched into fists, she tried to breathe through her anger. Not only had the bastard ruined dinner and damaged the art but he'd damn well stolen her drink too.

Her appetite gone, she forced the sandwich down, regardless. A glass of tap water did nothing to sate her thirst. She'd wanted that wine. Like an alcoholic, she knew nothing would soothe the craving she had until that first sip of wine was past her lips. She'd drunk like a madwoman after the rape; it was the only way she could sleep, eschewing the sleeping pills her doctor had prescribed. She preferred self medicating with wine. Lots of wine. With great difficulty, she'd weaned herself off her bottle a night habit after seeing the recycling bin full one morning. Full to overflowing, and not with milk bottles or jam jars, but of sour smelling empty bottles of pinot noir and cheap shiraz. She needed a drink.

Opening cupboards and shifting jars around in the pantry uncovered no wine. It wouldn't surprise her if the bastard lawyer had whipped it before she'd arrived. She slammed the cupboards, hoping the sound would make its way upstairs and wake him.

"Stuff it," she said, before flicking the lights off, too upset to worry about the near total darkness in the hallway. She almost turned the foyer light off, but self-preservation stepped in. Leaving it on, she hurried upstairs, slamming her bedroom door shut. All pretence of polite civility absent now.

And in the study, a man sat at the desk, savouring the taste of the wine on his tongue. A newer vintage than him, but old enough that it could be savoured, the echo of long summers captured in the glass. He gazed at the unframed canvas propped on the bookcase. It's not his best work. Nothing done in haste is ever truly great, but it is a fair likeness. He was particularly proud of the eyes, they held the right shade of surprise.

On the floor, the little girl in the white dress doodles with a silver ballpoint pen, fascinated by the sound the spring makes every time she presses it.

They pass their time in companionable silence, the clicking of the pen the only distraction.

CHAPTER 20

Winter sun filled the bedroom, cloaking the room in a false summer haze. The insinuation of warmth was enough that Anita woke up happy. The trauma of the previous day left behind to the terrors of night.

She climbed out of bed. Today she'd ignore Alan. Losing her cool with him was unprofessional. She was not a toddler; she was a grown woman doing a job.

Comfort won out over glamour. A chunky jersey, the woollen socks she'd worn yesterday, jeans. Nothing fancy, just warm. She hoped the rest of the team would arrive soon with provisions. She considered the contents of the kitchen as she walked downstairs. Alan's door was still shut. Good, he could make his own breakfast. She wasn't a scullery maid nor a housekeeper.

There wasn't much left worth eating, as far as she could recall, and a scout through the fridge confirmed it. She uncovered a container of oats of unknown age. Adding milk and a liberal serving of sugar might make a palatable bowl of porridge, leaving enough milk for her coffee.

Tipping the milk into the saucepan and mug, she placed

the empty bottle next to the wine bottle. That'd teach him to finish her glass of wine. The stovetop made quick work of the porridge, and the sugar improved everything. Her stomach full, she made her way back to the dining room to start work before remembering her laptop was in the study.

Spinning on her socks she set off down a different corridor, the hallway Alan had last walked.

In the poor lighting she didn't see the overturned plant stand until a shard of pottery pierced her woollen sock, sinking itself into her soft heel.

"Christ!"

Her eyes adjusted to the dim light, the soil and broken pottery littering the hallway like the rubbish from a dorm room after party. She righted the wooden plant stand, piling the larger pieces of broken pottery on top. There wasn't much she could do about the dirt, especially since her heel hurt so much. She limped into the study, sinking into the nearest armchair.

The lamp wouldn't work because her laptop was using its power point so, unplugging her laptop, she replaced the plug for the lamp. The light was meagre but enough to see the spread of blood on the bottom of her sock. Peeling it off, she checked the wound. It felt worse than it looked despite the blood pulsing from the small puncture.

Pressing on the wound with the bloody sock, she cast her eyes around the room. She'd love a room like this one day. Her parents had bookcases filled with modern thrillers, Clive Cussler, Stephen King, and a few high-fantasy epics her mother preferred. But this was a library, filled with true classics. First editions, rare folios, and, another portrait? How had she missed that? Another one of Alan's games, moving the art around the house?

She checked her laptop, its full battery bar a reassuring sign that charging it overnight had worked, now she'd be able to scroll through the images until she found the ones where the subjects weren't missing. She was over being played and arming herself with evidence was the best defence. If it wasn't Alan, it had to be someone he was in cahoots with. Although god knows why someone would want to stall her or try to scare her. The job she was doing would only benefit the lawyer in the long run and it went against every moral code and business code for him to derail her work.

Speeding through, she couldn't believe she'd done as much as she had. She'd forgotten how much she'd achieved with all the drama from yesterday. She smiled. There were lots of rooms to do, but she'd broken the back of it. And fingers crossed, her colleagues would arrive today. Hopefully the snow ploughs were going this far out, the farmers still had to get to town.

Image after image flashed by, she tried not to think about the people missing from the portraits. She persuaded herself that those paintings were sketches of the final sitting, done so that the subjects in the portraits didn't have to sit for too long. She couldn't concentrate. Her eyes kept sliding around the study. She stabbed at the keyboard again, scrolling, scrolling. Her eyes blurred. Too many photos going past, she must have missed them. She scrolled up to the top, admonishing herself to be slower, when a sudden hammering at the door jolted her from her chair.

The farmer thought Anita, and she limped back to the foyer, laptop under one arm. It sounded like he was trying to break down the door so she hobbled faster, grimacing each time her heel hit the floor.

Awkwardly balancing on one foot, and the ball of the other, she tugged the heavy door open. It wasn't the ancient-lined face of the farmer who greeted her.

✳

Lined up on the steps, laden with overnight cases and an assortment of grocery bags were the rest of her team from work. Surprise gave way to relief and she flung herself at her colleagues, who laughed awkwardly. None of them had ever seen any form of emotion from Anita. She was a closed book which they'd discussed at length on the drive and the enforced overnight stay at the nearest town due to the heavy dumping of snow.

"Thank god you're here. You've no idea how much there is to do. Although I've done a lot, and I was running out of food, and wine," Anita laughed, before whispering, "And the lawyer for the estate is here. He's still in bed but he's an odd one, wait till you meet him. I burnt his legs, but it was an accident, and I finished the milk today, and, oh, thank god you're here." Anita tapered off, her hand straying to her ear, twisting the small diamond, round and round.

She didn't know these people well, about the same way you'd be familiar with a neighbour on the other side of the road. You waved at them, could recognise the car they drove, had an inkling about how many people lived there and noticed they used a cleaner once a week. But Anita knew nothing more than surface facts about her colleagues. She'd never asked. Rarely attended social engagements. Wasn't part of the work social club, and other than a lukewarm involvement with the once-a-year Secret Santa at work, she didn't socialise with them. Yet here she was, sharing her thoughts, and feelings, and hugging them. She stepped back.

"Please come in. It's freezing out there."

The trio traipsed in, three pairs of eyes scanning the cavernous foyer. Calculating eyes counting the frames stacked against the walls. Judgemental eyes taking in the tray of food Anita had left on the floor outside the dining room and Anita's dishevelled appearance.

Blushing, Anita realised she'd not had a wash or brushed her teeth since the day before. She wasn't vain but her hands fluttered to her hair and clamped her lips over her teeth, mortified she'd gushed over her colleagues with sour morning breath.

"My god, I never realised there were so many paintings," said Yvonne Hamilton, her high pitched voice at odds with her age and appearance. Yvonne peeled off her coat and scarf, hanging them on the hall stand. "Such a shame these are ruined," she said, holding up one of the damaged paintings. The same paintings Anita suspected Alan of standing on, which was why he was hiding in his room, because he didn't have the courage to face her wrath.

"This is half of them," Anita said, closing the door behind them. Not that it made much difference to the temperature.

"Christ, it was tropical in the car compared to here," said Scott Jacka, shivering in his lightweight crewneck jersey, his jacket on the backseat of the car still.

Anita nodded. Scott was around her age. Good looking, the sort who knew he was, so made no effort to be friendly. He didn't have to, for all his vanity, he had an encyclopaedic knowledge of books, stamps, coins and other such collectibles, and travelled the country at the beck and call of wealthy collectors and institutions.

"Sorry, I've not been able to figure out the heating. Come through to the kitchen where it's warmer and I can make coffee, as long as you've brought milk?" Anita limped off towards the kitchen, trusting they'd follow her. The third member of the team hadn't bothered to say anything, he stood there taking it all in. Callaghan Webb, Furniture Division. Stocky, silent, his hands stained with furniture polishes, stains and dyes. Anita had rarely spoken to him at work other than the usual morning greetings and small talk in the office kitchen, so wasn't surprised he'd held his tongue in the foyer.

"I don't know when Alan will appear," she burbled. "He's the lawyer," she added. "Where's Warren?" Warren Taylor, her manager. He'd told her he'd come too. A friendly face who was missing.

"Something came up, a great aunt died. He's the closest relative, so had to arrange the funeral and things. He left you a message, didn't you get it?" Yvonne flittered about the kitchen, peering in cupboards, drawers, and out the frosty window. "This place is a time warp," she said, stroking the wooden bench and fiddling with the bakelite knobs on the transistor. Roaring static filled the room as she turned it on. "Doesn't even work," she said, flicking it off.

"No coffee machine?" Scott asked, watching as Anita coaxed the old stovetop into life to boil the kettle.

Anita buried her frustration at the mirrored questions Scott was asking, so like Alan, it was unsettling. Where Alan was pasty and overweight, Scott had a runners physique. She'd seen him taking off from work, backpack on, jogging home. He'd no more end up as unfit as Alan Gates as she would become the President of the United States.

"No coffee machine," she replied, busying herself with mugs and spoons, amused by the look of anguish on Scott's face.

Callaghan fished out the milk, unscrewing the lid before handing it to her, all without catching her eye. His eyes flicked over the kitchen, homing in on the little pot of change on the bench. Callaghan tipped it out, discounting the coins which skittered across the table and onto the floor.

With his finger, he pushed through the pile. Intermingled among the coins were milk tokens, a tin Saint Christopher's medal and a cufflink. The matching cufflink to the shirt stud Anita had found in the dining room.

"This is a nice one Yvonne," Callaghan said, pushing the lone cufflink across the table.

Yvonne pulled a loupe from her cavernous handbag, fitting it into her eye socket with precision, freeing her hands to hold the cufflink.

"Such a shame there's only one, such a lovely piece, the enamel work is in perfect condition. Usually you'd see tiny chips, but there aren't any," said Yvonne, her face a mask of concentration.

"May I look?" Anita asked.

Yvonne's loupe slipped from her eye, and she caught it expert-like before handing over the cufflink.

Anita examined it, "I found a shirt stud last night which matches, in the dining room, where I've been working, wedged under the table."

"Marvellous," Yvonne gushed. "Where is it?"

Anita blushed. She'd left it on the tray amongst dismembered broccoli and stagnating rashers of bacon adorned with fluff and detritus from the floor.

"I'll go grab it, you guys drink your coffee, and I'll be right back." Anita fled, skidding on the foyer's tiles as she reached the tray. She couldn't carry this into the kitchen. What would they think of her? She never once considered that they'd arrive so early, counting on them not arriving till after lunch at the earliest. She'd have to hide it until later, when they were all in their rooms.

Casting about for a suitable hiding place, she felt like an utter ninny, and didn't want word getting back to Warren that she was lazy. She was already embarrassed by the pile of dishes in the sink. God, they must think she's an uncouth slob. She shot up the stairs with the tray. She'd leave it in her room and would clean it later. Swiping the stud from the tray, she gave it a good rub with a handkerchief from the top drawer. The faint smell of talcum powder still clung to its pressed cotton folds. Closing her bedroom door, she hammered on Alan's door, telling him the team from Nickleby's had arrived, complete with provisions.

There was no answer. Fine, let him sulk. At least they'd be able to get a start on things without him interrupting. He could stay there all day for all she cared. She felt a touch of anxiety as she walked away from his room. A touch which she shrugged off. She needed to show Yvonne the enamelled stud.

CHAPTER 21

"Could this house be any creepier?" Yvonne exclaimed, the coffee kick-starting her brain. The others in the kitchen nodded their agreement. "Did you hear about what happened here? Do you think Anita knows? Did anyone tell her?"

"Warren didn't want to tell her while she was here by herself," Callaghan replied, sipping the bitter brew. It wasn't the best coffee he'd had, but then again he hadn't made it and it was the only coffee on offer. Beggars can't be choosers, his life motto.

"Warren wasn't going to tell me what?" Anita replied, walking back into the kitchen.

Callaghan subsided into his mug, mute once more. Scott took up where Yvonne left off, his social skills as lacking as his modesty.

"The children who went missing, murdered probably. Their bodies never found. Complete scandal. Family claimed they drowned in a pond, but come on, a pond? They would have floated to the surface, or someone could have jumped in and saved them. If you read the local history pages, there's loads of theories about what happened. Murdered by the mother's boyfriend being one of them."

"That's not helpful conjecture," Callaghan commented, watching Anita's face pale. It was interesting observing her process this information. He felt a little sorry for her. She wasn't the most social of colleagues, but even being in this house the short time he'd been was unsettling. He'd no idea how she'd coped for the last few nights. Idly, he wondered how well she was sleeping.

"How many children went missing?" Anita asked, the gold stud held tight in her hand, its sharp sides cutting into her flesh.

Scott pondered the question a moment, "No idea, I remember reading it was children and not child. Still, tragic. Have you heard them wailing at night?" he waved his fingers in a poor attempt at imitating a spooky Halloween ghost.

"Stop it Scott," Callaghan said, tiring of Scott's childish play. "Have you finished your coffee? Good, let's get unpacked and finish cataloguing this house. The weather forecast is for more snow at the end of the week. We need to be done before the truck arrives to take everything back for the auction."

Scott, immune to the warning in Callaghan's voice, drained his coffee, grimacing at the artificial taste. It would be a long week if this was the standard of coffee he'd be drinking every morning.

The scraping of chairs, the rinsing of coffee cups and congenial chatter filled the kitchen. There was no way anyone would have heard the muffled cries from elsewhere in the house. Cries cut short with the sweep of a sable brush.

CHAPTER 22

The team of appraisers worked like a well-oiled machine; each had their speciality and knew where the boundaries between each discipline were and they weren't above helping each other either. Even Scott, for all his foibles, was a good team player, expert not only in his field but with passable knowledge in a dozen different areas.

"Hey Scott, can you come and look at this?" Yvonne called from the dining room.

Scott left the shoebox of stamps he'd discovered on a shelf in the drawing room. It amused him how people stored their stamp collections in shoe boxes. Of all the boxes ever designed, shoe boxes were the most common sort of storage repository he handled. Some of his clients kept thousands of dollars worth of stamps in boxes held together with yellowing tape.

"What have you got?"

"What do you think this mark is? I can't read it, and I don't want to take a stab at guessing," Yvonne passed over the small silver salver.

"Looks like *London*, there's an *F*, is that a crown on the top? Can't work out the second initial, an *H* or *K*. Sorry."

"It's a *K*, with a crown and definitely the leopard's head, but can't make out the year, *1770* or *1772*?"

"Could be. Who's the maker then, if it's an *F* and *K*?" Scott asked.

Yvonne tilted her head, like a squirrel determining the best way up a tree. *"Fred Knopfell?* His work is standard run-of-the-mill stuff, but this is a nice piece. He was a journeyman for *Paul de Lamerie*, but with none of his flair, unfortunately. Still it'll fetch a fair price at auction, because of *Knopfell's* link to *de Lamiere*."

Coding it with a sticker, Yvonne moving the small piece onto the table, to join the pile of other treasures she'd catalogued. It was easier to describe marked silverware than a stylised signature on an obscure piece of art.

Scott returned to the stamp collection. A glance showed a standard assortment of twentieth century stamps, all postally used. It wasn't worth his time sorting through the collection. He'd auction it as a box lot and good luck to the person who bid on it. There wouldn't be a *Penny Black* hidden amongst them, there never was. In his early years he expected every bulk lot was hiding a gem and that if he looked carefully enough he'd discover that rare postage frank or stamp and make his millions. But those days were long gone.

Callaghan joined him in the drawing room. As the resident furniture expert, his job was the easiest of the group. Older furniture is bulkier than modern pieces and more likely to come in pairs or suites, so it was faster to describe a set of twelve Gothic Revival dining chairs than it was to itemise the contents of a jewellery box or a box of stamps.

"Have you seen the lawyer yet?" Callaghan asked, taking a seat on the couch.

Scott shook his head before standing and stretching.

Hunching over the shoebox had given him an uncomfortable crick in his neck.

"One of us should get him out of bed. It would be a courtesy to us showing his face," Callaghan said. He had no time for laziness.

Scott abandoned his stamps, the gleeful little boy inside jumping at the chance to take a break. Walking through the dining room, he noted Anita hunched over a corner of a wooden frame. She was an odd one that one. Quiet, but intense at the same time. Aside from the ridiculously enthusiastic welcome she'd given them when they'd arrived, she'd pretty much not said a word since.

Giving Anita no more thought, he bounded up the stairs. They'd not even ventured upstairs yet, having got straight to work after the coffee conscious they had limited daylight hours. The hall stretched for miles, interrupted at intervals by tightly shut doors. He hadn't asked Anita which room was the lawyer's, so tried the first one. The door opened revealing clothing strewn across the floor and bed. A tray of what looked liked last night's dinner sat on the dressing table and the large bed was unmade, covers thrown back, pillows clumped together like a feathered nest. Ah, Anita's room. Unlike the rest of the house, these walls were empty. He didn't blame her for starting here. He hoped like hell she'd emptied his room too as he didn't fancy sleeping in a room full of long-dead, dour-faced portraits like the ones downstairs. God knows the dreams they'd conjure up. He pulled the door shut and moved on to the next one.

He raised his hand ready to knock. Something didn't feel right and his hand fell to his side. Scott looked down the hall. He could have sworn all the doors were shut, but now the one at the end was open. Mind you, it was an old house and these things happened. Probably when he opened Anita's door, the air pressure changed or... *Jesus*, now he was being paranoid.

Ignoring the open door, he knocked on the door in front of him, which was bound to be the lawyer's room, a forceful no nonsense knocking. The sound rang out through the house and the fronds of the nearest fern quivered with the reverberations. There was no answer. Scott tried again. Nothing.

Gripping the brass handle, he turned it and the door opened silently. He'd been right, this was obviously Alan's room. Placed on the floor at the end of the bed were the lawyer's ruined brogues and his trousers lay folded across an ancient wooden trouser press. Loose change and a cellphone the only adornments on the heavy mahogany campaign chest which served as the dressing table. Of the lawyer, there was no sign. He'd slept here at some stage, the covers loosely pulled up, as if he'd attempted to make the bed, but had lost interest halfway through.

Scott stepped into the room, his curiosity piqued. On the opposite wall stood a huge freestanding wardrobe. He admired himself in the mirrored middle section and self-consciously tidied his hair and tucked his shirt in, smoothing out the creases from the long car trip. He pulled open the left-hand side door of the wardrobe; the hinges protesting. Heavy winter coats hung in a line with military precision, sporting tiny holes, the victims of fashion conscious moths. Scott pushed the coats to one side, coughing as the movement disturbed decades of dust. The fabric fibres tickling his nose. He sneezed, the sound unnaturally loud in the room. Aside from an old pair of ice-skates, the bottom was empty. Scott turned his attention to the other side. He didn't expect to find the lawyer cowering there but instinct told him to check anyway.

Grabbing the tear drop door handle, he tugged hard,

expecting the hinges to resist as much as the other doors had. It opened smoothly.

The absence of dust and moth carcasses the most striking thing about this side of the panelled wardrobe. Pairs of polished shoes lined the base and wooden shoe lasts sat like prosthetic feet in every shoe. A line of men's suits hung smooth on their hangers. A black scarf wound around one hanger the only jarring note.

Scott closed the door and held it shut. For reasons he couldn't articulate, the suits and shoes struck him as wrong. The winter coats on the other side oozed the scent of decay, and the sleeve of his jersey was peppered with dust from where he'd moved the coats. Yet this side was pristine, cleaner than his wardrobe at home.

He backed away from the wardrobe as the door slowly swung open and hung like a slack-jawed idiot.

Scott froze. His reflected image could well have been a portrait. Like a startled rabbit, he hurried from the room without looking back, racing downstairs, taking them two at a time, he tripped as he reached the bottom and barrelled into the dining room. Heart racing, he grasped the back of a chair for support. He had no words.

Anita looked up from her laptop. The light from the chandelier reflected on the sheen of sweat on Scott's brow.

"What's wrong?"

"Nothing, just ran down the stairs, thought I was fitter than this," Scott coughed, covering his discomfort. His knuckles white, he unclenched his hands and stretched his fingers before wiping the perspiration from his forehead.

"Was Alan still asleep?"

"He wasn't in his room." Scott said.

"Maybe he was in the bathroom?" she said.

Scott grunted. It was possible that the lawyer had been in the toilet but there was no way he was going to look.

Irrational he knew, but he wasn't going back upstairs unless someone came with him. Not that he'd ever say that to Anita, or to anyone else.

"He'll turn up I'm sure, anyway I've got heaps to carry on with in here," he said, pointing to the drawing room.

He looked out to the shadowy foyer, before darting back into the drawing room. Anita's eyes followed him, before she too looked out into the familiar foyer. She couldn't see, or hear, anything out of the ordinary.

CHAPTER 23

"What did the lawyer say?" Callaghan asked, dropping heavily into an armchair.

"He wasn't in his room," Scott replied, not meeting Callaghan's eyes.

Callaghan observed his colleague for a moment, noting his flushed cheeks and the throbbing vein at Scott's temple. "That's weird."

"Ah huh," Scott said, his head bent low over the box of stamps. Stamps he'd not normally have paid any attention to.

"Did you look around?"

"No," Scott replied abruptly, putting an end to the conversation.

Callaghan's eyes travelled around the room, taking in the voids on the mantelpiece, and the gaps on the walls where Anita had removed the art. It was an interesting collection. The contents ranged from early Victorian, right through the Arts and Crafts movement. Colonial American was well represented. The silverware seemed to be mainly from Continental Europe and there was a smattering of Oriental and Islamic pieces — large Cloisonné vases and Persian fritware bowls. He leaned forward in his seat, he'd recognised a small glass-fronted bookcase in the corner, an oak Craftsman bookcase by Gustav Stickley. It wasn't filled with books, only half the shelves had leather clad tomes on them. The others, an assortment of tiny ornaments - Japanese *netsuke*.

"Did you see the bookcase?" Callaghan asked, pulling on the arrowhead drop handles to open the doors.

Scott didn't answer but Callaghan didn't care, entranced not only by the oak bookcase but by its contents. He'd spied *netsuke* carved from amber, ivory and nephrite jade. Running the gamut from stylised animals to simpler pieces, there must have been over two dozen carved pieces on display.

Reverently he held the first one up to the pale light, turning it over in his hands. Smooth to the touch, cool, the amber fox radiated an ethereal light, beautiful. Laying it to one side, he picked up the next one. Pale jade, it was in the form of a dog, torturously twisted upon itself. The workmanship was exquisite despite the grotesque nature of the piece.

"These are amazing, Scott. I'm surprised you haven't looked at them yet," Callaghan said. Again there was no answer. "Scott?" Callaghan turned around. Stamps lay across the coffee table where Scott had been working, but there was no sign of his colleague. Weird. He hadn't even noticed him leaving the room. Shrugging it off, he emptied the bookcase of the *netsukes* and lined them up on the mantelpiece, moving the old clock to one side, smudging the empty dust rings.

Out of the bookcase, the exquisite sculptures captured the light and glimmered with life. What a collection, not his particular area of expertise, but he could appreciate the skill which went into crafting these collectible pieces. Scott would know more. They'd fetch good prices at auction given the quality of the carving, garnering better prices if signed, which, in this light, he'd never be able to discern.

"Scott?"

Callaghan walked into the dining room, one *netsuke* clasped in his hand. Anita was where he'd last seen her, the pile of frames stacked around her testament to her work ethic.

"Where did Scott go?"

Anita looked up from a portrait of a woman kneeling in a wooden pew, hands in supplication. For a moment, Anita's face mirrored the haunting features of the woman in the painting. Callaghan blinked, and Anita returned to herself.

"Sorry, I wasn't paying attention. Did he go to make a coffee?"

Callaghan murmured under his breath and leaving Anita to her task, he walked towards the kitchen. Yvonne had based herself at the kitchen table, in the warmest room in the house, and the one with the best lighting — natural and electrical. The table covered with baubles and trinkets, covering the spectrum from precious metals to fairground kitsch. She'd come prepared with hundreds of various sized zip-lock bags, and a stack of small boxes which she assembled as required. She had a particular left-to-right arrangement going, and for only having been at work for a couple of hours, she'd made huge headway.

"Looks like you've got things under control here," Callaghan said.

"This is from a quick once round downstairs. I've not even bothered going deep yet. Nothing too spectacular, more silver plate than silverware, but still some nice pieces. Mind you, it was the art we're here for. Anita has a big job ahead of her. I don't envy her that."

"Have you seen Scott?" Callaghan asked.

"No, I thought he was with you?"

"He was, but now he's not. I thought he'd come in here for lunch."

"It's just been me in here. Has the lawyer shown his face yet? Maybe Scott's found him and they're upstairs having a chat?"

Callaghan nodded, fingers dancing over the carving of the dog, the smoothness unnatural yet calming, soothing.

Yvonne caught sight of the jade in Callaghan's hands.

"What have you found?"

Yvonne scraped back her chair and reached for Callaghan's hands. In the briefest of moments as she fought to open his hand, the tiny jade creature fell through his fingers and the pearls on Yvonne's finger flashed like lightning. The jade dog tumbled in slow motion through the air before its tortuous body crashed to the kitchen floor. The second it hit the ground, a howling rent the air.

CHAPTER 24

The sound echoed through the house causing Anita to look up from her work. The lawyer had mentioned a dog. Checking the window she saw nothing but snow outside. Walking through to the drawing room, ignoring the stamps, she crossed to the patio doors. Outside was a mess of paw prints in the snow, large paw prints, heading past the house towards the mausoleum. Was that where the dog was sheltering?

She was hungry and couldn't see the dog, so gave it no more thought. Checking the clock on the mantel she was surprised it was already two o'clock, it was no wonder she was starving.

Carrying the pile of completed art into the foyer, she stacked them with the rest. The stacks were growing at a satisfying rate although the damaged pieces stared at her from their resting place by the wall. She picked up the mutilated painting of a child; one of the boys, hard to tell now which one. Turning it over to check the name, and a tiny bundle fell out — a lock of blonde hair, tied together with a thin black ribbon. A lock of the boy's hair? Unusual for something like this to be hidden between the canvas and the sarking.

Anita fingered the hair and looked back to the damaged frame. The two needed to be together, but if she tucked the small bundle back into the edge of the frame, it might come adrift again when the packers turned up. She slipped the package into her pocket, she'd find a bag in the kitchen for it and would tape the bag to the back of the frame. She doubted the auction house would pay for restoration, but someone had gone to the trouble of keeping the child's hair with his portrait, so the least she could do was to ensure that they stayed together.

She found Yvonne and Callaghan, heads together, peering out the window.

"Are you looking for the dog?" she asked.

They spun around.

"Did you hear it too?" Yvonne asked.

"I heard it from the dining room but I think it's gone down the back of the property. Its footprints are outside the patio door, in the snow."

Relief flooded Yvonne's face. "So there really was a dog?" she said.

Anita started to reply when Yvonne laughed. A laugh which didn't quite make it all the way to her eyes which were directed towards Callaghan, who hadn't moved from the window.

"Alan said there'd been a dog here before the owner passed away. He said he hadn't seen it. My guess is that someone else has been caring for it and it's run off and has finally found its way home."

"Sounds reasonable," Callaghan said, bending to retrieve a tiny piece of jade on the floor, adding it to a small pile on the counter.

"What's that?" asked Anita.

"I broke a *netsuke*," Yvonne replied. "Bloody stupid of me. A *netsuke* shaped like a-"

Callaghan interrupted, "It was an accident, and doesn't matter now. I'll clean up and then we can have lunch."

Yvonne pursed her lips and retook her seat at the table.

Anita sensed something was unsaid in the room, but asking those tricky social questions had never been her style. Brushing it off, she asked "I'll track down Scott then, and Alan. They're probably upstairs in the turret. Okay?"

The two other people nodded, the silence uncomfortable.

After Anita had left the kitchen, Yvonne turned on Callaghan.

"Why'd you interrupt me? It doesn't matter that it was a carving of a dog, I was making an observation."

"Anita doesn't need your observations, the dog was a coincidence that's all."

Callaghan thrust his hands into his pockets and caressed the undamaged dog head he'd pocketed when he'd cleaned up the broken *netsuke*. It remained a piece of exquisite carving and while the rest had shattered, he couldn't let this fragment go in the bin. He returned to the window.

Yvonne interrupted his musings by announcing her gnawing hunger pains. Callaghan stepped back just as a dark shape shot through the undergrowth at the end of the garden. Catching movement from the corner of his eye, he turned an instant too late. Whatever it was he'd seen had gone and outside everything was still, the landscape silent. Even the gulls were absent from the skies.

CHAPTER 25

Anita limped upstairs, her heel aching more now. She joked to herself that she'd have supermodel thighs if she did this for a few more days. Ignoring her own door, she paused outside Alan's. It was ajar, but still she knocked before pushing the door open. The room was empty. Alan had laid out a suit on the bed. She hadn't realised he'd brought a change of clothes with him. Maybe that's what he'd been doing today; grabbing clean clothes from his car, having a bath, trying to be a better companion given how long they'd been forced to stay together?

She wandered along the hall, pausing at the bathroom door. She knocked, then turned the knob. The door opened to the bathroom she'd come to love. The empty bathroom, her toiletries poised by the basin and beside the porcelain bath. If he'd had a bath, he'd cleaned up after himself. There were no telltale damp patches on the rag rug nor was the mirror fogged with steam.

That only left the turret room. Anita hesitated. She reached the door and pulled it open and heard the quiet tones of someone's voice. Too soft for her to make out who was talking, but loud enough to boost her confidence.

Taking a deep breath, ignoring her memories of the last time she was up here, she mounted the stairs. And there, lolling on the window seat, legs stretched out, was Scott on his cellphone. He held up a finger so Anita paused on the top step. The rest of the room was empty. She wasn't disappointed but there was something peculiar about Alan hiding from them.

"Hey sorry, you know what girls are like. Had to call her and couldn't get any reception anywhere else in this place." Scott shoved his phone into his pocket and stretched.

"We were going to eat lunch," Anita said.

"Excellent I'm starving. Has your lawyer appeared yet?"

"No, I thought you were with him," she said. "Up here."

"Nope, just me," he said. "Come on then, let's eat."

Shooing her downstairs, Anita never had time to see the painting on the easel. Flexing her fingers, she tried to ignore the peculiar tingling in her fingertips, pinched nerves she thought.

When Scott and Anita joined the others in the kitchen, the tension between Callaghan and Yvonne dissipated. With the coffee brewed and the bread sliced, the tangy scent of pickle and yeasty bread filled the room.

Anita joined in with the light-hearted banter. She still felt somewhat like an outsider, the youngest on the team and the least experienced but at least the others treated her as an equal and for that she was grateful, and together they would shoulder the mammoth task ahead of them.

The main topic of conversation was the whereabouts of the lawyer. Scott's contribution muted. He wouldn't be drawn on theorising about where the lawyer might have gone. Callaghan had stood at the bottom of the staircase with his coffee mug bellowing out the lawyer's name, before returning to the kitchen and shaking his head.

"We should check outside," Yvonne suggested.

"He's been outside, because he's laid out clean clothes on his bed," said Anita.

Scott looked up from the crumbs on his plate he'd been playing with.

"There was nothing on his bed when I looked," he said.

"So he went out to his car, came back in and then went back outside to grab something else. I'll look. He could have slipped over." Callaghan said.

Yvonne leapt up and made to join him.

"It's freezing outside Yvonne, you stay here. I'll just go get my coat."

Of the three people in the kitchen, only two were talking. Scott sat silently at the table, his leg twitching under the table. There had been no suit on the bed. Suits were hanging in the wardrobe, but they weren't laid out on the bed. Mind you, he'd been upstairs talking to Shelby so could have missed the lawyer going back into his room.

Somewhere in the house a door banged shut.

Scott jumped as if shot. Yvonne laughed at his reaction.

"Come on Scott, it was just a door," she said.

Anita looked at Scott, unnaturally reserved, pale even. A bead of sweat appeared on his brow. Fascinated, Anita watched it quiver before it slipped down his face and fell unheeded to the table.

"What's wrong?"

"Huh?"

"What's wrong? You look like death warmed up," Anita observed.

Scott shrugged, before finding his swagger. It wasn't his style to be morose but this house had that effect.

"Ah, it's nothing. This fresh air is getting to me. I'm a city boy, give me a polluted city with free flowing espresso, and I'll be fine."

"Do you think Cal locked himself out?" Yvonne asked. "When the door slammed?"

"It was probably a door upstairs. The front door is far too heavy, anyway the doors here swing open left, right and centre and none of the windows seal properly," said Anita.

"Come on, let's see what's going on out there." Scott was full of bravado now, concealing his true anxiety. Persuading himself that the lawyer had laid out the suit on the bed.

Yvonne and Anita exchanged bewildered glances as they hurried behind him.

The front door was open, ushering the subzero temperatures into the house. Callaghan was stomping around outside in the snow, head down like a bloodhound, hands deep in his pockets. The trio trooped out onto the steps to watch.

"Find anything?" Scott asked, shivering on the porch.

Callaghan shook his head. Pacing around the lawyer's car, the blanket of snow a giveaway that no one had touched the little red sports car since the snow had fallen. Callaghan rubbed his forearm against the driver's window and peered in.

"What's he looking for?" Anita whispered to Yvonne.

"A body?" Yvonne offered.

"Stop it you two," Scott snapped, before turning around and vanishing inside.

"What are you looking for?" Anita called out to Callaghan. Regardless of the fact it was freezing, Alan going missing made her uncomfortable. The others hadn't even met him. What if they thought she'd done something to him?

She huddled further into herself. Her ankle aching in the cold, and on her opposite foot, her heel throbbed from standing on the broken pottery. It wasn't helping her mood any that Callaghan had vanished from sight.

He reappeared, his cheeks rosy from the bitter weather, his breath puffing out in great plumes. He climbed the steps, his face a picture of confusion. Turning to look at the cars in the driveway, he finally answered. "He's not in his car, and he hasn't been out here. The only footprints out here are mine. There were paw prints going around the side of the house but no sign it's attacked a grown man out here, so we can safely discount that theory. He's got to be inside." He looked at Anita, holding her gaze a moment too long until she dropped her eyes. "Do you think he's hiding from us?" he asked, his question barely audible over the waves at the bottom of the cliffs.

Anita shook her head, inexplicable shame infusing her cheeks. "No, sorry, I don't know," she said, avoiding Callaghan's eyes, looking instead towards a sky slicked with flickers of pink and yellow. The sun set early at this time of year. She stretched out her hand and rubbed her tingling fingers, the pins and needles sensation now travelling up her arm.

Callaghan continued to stare at her. "We'll do a proper search inside," he said, walking inside, leaving the girls on the doorstep.

Anita and Yvonne followed him, grateful to be closing the door on the cold behind them.

If they'd looked up they would have seen two figures behind the windows of the turret, staring at them. Conferring between themselves before the sun sank too far below the horizon for anything to be seen other than shadows.

CHAPTER 26

It was a subdued group who convened in the drawing room but the sight of the beginnings of a fire inflated the mood. Scott had coaxed one up using the pine cones and kindling and the team mingled uneasily within reach of its warmth. Anita focused on a cone tottering atop the pyre. It brought back memories of one portrait she'd catalogued. She imagined the man from Jerusalem laying his pine cone on the fire, watching the flames lick at the scales, charring the edges until the fire took hold and the cones surrendered to the heat.

Pained howling of a dog saw four heads swing towards the window. The flame's reflection distorting the view outside, making the landscape buckle and dance. The depth of the blackness swallowing any sign of the howling creature.

"Did he go out this door?" Yvonne asked, hand on the door handle. It turned easily and ushered in a gust of icy tentacles which whipped around the room. The fire spluttered in the hearth and Anita shivered. The anguished howls of the dog echoed through the room. No one moved, the spell of the hound holding them motionless.

"I went out through that door, before," Anita said, breaking the silence. Normality struck the room.

"So the lawyer could have gone out here then?" Callaghan said.

"And he's out there, with that dog, who's starving to death, ripping him to shreds as we speak…"

"Yvonne, that's not helpful. Come on Scott, we'll have a look. Keep the door shut after us and don't let the dog in if it comes sniffing around." With that, Callaghan ducked outside, still wearing his bulky jacket. Scott trailed behind, his expression thunderous.

Anita pushed the door shut behind them and pressed her face to the window, her forehead leaving an oily imprint on the thin glass.

"Can you see anything?"

"No," Anita said.

Yvonne cupped her hands around her eyes and peered out into the gardens, ignoring her obese rings which scratched against the glass. A dog hurled itself against the fragile doors — a furious baying bundle of fur, teeth, paws and tail.

The old brassware strained under the assault, threatening to give way. The flames of the fire reflected in the dog's wild eyes. Its teeth stark white against its black coat. It threw itself again at the glass, snarling. The doors rattled, their wooden frames flexing under the weight of the huge animal.

A crash of statuary, a yelp and the dog ran off. The shouts of the men yelling at the creature echoed out through the night.

Yvonne and Anita fled to the safety of the far door when the dog appeared, screaming like schoolgirls. Their screams gave way to embarrassed laughs. It was just a dog. Scott and Callaghan had thrown something at it, something heavy which smashed on the paving stones.

They pushed off from each other and crept away from the window, as if the mere sound of their voices would tempt the dog back. The door handle turned and the men hurried inside stomping snow from their shoes. Mid conversation, they didn't acknowledge the others.

"You didn't hit it."

"I did. Didn't you see it limping as it ran off?"

"You should've let me throw the bloody statue," Scott said, slamming the door shut behind them.

"There wasn't time to agree on a plan," Callaghan replied.

"It could've turned on us you know. You should've told me what your plan was. Damn stupid thing to do, What if you'd missed? We'd be dog food now?"

"I didn't miss. Anyway, it's gone now." Moving over to the fire, Callaghan rubbed his hands in front of the flames, "Christ it's cold out."

"Did you hit the dog?" Anita asked.

"He didn't hit, just scared it off. It'll come back. Meaner than before," Scott said.

"Stop it," said Callaghan.

"Stop what? I'm just saying what the others are thinking. That the dog attacked Anita's lawyer, and now it's hungry for more. When a dog attacks a sheep, the dog gets put down because once it's tasted a sheep, it wants more. Same thing here."

"It is not the same thing. We found nothing to show the lawyer had even been outside, let alone attacked by a starving dog. Now give it up. I've got work to do and you should carry on with yours, too. I don't give a toss about the lawyer. He's a big boy. He can sort himself out. If his leg is as sore as you said it was Anita, maybe one of his friends came to pick him up. I for one will not worry about it. Now excuse me." Callaghan marched off.

Anita rubbed her arm. The tingling hadn't abated. It had worsened.

"I'll be in the dining room," she said, and returned to her seat at the table, hopeful that a fraction of the fire's warmth would follow her into the room.

Yvonne was next to leave, back to the kitchen to work on the selection she'd gathered earlier, leaving Scott standing by the fire.

Scott took a brittle pine cone out of the wood box and pulled out the scales, tossing them into the flames one by one, the sap spitting and sizzling in the heat. His watch said it was only four o'clock, yet it felt closer to eight. This job would be a long drawn out one. It was then he noticed the *netsukes* Callaghan had left on the mantel. Such tiny pieces of workmanship, each figure its own work of art, mostly macabre. There was a miniature skull entwined with a serpent; a stylised dog, standing over another skull, which was particularly disconcerting... And the last one which took his eye was a heaving morass of rats gnawing at a decomposing skeleton.

Scott imagined he could feel the hungry rodents chomping at his shadow. Shuddering, he moved back into the dining room where Anita was hunched over her laptop, someone else could pack the gruesome *netsukes* up, he wasn't going to touch them.

"How many portraits are left to do?" Scott asked.

Anita thought about it for a moment, "I haven't dared to count them. I'm doing one room at a time. There are so many, I don't think I've even scratched the surface." She considered her next words. She didn't want her colleagues to suspect she was losing her marbles, but Alan going missing was eating her up. "What do you think happened to Alan? I mean, I know you didn't meet him, but I don't understand why he left without saying. And without his car?"

"Did you scare him off?" Scott asked, laughing at his own joke.

"No, but he damaged some of the art, and I'm worried he's taken a few of the pieces. At least three I can work out."

"There you go, he worked out they were more valuable than the others and whipped them from under your nose. Case closed, Sherlock."

Anita shook her head, it wasn't that simple. Scott laughing it off made her doubt herself more. Maybe it was that simple?

"The missing pictures aren't valuable, I don't even know who the artist is yet. They're responsible for at least a third of the pictures here, but…"

"I wouldn't worry about it," Scott sniffed. "I'll go work in another room and leave you to it. He'll probably waltz back in at any moment. Don't even think about him. I won't be."

Scott walked out, his back straight, hands in his pockets. Hands clenched tight. He may have put on a brave face for Anita, but the missing lawyer and his experience in the lawyer's room unsettled him more than he wanted to admit.

The clock in the drawing room struck six o'clock. Its melodic chimes reverberating around the house. Four heads lifted and as one, they made their way to the kitchen. The darkness outside was complete, and the chill inside pervasive.

The Nickleby's team had brought with them the required ingredients for any great dinner: Wine, cheese, crackers, quality eye fillet steak, and readymade salads. Anita coaxed the ancient stove into life, the flame sputtering with the strike of a match. The hiss of the gas filled the room, followed by the heat from the flames.

Scott wielded a heavy duty iron skillet he'd found buried

beneath a mountain of baking trays, whilst Callaghan pulled the cork from a bottle of wine. It was a convivial setting, four friends eating together, unencumbered by modern life, no one checking their cellphones, or firing off a quick email. There was no one saying I've just got to make this quick call.

The aroma of well-cooked steaks filled the kitchen, as did inane gossip about coworkers and pay rates, the art market and the president. Normal topics of conversation — the gold price, the cost of food in the staff canteen. The weather. By unspoken agreement there was no mention of the lawyer, or the dog. During the dinner, somewhere through the second bottle of red, one of them would pause, gaze into the blackness outside, and strain for any sound of the dog, or the sound of anything troubling. An impartial observer may not have noticed the sudden dip in conversation as each of the participants trailed off at different times, their thoughts elsewhere.

The phone rang.

Not an iPhone, a Nokia, or even a Samsung ringtone, but an old fashioned one with a cord and a bakelite handle. A phone you only saw in the movies or museums. The phone in the study.

"I'll get it," said Yvonne, and shot out of the kitchen.

The others lapsed into silence as if the absence of their lynchpin had rendered them incapable of conversation. Callaghan fiddled with the jadeite dog head in his pocket. Scott pulled out his redundant cellphone and scrolled through the pictures he'd taken during the day. Sideboards, bookcases, balloon backed chairs, plant stands and campaign chests. All nice and all saleable, nothing extraordinary though, just run of the mill good quality stuff. It bored him senseless.

Yvonne returned, a curious look on her face. In one hand she held an unframed canvas, her other she held in front of her, rubbing her fingers together as if she trying to rub away a foul substance she'd accidentally touched.

"I found this in the study," she said, offering the canvas to the others. "The paint's still wet, so which one of you painted this then?"

Anita reached for the canvas, her fingers smearing the edges of the still wet paint. The likeness was unmistakable. It was a perfect rendering of Alan Gates, the lawyer. His eyes wide, mouth held open as if he were mid shout, or scream.

Her own mouth froze open and her legs crumpled from underneath her.

CHAPTER 27

"It's Alan, Alan Gates, the lawyer," Anita said. "Where did you find it?"

Callaghan and Yvonne struggled to lift Anita from the floor and onto the chair. Yvonne's fingers leaving smears of red oil paint on Anita's sleeves.

"It was in the study," Yvonne said.

She'd emptied the study of all the portraits. This one hadn't been there. Unframed, just a stretched canvas. Her nostrils flared at the smell of fresh paint, panic poured off her. She dabbed at a corner. Wet white paint transferred to her finger, like some hideous skin condition. Alan must have painted it. He was toying with her. It couldn't have been anyone else. As much as she tried to make sense of it, her body wouldn't react to any of her signals. It wanted to run, far away from this house, and the art which filled it.

Scott sat nonplussed at the table. He didn't know Anita well but this portrait thing was taking things too far. Doubts crowded in upon his head. Was this girl for real? What game was she playing at?

"Who was on the phone Yvonne?" he asked.

Irritation flashed across Yvonne's face. She and Callaghan were still trying to manhandle Anita into the chair.

"What?"

"Who was on the phone? Remember, you ran off to answer the ringing contraption somewhere in the house?"

"Does it matter? God, can't you see Anita is unwell," Yvonne spat.

Callaghan filled a glass from the tap. The ancient pipes shuddering with the sudden shut off of the flow of water. He passed it to Anita, whose trembling paint tainted hands struggled to hold it.

The portrait stared at Anita. The eyes of the man open wide, catatonic with paint. Anita reached out one finger, as if she were trying to close his eyes, the way you would with a corpse.

"How do we know that's a painting of the lawyer?" Scott asked, his voice dripping with sarcasm.

Anita snapped from her reverie. "You don't, but I do. And it is Alan. He's playing with us. Trying to scare me. I don't know why, but he is." She looked at her hands, streaked with oil paint, wiping them on her legs, leaving a rainbow of doubt on her jeans. "I can't deal with this, sorry. I'm off to bed, see you in the morning."

"Unless you disappear too," Scott said as Anita left the room, leaning back in his seat, hands linked behind his head, a smile on his face. What a farce this whole thing was.

Yvonne dumped the dirty plates into the sink, running the water and wielding the dish brush as if she were imagining it was Scott she was beating with the brush and not the serviceable ceramic plates and crystal glasses. "You're an idiot," she said, thumping the dishes into the drainer.

"Not an idiot, just wise to her tricks. Don't know how you two have fallen for it. She's playing us like a puppet master. I've no idea why. It's ludicrous. But let her have her fun. I'm going to bed, too. I take it that our rooms are upstairs too. See you in the morning." Stretching, he smiled at the others, grabbed his wineglass and sauntered out of the kitchen, scooping up his bags on his way through.

Yvonne paused in her violent scrubbing of the dishes to look at Callaghan. In his usual verbose way, he raised his eyebrows and sipped his wine. The whole performance had shaken him. He didn't know what to think about Anita, and the painting, and the rabid dog outside. There were too many coincidences, but maybe they were just that, coincidences. He couldn't explain why the paint on the portrait was still wet, but he'd only been here for less than a day. In this weather it would take a good number of days for oil paint to dry. Anyone could've painted it.

Callaghan picked the portrait off the floor. The edges were indistinct, and the eyes smudged beyond recognition as if someone had tried to gouge them out. There was no salvation for the painting now. If it was a portrait of the lawyer, no one could recognise him now.

CHAPTER 28

Anita thrashed about in bed, struggling against the heavy covers pinning her down. Fighting imaginary assailants, their faces in shadow, stalking her through her dreams, her nightmares.

The man in her room stepped forward and reached out for the feather comforter. Pulling it back, he released her from her baseless fears. She quieted, unaware of the presence of another. Her breathing slowed. The cold air washing against her exposed skin brought out goosebumps. She shivered, burrowing further into the soft mattress. He hesitated a moment before picking up the light throw hanging over the back of the nursing chair in the corner of the room and laying it over her.

Turning his back to her, he looked over the jewellery Anita left on the dressing table. Reverently he touched each piece until he came to the star brooch. This he picked up. Its pointed corners pressing into his flesh. He'd not seen it for a long time but he remembered it well. It had caused so such misery, and yet it was worthless. Thirty-six paste stones, backed with silver foil. A tiny safety chain which had been broken and repaired more than once. Yet how many people had lost their lives over it? It would be better for everyone if it disappeared, again. He slipped it into his suit pocket. The threads of the silk lining snagging on the misshapen pin at the back.

He looked back at Anita. She was still now, her breathing steady, her face relaxed. He left her sleeping and walked back into the hall. He could join the others upstairs, but he had no desire to revisit those wounds. This wasn't a life he wanted to lead. It wasn't his life either. That was over.

CHAPTER 29

Scott woke in the morning, disorientated. The bed lumpier than he preferred, surrounded by sour-faced portraits, with an arctic breeze moving the moth-eaten curtains. The billowing curtains allowed the morning light to fall across his face and it was a combination of the light and a blinding headache threatening to split his skull, which woke him.

He stumbled from the bed, fighting his way to the bathroom. The pain from the headache so intense he could barely see. Wrenching open the door he fell into the bathroom, sank to his knees and heaved into the toilet. Great gushes of vomit splashed into the water. Again and again he threw up until there was only foul tasting bile left.

He rested his forehead against the porcelain seat, the chilly ceramic helping to ease the pain radiating through his head and now his hands. He flexed his fingers, rubbing the sensation away. Pushing himself up, he stood in front of the foxed mirror. Broken capillaries flushed his cheeks, his eyes more bloodshot than after a boozy night out with the boys. He was a wreck.

A clean towel beckoned to him from the rail and he

looked around for a shower. A decent shower would wash away most of his headache and the pain. Damn it, only a bloody bath. He couldn't recall the last time he'd had a bath, maybe when he was eight? It was his only choice.

The antiquated taps rewarded him with the gushing of hot water and the room filled with steam. He sloughed off his clothes, keen to wash away the pervasive scent of vomit.

The water temperature bearable, he climbed in, curling his lanky frame into the tub. The problem with bathtubs was that one end of you was always cold. You could either submerge yourself under the water but then your legs would freeze. Or you could have your feet and legs warm beneath the waterline but then your shoulders felt the chill. Only a contortionist could fit all of themselves under.

Scott submerged himself, hot water flooding over his face and through his hair taking with it most of the pain. He rubbed his face, the vigorous splashing sending rivulets of water over the bath's edge. Oblivious to the minor flooding, Scott grabbed a long handled brush from beside the bath and a cast around for body wash. A well used, long forgotten bar of soap lay on the edge of the bath. He tried not to imagine who may have last used it, and gritting his teeth he scrubbed at the imagined grime covering him from head to toe. It wasn't as good as a shower but it was hot and there were no random hairs stuck to the soap… He submerged himself again, eyes closed, the water blocking out the world.

The hot tap turned on. Scalding water trickled out, the flow becoming stronger the more the tap turned.

Scott shot up, spluttering and swearing and scrambled out of the bath in a flood of expletives and tried turning the tap off. He jumped back shrieking as his skin made contact with the super heated brassware.

Hopping around the bathroom naked, he was in no position to notice the lock on door disengaging as he was bathing his hand under the tap in the sink. And then the door opened.

"Oh my god, have you never heard of locking a door?" Yvonne squealed.

"Christ almighty, I'm naked here, give me a moment," Scott yelled, his hand still under the running water. The towel too far away for him to reach without leaving the soothing cool water. Even to the casual observer, it was clear Scott was in some discomfort.

"It's nothing I haven't seen before," replied Yvonne, walking in and handing Scott the towel to cover himself. "What happened?"

"Seriously Yvonne, this is not okay," said Scott, wrapping the towel round his waist.

"You'll need cream on that," Yvonne said after examining Scott's hand under the tap.

"No shit," Scott said. "I can't believe there's no safety valve for the temperature."

"It's an old house Scott, what did you expect, the Hilton? Come on, get out, I need the toilet."

Mumbling under his breath, Scott returned to his monastic room to get changed. At least his headache had mostly gone and a couple of painkillers would take care of the remnants. Pulling on his sweater made more awkward by the scald on his hand, which hadn't disguised the unusual pins and needles radiating up his arm. The bed was to blame, for sure. He tried not to look at the scowling portraits on the walls, watching him, judging him.

"What are you looking at?" he asked, pulling a portrait of an elderly matron off the wall. He stacked three other portraits of relatives or descendants on top of the old woman's picture. Each time he lifted a painting from the wall, his hand smarted more than the initial burn but there was no way he'd sleep another night with these people on the walls.

Finally the walls were bare and the bed laboured under the weight of a dozen oak framed portraits. Telltale lines of decades of dust showed where each portrait had hung, with spider carcasses littering the floor.

He wiped his dirty hands on the eiderdown, leaving two hand shaped prints. Hefting one pile of frames up, he made his way down to the dining room, and dumped them on the table, wincing at the uncomfortable scratching sound the frames made on the table underneath the protective cloth. That wasn't good. Still, not his problem. He'd done Anita a service by bringing them here. If she'd been more onto it, she would've had this lot catalogued and ready for the packers. He had real doubts about her now. All that talk about the lawyer, yet apart from a red sports car in the drive, which could've belonged to the original owner of the house, there was no evidence of anyone else having been here. Scott discounted the stuff in the other bedroom, coincidental. The more he thought about it, the more he believed Anita had used the lawyer as an excuse for slacking off.

There was no coffee ready or breakfast, so he tried to light the belligerent antique stove. After several failed attempts, and a dozen broken matches, he got the gas going, and thumped the kettle onto the stove.

Outside the sun pushed through the clouds, the diamond-like snow glistening, highlighting the deep paw prints from the dog from last night. He could've been bitten, dying a painful death from rabies in bed. It was damn irresponsible of Callaghan to force him to hunt a mythical lawyer. Anyone could see the girl wasn't all there. She was nice enough, but something was off.

The kettle whistled, just at the same time as he could've sworn he heard a child screaming outside. Screaming? No, it was his imagination. Stirring his coffee he looked out the window. There was that sound again. Faint, but it sounded like a child. Not a scream, a yell? If that dog was still out there that child would be in trouble yelling so loudly. *Jesus*, look at the position that put him in.

Moving to the kitchen doorway he called out for Callaghan. No answer. Shit, he'd have to go outside. Why him? He didn't even have a coat, and there was no way a child should be out there alone, not with a crazed dog loose. He'd never forgotten when a boy at school was attacked on the lower field one lunchtime. Two dogs had run riot before pouncing on a boy, tearing great strips from his face. Flaps of flesh hung down like a cascading waterfall. He'd avoided dogs since then. Even as an adult he steered clear of dog walkers and often crossed the road to avoid a dog coming the other way. It didn't matter if it was a labrador or a poodle, dogs scared him.

Turning the gas off, he picked up the skillet from the draining board, wincing as the cold metal hit the fresh scald on his hand. Still, brandishing it like a sword, he opened the back door. Winter swamped the kitchen, and he stepped over the threshold, eyes darting left to right. Scott contemplated calling out to the child, but didn't want to attract the dog. He crept forward, feet crunching on the path. Snow blown in by the wind covered up his footprints. The tree branches braying like fairground donkeys under the weight of the snow.

His head snapped to the side, it was less distinct now but still the sound of a child. He pushed past the trees, snow avalanching around him. The calls of the gulls above cohabiting the air, confusing his sense of direction. Scott turned around, and turned again, uncertain as to the true direction of the child.

"Hello?"

A faint echo came back. Scott froze, straining to figure out the direction, the skillet heavy in his hand. He hefted it to the other side. God it was cold. He took a step forward. Paused. Another step, the pan dangling from his weaker left hand. A howling shook more snow from above. A howling which cut off. Scott panicked, running through the shrubbery, thrashing at the brambles tearing at his clothes. He was about to be mauled.

"Help!"

Melting snow drenched his hair and ran into his eyes. The pain which had crept up his arms all morning, exploded through his shoulders, crippling him. He tripped. The skillet clonked on a tile concealed by the snowy blanket. Crawling on his knees, his trousers soaked through, Scott cried out for help. His cries echoing those of the child he'd forgotten.

Snot bubbled from his nose, joining the salty tears and sweat pouring forth. Lurching to his feet, he tried to get his bearings. He wiped his face, smearing grit from the ground through his stubble. It had fallen silent around him. Even the gulls above had vanished. The soothing sound of trickling water emerged from the silence. Melting snow or a virgin stream? His arms and shoulders ached more than he thought possible. Pain coursed through his neck, radiating up to his skull. His lips were numb. Was this the onset of a stroke? Where the fuck was the house?

The child cried out again. She sounded closer than she had before. Petrified the dog would find him, but it could just as easily attack the child, he took a deep breath and followed the sounds of the child's cries. Freezing in saturated clothes, and with a migraine he wouldn't wish on his worst enemy, it was tempting to give up. But he wasn't callous, he wouldn't let a rabid dog maul a child. He was a grown man.

One more step, and then he slipped down an incline; the reeds disguising the start of a body of water. Scott backed up.

Brilliant, bloody brilliant, now sludge from the muddy edge caked his suede shoes. They were unsalvageable, but he had no time to worry about them now. Where the hell was the girl?

There was no sign of her, or the dog. And there was no way to cross the water to get to the building in the middle. How did a child get there? It made no sense. He inched his way along the bank, looking for a causeway or stepping stones, a bridge or anything. The cries had turned to sobs, hiccupping across the water.

"I'm coming, hang on," Scott called out.

Dimly remembered swimming lessons reminded him that swimming with shoes on was ill advised, so he pulled off his ruined shoes. He grabbed hold of a clump of reeds and probed the edge of the pond with his feet.

The water shot ice into his veins, too cold to cry out, he clamped his teeth together to stop them from chattering. The sludge under foot provided no grip. There was no sign of life within the watery expanse save for the drowned moths floating on the surface.

Putting all his weight on the reeds, it was no surprise when they pulled free from the earth, sending Scott tumbling into the water. He scrambled to find his footing on the silty bottom and coughing and spluttering he fought his way to the side, the frigid water clinging to him the way the icicles clung to the bushes around him. Using the last reserves of his strength, honed from too many hours in the gym, Scott hauled himself out of the water.

Pants ruined. Shirt ruined. His wristwatch, ruined. The watch he'd bought with his first substantial commission from Nickleby's, and of the numerous things he'd bought over the years, it was still his favourite possession. The 1942 rose gold *Breitling* the one thing he'd save from a burning building. The only silver lining being the house was visible through a narrow line of sight from his prone position in the filth of the water's edge. Gloomy forgotten windows stared at him, void of light. He couldn't see the bottom floor, only the second floor and the turret... awash with light There was a man in the turret, his face concealed by the easel. A man he didn't recognise. The lawyer?

Then Scott cried out and pulled himself into a foetal position as pain coursed through his body, radiating down from his head, engulfing him in a pain so intense Scott stopped functioning on any rational level. His legs shot out as if great volts of electricity were running through them. His bowels gave way. Somewhere in his mind he appreciated the warmth of the urine, but that flicker of humanity was snuffed out as his jaw locked in a macabre approximation of a grimace.

And then as abruptly as his death dance began, it stopped. And the carefree giggles of a child, a girl child, danced across the water from the middle of the island.

In the turret the artist applied the final touches to the background — water reeds flowering in a summer haze, sprinkled behind the man in the portrait. His dark hair mussed by an invisible wind, his hand hanging limply in the still water from the confines of a gaily painted wooden dinghy. Concentric ripples radiated out from his hand, the strap of a wristwatch visible below his shirt sleeve, the brand of the watch unmistakable despite the tiny writing. *Breitling.*

CHAPTER 30

Anita woke up and stretched. Mid stretch she froze, legs fully extended. She'd become used to the extraordinary weight of the comforter on her legs and it wasn't there. Instead her legs were covered by a soft throw. The throw which had been hanging on the back of the chair.

Anita pulled herself up, the lightweight blanket coming with her. Her duvet folded back upon itself although she had no recollection of pushing off her covers; of getting out of bed to drape the lighter blanket over herself. She shivered. Any comfort she'd felt when she first awoke gone. She'd drunk some wine the night before but not enough to have suffered any memory loss. Nothing else in her room had been moved, she didn't want to move either, but her bowels gave her no choice.

Lowering her feet to the floor, she eyed the duvet, its feathery warmth suddenly so sinister. Why couldn't she remember folding it back? The room was freezing during the day and glacial at night, she'd would never have exchanged the heavier comforter for a summer weight throw. She pulled the blanket around her shoulders and padded over to the dressing table where the sight that greeted her was reminiscent of how she'd looked in those early days after her attack. Dark rings pulled her eyes downwards into her pale skin, as if sunlight was a foreign concept. Even her hair had lost its shine.

She felt dirty, unkempt, and worst of all unsafe. She'd moved beyond enjoying the solitude so many took for granted, to looking over her shoulder and jumping at shadows. She thought she'd left all that behind her but now darkness had resettled upon her shoulders. And once again it was a man who'd done this to her. He'd ruined her solitude, destroying the carefully reconstructed world she'd built for herself. A world in which she could function as an adult, doing grown up things, like finding employment and performing at an acceptable level within that job. She couldn't let it happen again, to be constrained by the emotional, or physical, subjugation by a man, against her will. She needed to speak with her mother. After that she'd straighten her shoulders, push her sleeves back and present herself to her colleagues as a more than competent art appraiser, one destined for great things.

She grabbed her cellphone, again no signal showed but there was enough battery left she knew she could quickly call her mother. If Scott had found a signal upstairs, then she could too. But a bath and breakfast first, otherwise the others might come looking for her and she wanted to talk with her mother with no one hovering around. All girls, no matter their age, whether they are broken or whole, need their mothers.

Yvonne and Callaghan descended the staircase at the same time with Yvonne regaling him about her eyeful of Scott in the bathroom and it was a merry pair which made their way into the kitchen.

If the foyer and staircase were frigid, the temperature in the kitchen was subarctic. With the door wide open, wind flew in across the open fields and a small drift of snow had spread its icy tentacles across the tiled floor.

Yvonne and Callaghan exchanged glances. The door had been shut when they'd gone to bed. Yvonne shrugged. It was an old house and she pushed the door shut, thumping it with her hip until the latch engaged in the doorplate.

"You didn't want to kick that snow outside first?" Callaghan asked, nudging the snowdrift with his boot.

"Ah, not using these," said Yvonne, pointing to the slippers on her feet, decorated with cartoonish sausage dogs. "It's far too cold in this house to wear anything else. I had to wear most of my clothes in bed as it was. Can you try to get the furnace working?"

"Sure, after breakfast," Callaghan said, opening the fridge, looking for the milk.

"Milk's here," Yvonne said, holding up the bottle Scott had left on the bench. "At least there's no chance of it spoiling in the heat," she joked before sniffing it for any sign it had gone off. "Trust Scott to have made himself a coffee and not one for the rest of us. Bet you he's upstairs on the phone to his girlfriend trying to ignore that I've just seen him naked," Yvonne laughed.

"He didn't finish his coffee though," Callaghan said, tipping the mug of cold coffee into the sink. The brown liquid raced down the plughole.

Yvonne didn't seem fazed, she'd become distracted by an oblong silver tube she'd discovered under the teaspoons in the drawer. "Look at this." The cigar cutter wasn't remarkable but Yvonne seemed happy, pulling out her loupe to read the hallmarks, her own coffee cooling by her elbow.

"Breakfast is ready," Callaghan announced. "Where's Anita?"

Yvonne hadn't even registered the breakfast Callaghan had laid out; bread rolls, juice, three different cheeses, ham, smoked salmon slices and cherry tomatoes. She clapped her hands happily as she spied the spread in front of her. "This looks fabulous."

Yvonne pushed her treasures to one end of the table, and was already lathering butter onto her bread rolls as she chatted about her home ownership dreams and how this was exactly the type of house she hoped to own, except less haunted than this one.

"Seriously Yvonne, a haunted house? Have you seen any ghostly apparitions?" Callaghan said.

Yvonne rolled her eyes and took a mighty bite out of her bagel, mumbling through the doughy mouthful as Anita appeared in the doorway.

The standard morning pleasantries done, Callaghan poured Anita a coffee and ladled a serving of the still warm eggs and tomatoes onto her plate. She sat next to Yvonne and sipped her coffee.

Callaghan lifted the ruined portrait off the other chair and onto the kitchen bench to make room for himself, just as Anita cut into a tomato and forked it into her mouth. The sight of the man in the portrait and the acidic flesh on her tongue nudged a memory to the surface so vivid, so recent, she started choking on the tomato.

Anita tried to cough and tried again, the tomato wedged in her throat. She clawed at her throat and made frantic gestures towards the others.

Yvonne leapt into action and a hearty slap on Anita's back

dislodged the fruit and Anita spat the masticated pulp onto her plate. Eyes watering, the taste of tomato replaced by bile and a previously buried memory of her attacker.

He'd eaten a tomato like an apple, after her rape. His first bite of the fruit had left a trail of watery red juice running down his chin as he'd stood there in the kitchen doorway. Oil stained hands holding the half-eaten tomato. Such an innocuous fruit. At the time she thought her insides had turned to pulp there was so much blood, yet he'd watched her bleed out while he calmly ate a tomato. A tomato from her kitchen, from her grandfather's glasshouse. Rich red skin, tart juice, larger than the insipid tomatoes at the store, more flavoursome. He'd stood in the doorway eating the whole thing, even the centre, and when he finished he'd wiped his juice-stained hands on his jeans before smiling and tipping an imaginary hat towards her. How could she have forgotten that?

"You're meant to chew it," Yvonne said, returning to her chair. She'd moved on from the cigar cutter and was stacking a set of sterling silver coffee spoons she'd rescued from the cutlery drawer, while tearing into another roll with her other hand.

The foul taste of tomato in her mouth, Anita took a gulp of the coffee Callaghan served her. Her stomach roiled at the bitter brew but not as much as it had with the tomato. She tried to recall if she'd eaten a tomato since the rape, she must have, so why the issue now? She couldn't even recall telling the police about him eating a tomato. Would that have made a difference? She doubted it.

"I think I'll carry on with my work. I'll be in the dining room if you need me," Anita said, pushing back her chair. The others didn't bother answering. Yvonne, absorbed with her spoons, had pulled out the entire drawer, and Callaghan had moved to the back door, staring out the window, coffee mug held between both hands, warming them. What he was looking at, or thinking, was unreadable.

The portrait on the kitchen bench, the portrait of Alan - his eyes smeared permanently shut, screamed blindly at Anita as she left the kitchen.

Back in the dining room Anita struggled to concentrate. She peered out the windows, checking their locks and then went through to the drawing room, where she double checked those doors and windows. Shut and locked. Outside a cliche of beauty; snow-covered branches and brittle blue skies, a picture of innocence. She leaned against the glass, there was no sign of a dog or Alan. The kerfuffle the night before obliterated by the winds which had dropped to a whimper, with Snowdrops bobbing their slender necks in the ghostly breeze which remained.

The silence was shattered by a plume of black which rose scowling and squawking from behind the trees. From the crypt, an unkindness of ravens filled the sky with feathery black wings, their cries both haunting and disturbing. They wheeled in tight formation and disappeared from sight, their cries becoming fainter until their sound faded. Had the dog disturbed their slumber or something else?

The portrait of Alan worried her, it needled her as she sat at her computer rubbing her fingers. It was only now she realised the pins and needles had abated despite being her constant companion the day before and yet she hadn't noticed their absence until now. She put the pains down to too much typing. One more day and she'd have finished. One more day of typing and photographing, then the packers would arrive and she'd help them load up the art, label each crate and wave them off.

She couldn't imagine this house empty. The rooms would be too big, the echoes too old. The act of removing the portraits from the walls as if she was stripping the house of its identity. That somehow she was removing decades of memories and destroying the house's narrative. She knew it was unavoidable but to what end? To line the pockets of the lawyer? To enrich the obese auction house? She was complicit in the rape of the house; she was part of the machinery stripping it bare and she didn't like how that made her feel.

A shadow flew across the pale sun, the ravens returning to their roost. So many that their outstretched wings blocked the sunlight. For a moment the light in the drawing room dimmed, the colours turning to every shade of ash, and then the birds passed. Dropping out of sight, their cries cut off, as if they'd found something else to focus their beaks on.

CHAPTER 31

Callaghan prowled the house. Scott hadn't shown his face and it was out of character for him to dwell on embarrassment. In the past he'd even laughed off the fallout from his drunken debauchery at a work Christmas party. Photographs of his exploits were posted anonymously on the intranet, leading to a complete overhaul of the IT security system. Scott only just kept his job, but still joked about it. His co-conspirator lost her job and husband — another manager who hadn't thought much of Scott taking up with his wife in such a public forum.

There was no sign of him in the upstairs bathroom. His bedroom was empty. Only Anita was in the drawing room. Callaghan poked his head in and watched her fidgeting at the window, checking the locks and trying the door handle. Leaving her to it, he wandered the panelled hallways.

Callaghan noted the luxurious foliage of the indoor plants. He'd noticed but hadn't given them any thought until he came across the mess of the plant stand knocked over by Alan. The razor-sharp shards of broken pottery now brushed against the wide skirting boards but dirt and the desiccated roots of the fern still littered the floor. The wooden stand leaned drunkenly against the wall, one leg twisted at an angle, its shaft split lengthways. Only good for the fire now. Walking past the mess Callaghan tried the next door. It opened onto a nursery decorated with teddy bears and prancing horses galloping around the walls.

White curtains adorned the windows, tied back with velvet cords threaded through creamy pearlescent shells. Old ash still lay in the hearth and in the corner a brave spider spun a lazy web, nothing intricate, mere lines — a way of getting from A to B, no convoluted patterns. An unfortunate moth was caught by its wing and fluttered against the iron-like thread the spider had spun.

Callaghan walked around the room, hands in his pockets, not wanting to disturb the layer of dust which clung to the furniture and toys. How this one room had escaped the ministrations of the cleaner was a mystery.

A set of half built *Meccano* lay scattered across the floor, the green and red strips as distinctive today as they had been when they were new. Someone had been building a complicated bridge, a replica perhaps of Tower Bridge or the Brooklyn Bridge. In its half finished state it was impossible to tell. His eyes travelled to the desk, a large adult sized desk with four chairs around it, two of which sported badly moth-eaten bulbous cushions, probably caused by long dead ancestors of the moth still struggling in the clutches of the web. Callaghan watched the slow onslaught of the spider as it appeared from nowhere and minced its way towards its prey. He shuddered. It was just a moth but the death of any creature at the hands of another was disturbing.

Callaghan returned his attention to the desk. The papers strewn across the top were covered in childish script and the joins and curvature of the cursive letters became messier the further he read. Someone who'd become bored with their classwork? Curious, he turned the pages, rousing decades of dust. He sneezed and the sheaf of papers flew off the desk and onto the floor.

"Damn it," he muttered. Scrambling around to gather the paper he couldn't help but notice the different handwriting on the rest of the pages, which struck him as off. The handwriting, and the repetition of one word. *Sorry.* Written over and over, the words becoming larger on each subsequent line, until at the bottom of every page was the sentence *'I'm sorry Daddy. I'm sorry.'*

The door to the nursery swung shut. Callaghan shot up, banging his head on the underside of the desk. Grimacing, he dumped the papers into the overflowing waste basket, causing the whole thing to tip. Callaghan swore. Childish watercolours spilled from the bin and page after page of blonde children stared up at him. Half finished, missing limbs, smeared with dissatisfaction, they showed promise but not yet mastery. The artist had attempted to capture different emotions but their talent lay more with misery than with joy. There were no complete faces showing happiness and the few portraits where the artist had almost captured a smile were slashed though with broad pencil strokes.

The door slamming did not concern him, the draughts running through this house were enough to ventilate the most noxious of environments. He focused on his work and shoved the watercolours into the bin and righted it. He rubbed his head and took one last look around the room before opening the door. It didn't open. He twisted the handle. The mechanism moved but the door remained shut. Callaghan kicked it with his boot, pulling firmly on the handle, and it swung free. Old houses and cold weather. Every time.

Further along the corridor there was no sign anyone had been in these rooms other than a cleaning service. The remaining rooms were as devoid of dust and opportunistic spiders as they were of Scott. The daylight delivered an appreciation of how nothing of value was left in this part of the house. All that remained were redundant pieces of furniture, more portraits and empty hearths. It wouldn't take him long to finish this end of the house after he'd located Scott.

He strode back to the foyer and noticed that the stacks of portraits had increased. Anita had been excessively productive over the last few minutes. He checked his watch. It hadn't been a few minutes, it had been two hours. He tapped at his watch; the second hand swooped unheeded in a continuous march. The minutes ticked by and Callaghan stood transfixed. It wasn't until he heard Yvonne call to him as she walked down the stairs that he snapped out of his reverie.

"Find him?" she said.

"Not down here. Was he upstairs?" he asked.

Yvonne shook her head, fully focused on the piece of art she held in her hands. "Look at this," she said, waving the frame towards Callaghan and hollering for Anita.

Anita emerged from the dining room. Callaghan took in her bleary-eyed appearance, how after only two days she appeared haggard, as if she hadn't slept for a week. Last night's mascara sagged around her cheeks and her hair had passed the electrification stage, edging towards the unkept homeless style more commonly seen on the streets of the city.

Callaghan reached out to pat Anita on the shoulder, "Are you okay?"

Anita shrank back, her eyes widening.

"I was just asking if you were okay." He withdrew his hand, shoving it into his pocket, casting around for the jade head he'd found himself caressing during the day. The smooth planes of the dog's broken head soothing. Stepping back, he checked his watch again. Time had settled into its expected pattern, sixty-seconds to a minute, sixty minutes to an hour, twenty-four hours in a day. There was no explanation for the time he'd lost in the playroom, none at all.

Yvonne was oblivious to the carryings-on of the others and thrust the frame into Callaghan's hands and waited.

CHAPTER 32

"Well?" Yvonne asked Callaghan.

There wasn't much he could say, he was at a complete loss about what she was expecting from him.

"Look at the picture, see what she's wearing. We have to find it," Yvonne said, gesturing at the portrait, frothing with excitement, eyes gleaming as she hopped like a marionette from one foot to the other.

She watched him examine the small portrait, its gilt frame gleaming under the foyer's electric lights. The cleaner had been overzealous here. Not a speck of dust marred the hand-applied gold leaf flecked gilt frame which surrounded a blonde-haired woman, perched on the edge of a day bed. Her formal outfit in stark contrast to her surrounds. A hound at her feet and a book by her side, yet she was in an evening gown, hair swept up, a touch of red on her lips and rouge on her cheeks. Pinned to her chest was a magnificent star-shaped brooch. The artist had captured the rainbow refractions shining through the gems with such clarity, it could have been a photograph.

"They're diamonds, that's a diamond brooch. Look at the

size of them!" Yvonne gushed, grabbing the frame from Callaghan before he'd commented. She thrust it at Anita, who stumbled at the suddenness of the movement. "Anita, look at it."

"Where'd you find this?" Anita asked.

"What does it matter? It's the brooch I want. It's marvellous. The colour, the lustre, imagine if it's still here. Have you found any jewellery boxes yet? Or a safe? Was there one in the study?"

Anita shook her head.

"Damn," Yvonne said, ripping the painting from Anita, oblivious to the glance between Anita and Callaghan. Yvonne stalked around the foyer peering through doorways, nudging Anita's stacked frames with her feet.

"Hey," Anita shouted, before shutting her mouth.

Yvonne turned and frowned, "What?"

"The frames…" Anita replied, straightening a stack Yvonne moved.

"I was looking for other pictures with the same brooch in them, calm down."

Anita looked back towards Callaghan, who was standing with his head cocked to one side, looking up the curved staircase, hands in his pockets. She turned back to Yvonne, who was stroking the brooch in the painting.

"You can't touch the painting Yvonne," Anita said, her training overriding her normal deference. "The oils from your skin could damage it. Come on, bring it into the dining room, the light's better there."

Yvonne broke from her trancelike state and nodded. Shaking the confusion from her head, she followed Anita and laid the frame on the padded table, before slipping into a chair.

"God my arms hurt," she said, stretching them up and out, before cradling them in her lap.

Anita ignored her, instead peering through her loupe at the brooch in the centre of the picture. The woman looked familiar, as if she'd seen another portrait featuring her, or at least a relative. Casting her mind back she couldn't think of any of the portraits she'd already catalogued which matched, except for... maybe the children. The woman in the portrait had the same blonde hair and blue eyes as the children, but she was sad. Beautiful and sad. The way she'd placed her feet, clasping her hands as if she wanted this ordeal to be over as soon as possible, the sitting done under sufferance.

"Did she live here? Was that painted here?" Yvonne asked, flexing her decorated fingers. Fingers adorned with an array of rings, both modern and antique. One, a band of silver with a pyramid-shaped dome awkwardly attached. Another, a cluster of pearls — meant more for decorative wear than day-to-day use, but Yvonne wore it every day, rain or shine. The third, a belt shaped gold band — popular in Victorian times as mourning jewellery, plain and embellishment free, far more practical than the pearl monstrosity. And an ugly opal ring — designed in the Seventies, with heavy gold shoulders and a huge oval. The stone needed a good buff by a jeweller to remove the scuffing, but the ring itself had the ability to inflict real damage should she ever need to wield it as a weapon. Each ring had its own story and she couldn't bear being parted from any of them. For the moment though their inconsequential weight was exacerbating the pins and needles in her fingers and hands. She slipped them off, lining them up on the table. "So, any clues, oh resident art expert?"

Anita sighed and folded away her loupe, rubbing her eyes before replying.

"From what I can tell, yes, it was painted in this house. I don't think the furniture she's on is here anymore though, but I recognise the windows and the view. See here?" She pointed out the hills behind the house where an exceptionally tall tree stood sentinel in the middle. Even in the depths of winter, decades later, the same tree stood guard over the gap between the hills. "I've not seen any other portraits of her. There's no signature and I don't recognise the subject. She could be related to the four children in a series of paintings I've catalogued, but I'd be guessing if I suggested that."

Yvonne hung off every word, her eyes boring into Anita's. Anita fidgeted in her chair.

"The brooch though—"

"What?" Yvonne interrupted.

"I didn't recognise the brooch straight away, but I think I've seen it, upstairs. I'm sure it's just paste."

"It's not your place to decide what is or what isn't paste," Yvonne grabbed the frame and leapt up. She stumbled backwards before regaining her balance. "Where's the brooch?"

"In my room, on the dressing table."

"Let's go then," Yvonne said, already in the doorway.

Anita pushed herself up from the table, hobbling over to Yvonne.

"Why are you limping?"

"I hurt my heel yesterday before you arrived. Stood on some broken pottery. I thought I'd got it all out, but I guess I didn't," Anita replied.

Yvonne sniffed, she'd offer to help the other woman up the stairs but didn't want to relinquish the frame. Besides, her arms were feeling worse.

The women made their way upstairs. They reached the bedroom and Anita sank to the bed, struggling to pull off the sock she'd been wearing since before the others had arrived.

Placing the gilt frame on the mantel over the fireplace, Yvonne poked around at the bits and bobs strewn across the polished wood.

"You said it was on the dressing table but I can't see it anywhere, it's not here." Yvonne said to Anita, narrowing her eyes. She didn't want to suspect a colleague of pocketing such a thing, but it wouldn't be the first time someone had stolen a valuable item before it got to the auction room floor.

"It was in a purse in the drawer. I tipped it out to look through it, then left it there, even the purse. Oh!" Anita broke off and was probing her foot.

Distracted, Yvonne glanced at Anita's foot, "That's infected, girl." Yvonne switched from heartless auctioneer to saintly nurse in a nanosecond, the brooch momentarily forgotten. "Lie down now, leg up." She bustled around, calling for Callaghan and Scott to come and help.

Callaghan appeared at the door, taking it all from the doorway. Unreadable as always.

"Don't stand there like a piece of furniture. Look at this and tell me what you think?" Yvonne instructed.

Anita tried to object, but Yvonne shushed her. If Callaghan noticed the discomfort on Anita's face at Yvonne's words, he said nothing.

"No wonder you weren't looking well downstairs," was as much as Callaghan offered, although to his credit he appeared concerned.

"You can see the infection spreading up your ankle," Yvonne said, prodding at the offending red lines radiating up Anita's foot. "I guess we need to bathe it. Any thoughts, Cal?"

"I'll find a bowl of water," Callaghan replied, before disappearing again.

"Where the hell is Scott? I need him to light the fire."

"Why do we need a fire?" Anita asked.

"Because it's freezing in here that's why." Yvonne walked out to the hall, "Scott? Come and help you lazy bastard."

She massaged her arms, the pain spreading further up, tightening its grip. The last thing they needed was for another one of them to get sick before they'd finished. She couldn't wait to get out of this place. Once she found the brooch she'd be done, and when the packers arrived anything she hadn't catalogued could be packed up and itemised by the team back at work. That's what they got paid for.

CHAPTER 33

Anita couldn't tell if Yvonne was more annoyed at Scott disappearing, at her injury, or whether it was the missing brooch which made the jewellery expert huff like a train as she tried to light a fire.

Anita felt more light-headed in bed than she had working at the dining room table. Her leg was propped on a tower of old pillows Yvonne had nabbed from elsewhere in the house, so every time she moved her leg, the scent of neglect wafted through the room. The chilly air permeated her whole body, forcing involuntary tremors through her limbs.

Anita watched Yvonne drop the matches at least four times while listening to her running commentary about the dearth of firewood in the house. She'd sent Callaghan to source wood, pinecones, paper, or anything she could use for a fire. The absent Scott bore the brunt of Yvonne's vitriol and the colourful language a grateful respite from Yvonne's earlier behaviour. This was more the person she knew.

"Sorry about causing so much trouble," Anita said.

"Its fine, it is not your fault, it's Scott I'm pissed at. You don't just up and disappear because someone saw you in the nude. So childish. He's avoiding us. It'd be helpful for him to show his face, no one cares about what's in his pants that's for sure." She struck another match. This time the flame flared and, cupping it carefully, Yvonne lowered it to the paper she'd scrunched into the hearth. The fire caught, the draughts in the room helping fuel the flames as they took hold of the brittle newspaper. "Did it! Didn't need a man," Yvonne said sitting back on her heels. She gathered up the spent matches and threw them into the fire. "Nice tiles," she remarked, before stretching the aching muscles in her shoulders and arms.

Anita propped herself up to peer at the fireplace. The tiles were identical to the ones in the drawing room, decorated with pairs of ravens and Anita fancied the birds were whispering to each other before turning to look at her, hundreds of interchangeable heads swivelling her way, piercing her with their jet eyes. She tried to tear her eyes away, mesmerised by the glossy plumage leaping from the midnight blue tiles.

"Are you listening?"

Anita broke from her trance, "What?"

"I said, are you listening?" Yvonne replied, a towel slung over her shoulder and a bowl of water resting on a chair someone had dragged over to the bed. "I need to bathe your foot. Not the best job I've ever had, but Callaghan is useless, and Scott is having a tantrum somewhere, so you're left with me - Florence Bloody Nightingale." She dabbed at Anita's foot with as much care as a rat catcher.

Anita screwed her eyes shut, the minuscule splinter sending shots of pain through her whole body, as if Yvonne was stabbing at her foot with a hot poker fresh from the fire.

"Have you nearly finished?" she asked through gritted teeth.

"I think so, hard to know really."

The sound of Callaghan calling to Scott reached the girls.

"He's still sulking somewhere then?" Anita said.

"No idea, he isn't doing himself any favours behaving this way. He's always been a bit special. If he wasn't so good at his job Warren would've cut him years ago."

Callaghan's voice had a distinctive angry edge to it now; the solid slamming of doors another clue their colleague was well past being entertained by Scott's disappearing act. Every time another door slammed the glass rattled in the window frame and the delicate glassware danced on the dressing table and the pinecones in the fireplace jumped behind the iron grate.

"If he keeps doing that the place will collapse around us," Yvonne exclaimed. "Jesus, I can't handle any more of this." Thumping down the bowl of water, she stomped out of the room, adding to the cacophony echoing from the hall.

Anita's eyes returned to the hearth. The fire flared as it hit a vein of sap, and a pine cone popped and toppled from the fiery heap onto the tiles. The fire crackled and hissed, waking the ravens from their slumber. The ravens squabbled, feathers rustling like silk as they gambolled about the burning pine cone, the fire reflected a thousand times in their beady eyes.

The portrait of the woman Yvonne had left on the mantelpiece shimmered, and the stones of the brooch luminesced in the firelight, throwing brilliant rainbows across the woman's black dress. The painted dog whimpered, lifting its head to look up at the woman in the portrait who shuddered, her knuckles whitening in her lap. A tear trickled down her cheek. Her lips parted, whispering two words, "Help me."

Somewhere in the hall another door slammed shut and the ravens rose as one, their wings beating the air and fanning the flames of the fire, swooping and diving in furious coordination, amongst the maelstrom the gilt frame teetered on the mantel. And then it fell.

"No!" Anita screamed, reaching for the painting. Everything happened in slow motion, right until the frame hit the tiled hearth. There was an explosive cracking sound as the force of the fall ricocheted the painting into the fire. The heavy oils caught at once and blue flames devoured the edges of the portrait before licking at the woman in the centre of the canvas. Her sad face twisted in agony and a deep keening filled the house, reverberating through the barren walls and the empty rooms.

Anita blinked and the ravens vanished. Anita watched a jet black feather float to the ground and settle a breath away from the hearth. The door opened and Yvonne and Callaghan careened into the room. The sudden gust of air caught the feather and hurled it into the fire, where it caught alight, curled, and turned to ash.

CHAPTER 34

The farmer stalked across the barren fields, dog by his side. He cast the occasional glance up at the big house. Those kids were playing with fire up there. Nothing good came from that house. In fact, not much came out of it at all. He'd had few interactions with the old man but he'd seen him often enough up in the turret, hours on end, paintbrush in hand. He'd seen no one up there with him, just old Kubin and his easel.

The farmer's dog took off across the field, his loping gait leaving deep paw prints in the snow still hugging the earth.

"Oi, Ace, come back here. Heel."

Ace paid no attention, bounding through the undergrowth separating the fields and the Kubin house, disappearing from sight. The farmer whistled. The sound shrill in the empty countryside, startling the ravens from their roosting place. They took to the air in alarm, flying circles above him. He scowled at them. Harbingers of bad luck. They pecked at his crops and scared his animals. He couldn't remember them being around when he was a boy but they'd been a constant presence in the skies around the big house his whole adult life. There was no response to the whistle.

"Ace, heel!" he yelled, his voice hoarse in the cold air. He tugged the scarf tighter around his throat as he clambered over the stile at the back of the old house. His thick coat protecting his arms as he bashed through the thorny vines which grew unapologetically wild along the boundary. The farmer emerged on the banks of the icy pond, skirting the edge carefully.

The pond built before Kubin's time, back when planning permission meant getting approval from the lady of the house, or the man, before the work began. It certainly didn't mean obtaining consent from the local council. As a result, there now existed this body of water with a folly in the middle. A summer house which saw no summer, surrounded as it was by old trees towering above the ramshackle structure. The bridge to the island had long since decayed. Even as a boy, on the odd times he'd snuck through the fence to cadge a swim in the fresh water, the place had an aura of malevolence about it, one which as a teenager, he and his friends ignored. Diving into the pond and swimming across to the old summer house a rite of passage for the local lads; daring each other to stay overnight in the wooden summer house, the biggest dare of them all. He'd never done it. One of his friends had though. He'd spent the whole night there. Wouldn't talk about it afterwards and moved away a few months later. The local gossip was that he'd ended up in the loony bin. His own father caught him swimming there once. He'd received the biggest walloping of his life and was made to swear on the life of his mother, whom he loved more than life itself, that he would never swim in the pond again. It wasn't till he was much older that he heard the scuttlebutt about the children drowning in it and how their mother had taken her own life afterwards. How the big house changed hands a dozen times before the old artist turned up, then never left again.

"Ace, you come back here right now." He could see the dog worrying at something in the reeds by the water's edge. His whistle clamped firming between his teeth, he whistled again. Ace didn't even look up.

The farmer struggled around the edge of the pond, focusing on where he was placing his feet. Didn't want to get into the same difficulties as the girl up at the house. Finally he reached the side of his faithful companion, the only family he had now. His wife moved into the city to care for her mother and had never come back, succumbing to the same cancer which stole her own mother. It was him and Ace and his cattle, with a smattering of goats and chickens rounding out his life.

"What've you got there, boy?"

Reaching down, he pushed the dog's muzzle out of the way. The dog had been chewing at a pair of men's shoes. The farmer stepped back, his breath wheezy.

"Where is he then?" he asked Ace.

The dog sat on his haunches and looked up at the farmer. He was a good dog, an obedient dog. But he couldn't know what the farmer was thinking.

The farmer turned around, confused. This wasn't the spot where the girl had gone in, that was on the other side, the side closest to the house. But the ice behind him was broken, reeds floating at the water's edge, their uprooted tendrils reaching out and the soil was a messy smear of mud and bare footprints. Whoever had gone into the pond had made it out again. So where were they?

Bending to pick up the shoes, he pushed the dog away. Ace darted in again, barking, trying to get at the shoes, to bite them, tearing one away from the farmer's work-hardened hands.

"Stop it you daft creature, give me the shoe. Drop it."

Ace dropped it, but started barking again. A bark bordering on a whine. Ignoring the instincts of the animal, he picked up the shoes and made the precarious walk around the pond up to the big house. His father's decades-old warning ringing in his ears.

CHAPTER 35

Callaghan and Yvonne ran into Anita's bedroom in time to see the gilt frame engulfed in brilliant orange and blue flames.

Yvonne grabbed the bowl of water and threw it onto the flames. The fireplace exploded with a hiss and acrid smoke filled the room.

"Get more water," Yvonne instructed, in a futile attempt to rescue the frame from the fire.

Callaghan ignored her. There was no point going for any more water, the elegant woman who'd graced the canvas now reduced to bubbling pools of oil paint. All signs of the woman, and the brooch, lost. Only the lower half of the portrait remained free from damage. The old dog looking out from his edge of the frame, fur accented with purple streaks from the melted image of the day bed.

Holding the charred frame, Yvonne looked incredulously at Anita, "What did you do?"

"Me? Nothing, it fell off the mantelpiece. I think the doors slamming must have jolted—"

"Frames don't just fall," Yvonne interrupted. "They get

helped, by people who help themselves to valuable jewellery." It wasn't the heat from the fire making Yvonne's cheeks flush. Anger poured off her. Irrational, all-consuming, anger.

"Yvonne I don't think Anita would do—" Callaghan started.

"You know nothing about her. Go on, admit it. None of us do. We talked about it in the car up here, she never talks about her life. A closed book. A book where all the bad stuff is in the sealed section." Yvonne stood over Anita, spittle forming as she spat the words out. "Bet they never even ran a police check on you, you little thief."

Anita sat up, "I left the brooch on the dressing table. I don't know where it is now. Maybe Alan took it, or maybe Scott took it downstairs to give to you. The only thing I've ever stolen in my life was a butter knife from a hostel in Finland when I was nineteen, and I still feel guilty about that. The frame fell into the fire because this is an old house and you were both were slamming doors like it was an Olympic sport—"

"Oh, pulling out the Alan card? The mythical Alan, who none of us met. It's convenient to blame someone who was probably never here."

"His car is in the driveway," Callaghan added.

"We can't even be sure it's his car, Cal. So don't defend this thief."

"That's enough Yvonne, leave her alone. She's no more likely to throw a portrait into a fire, than you would swallow a bag of loose diamonds. It's an accident. One painting ruined out of the hundreds here will not make the slightest bit of difference to the price realised at auction for the lot. It's not like it was a Matisse or anything, was it Anita?"

Anita shook her head. "We'll find the brooch Yvonne, but I'm one hundred percent certain it was paste and not real diamonds."

"As if you'd have any idea. Forget it. I'm going downstairs and don't bother joining me, either of you." Yvonne abandoned the frame back into the fire, where the coals flared with the fresh fuel.

"How are you feeling?" Callaghan asked.

"Woozy. I wonder if the infection is making me see things."

"Really?" He moved closer, until Anita flinched. It was the smallest of movements but he noticed it immediately, kindling its own frisson of excitement within him. Hands in his pockets, he sought the comfort of the smooth jade head. Moving to the hearth, he nudged the damaged frame further into the fireplace with his toe. He watched as the dog at the bottom of the painting charred, then disintegrated, the ash falling through the grate.

Callaghan poked at the frame with a brass poker. "Why were you screaming? Was it because the painting fell in the fire?"

"I wasn't screaming," Anita replied. "It was the woman in the portrait who screamed."

CHAPTER 36

Yvonne locked herself in the bathroom where her tears flowed as water from the tap. She slammed her hands against the mirror; the face looking back at her twisted in anger. That stupid girl. Stupid, stupid girl. Wait till Warren heard about what had happened. She'd ring him as soon as she'd calmed down.

She splashed water on her face, washing away the hot salty tears. Reaching for a towel, she rubbed at her face, mascara transferring from her stumpy eyelashes leaving black trails across the white towelling. Not her problem.

"Why am I so upset about a bloody brooch?" she asked her reflection. No answer. Shame gripped her. She knew her behaviour was irrational, but the brooch was special. It was rare she came across a piece she wanted to own, and this one wasn't even that spectacular. She'd dealt with plenty of far superior pieces in her time but this one she had to have. She closed her eyes. She felt like a fool, the way she'd just behaved. Idiot.

With the hot tap on full, the ancient pipes protested at the amount of work they were doing. The bathroom filled with steam and Yvonne traced the shape of the brooch on the mirror. Without the portrait, her memory was already clouding over. Were there eight points to the brooch or twelve?

The pins and needles started their march up her arms again. Turning the water off, she unlocked the door. She rested her head against the wood for a moment as she composed herself and tried to swallow down the pain. She'd take some painkillers, finish her work, find Scott and fill him in. Then she'd ring Warren. He needed to be here, she couldn't let Anita get away with what she'd done today.

She opened the door and stepped into the hall. The houseplants casting shadows as Yvonne walked to her room. She ignored them. She didn't have the energy to jump at every shadow she saw lurking in a corner.

Hers was the largest bedroom, equipped with a kidney-shaped writing desk set up by one window and an occasional table and two armchairs by the second window. Her belongings laid out as if it were her own home. As diametrically opposite to Anita as possible.

She'd unpacked her toiletries bag onto the dressing table. Everything was laid out with military precision. Deodorant, perfume, her contact lenses solution, sleeping pills, painkillers and a beautician's counter worth of makeup and creams. Selecting a vanilla scented body lotion, she massaged the cool cream into her hands and wrists. She pulled off her sweater and her long sleeve t-shirt and set about rubbing the expensive lotion into her aching forearms, upper arms and finally her shoulders.

Rubbing the remnants of the cream into her hands, she realised she'd left her rings downstairs. Every one a connection to someone special — the silver one a gift from her father, long gone now, but his ring lived on. The gold buckle she'd earned from a summer job working for a family friend in a main street antique shop. The opal ring had been her mother's engagement ring. Considered ugly now, it was everything her mother had been — colourful, brash, larger than life. And the pearl one, six pearls for six wonderful years. He'd promised a diamond to replace the pearls, but that nirvana had been stolen from her. Lives are lost and so are engagements. Too many years ago to dwell on, but the ring was a reminder that love is like the grain of sand which forms a pearl. If you cosset love, if you feed it and protect it, it will turn into a pearl. If you don't, it runs through your fingers. Lost forever.

Chastising herself for not thinking to pack a muscle rub, her mouth narrowed as the pain made its way up into her neck. The discomfort from her self massage was worth it, to loosen up the muscles and relieve the tingling she was feeling. She ignored the chill in the room as she waited for the moisturiser to soak in. Popping two pills from their foil cells, she swallowed them dry. She'd get a drink downstairs.

She wandered downstairs, ignoring the voices she could hear in Anita's room. Callaghan was always so bloody measured. She'd never seen him lose his cool, or speak out of turn. He'd make a good politician, or lawyer. Trust him to weigh up the evidence first. She knew Anita had stolen the brooch and she'd prove it, as soon as the painkillers kicked in.

Her work in the house was almost done. She hadn't bothered going into half the rooms. Jewellery and silverware were her primary areas of ability so she hadn't looked in the nursery, the scullery, the bathrooms or any of the sheds and garages. She'd done the kitchen, the dining room, the drawing room and most of the bedrooms. Some of which contained only a bed and a set of empty drawers and they held no interest. She hadn't done Anita's room or the room the supposed lawyer had been using. Which only left the study. She'd get that done next, then hide herself away upstairs in the turret and admire the view while the others did whatever it was they needed to do. The turret would provide a nice secluded place to ring Warren and fill him in before the packers turned up. She knew she'd get a cellphone signal up there.

Like an idiot, she realised she hadn't even checked her phone. The thing probably wasn't even charged. The battery never lasted a whole day at the best of times and out here it would've wasted all its energy searching fruitlessly for a signal. Damn it.

Slipping her rings back on, she chose a now stale pastry from the kitchen, grabbed her work bag from the kitchen table and made her way to the study. Closing the door behind her was a relief, as it was doubtful the others would come in here soon. Ignoring the untidiness of the shelves, she switched on the banker's lamp and looked for somewhere to charge her phone. Just like Anita, she found that the only socket was the one the lamp occupied. No problem. She fished a double plug out of her bag and the battery icon appeared. Excellent.

She walked around the messy room, taking in the assortment of trinkets adorning the shelves. A copper and brass powder flask caught her eye. Beautifully polished, art nouveau style. A quick easy sale that one. These days anything military, in good condition, sold above its auction estimate. So many collectors were emerging from the affluent Far East that stuff like this flew out the door. Tagging it, she left it on the desk to be packed later. Two silver photo frames. The pictures inside the frames were less than inspiring. Prising open the backs of the frames, she slipped the photos out. Nothing written on the back to identify the people in the photos though — children on a picnic in one and a couple standing on the front steps of the house in the other. Given the stiff unsmiling poses and the clothing, the photos were early last century. The frames hallmarked London 1911, which tied in with the age of the photographs.

Yvonne froze. She carried the photograph of the couple over to the window where the light was better. The woman in the photo, there was something on her tailored coat. It was the brooch, there in all its glory. A manic grin spread across her face. Anita may have burnt the painting, but now she had proof that the brooch existed. She wasn't letting this one out of her hands. Excitement flared inside her. A movement outside distracted her — the flash of a man lumbering at the far end of the garden, a mutt by his side. She wondered if that was the dog from last night but was too entranced by the photograph to give it any further thought.

Turning away from the window, she lurched into the edge of the heavy desk. Pain coursed through her. Doubled over, she rubbed her sore thigh, which added to the dull throb running all the way down her right side. The painkillers had done nothing.

She hobbled to the foyer, leaning on the post at the bottom of the stairs for support as another wave of pain hit. Her hand tightened around the photograph. She had to force her fingers to relax before they ruined the photo. The picture was swimming in and out of focus, her eyesight blurring. Terrified she was experiencing a stroke, she waited for the sensation to pass. She needed to show the others this photo — validation of what she'd accused Anita of. Shaking her head, she crawled up the stairs on all fours; her weakened right-hand side causing a lopsided gait. Time and time again she crashed into the balustrades before changing direction and forcing herself up another step. The steps themselves multiplying and contracting as her vision played tricks on her mind. She needed to get to Anita's room — the closest door to the top of the stairs. Reaching the last step, she lay panting — half up and half down.

She had no energy to call out to the others, who were still enjoying their little tête-à-tête in the bedroom. She convulsed as another wave of pain traveled through her. Whimpering, she could barely breathe. Hearing a noise, she tried lifting her head. The pressure was incredible. At the end of the corridor was a man.

"Scott," she wheezed.

He walked closer, his black suit blending with the nocturnal shadows. It wasn't Scott. This must be Anita's lawyer making an appearance, except... he looked so familiar.

He stopped a little away from Yvonne, close enough for the hall light to illuminate his face sufficiently for recognition to set in. Yvonne pulled herself up, limbs sluggish, refusing to obey her. She tried to take a step, to make it to Anita'a room. Another wave of pain crashed against her and she fell against the newel post. Scrambling to stop herself falling, she caught her rings on the fretwork of the stairs. There are only so many knocks a ring will withstand before the metal weakens or a stone dislodges from damaged claws.

Knocked free from their setting, the jumble of pearls from Yvonne's ring bounced down the stairs, gathering momentum as they went, skittering across the floor in a hundred different directions. The tiny pings of their bounces growing fainter as they fell.

The man in front of her was the man in the photograph. Wracked with pain, she could do nothing as he leaned towards her and plucked the photograph from her arthritic-like hand. She tried to cry out, but had nothing left. She certainly had nothing left when he reached out and pushed her.

"It's better this way," she thought she heard him say.

CHAPTER 37

Up in the turret, a little girl threw herself onto the window seat and hugged her knees. She'd run up here like a rabbit after the loud lady had fallen down the stairs. Clicking her silver pen, she giggled to herself as she watched the last strokes applied to the painting on the easel in front of her.

This one made her laugh. What a silly lady, she'd looked so funny falling down the stairs, like a clown doing cartwheels at the circus. She wanted to gather up all the pretty little white pearls from the lady's ring, but he'd sent her away. Luckily she'd got back to the turret in time to see strings of those same pearls being strung around the lady's wrinkly neck, like a noose. She giggled again.

It was so funny adding something in that was never there in the first place. A joke no one else got, a joke just for her. Her brothers had never let her play with their *Meccano*, and now she had it all to herself, just like her sister's china-faced doll. Although she'd smashed that rosebud-lipped doll's face against the tiles outside. She didn't want it anymore; it reminded her of her sister. She didn't want reminding. She didn't want reminding about any of them. She wanted her

Daddy all to herself. Soon she would have him all to herself, again.

"Finish the other one now," she directed.

The artist flexed his knotted fingers. "My hands are too tired now, I need to rest them," he replied.

The angelic faced child scowled, her pretty mouth twisting into something ugly. She flounced off. She'd have to find something else to amuse herself with. It wouldn't be hard, there were still two other people in the house.

CHAPTER 38

Interrupted by the sound of an almighty crash followed by absolute silence, Callaghan had no time to digest what Anita said about the portrait screaming. Racing from Anita's room, with her limping behind, he cast around for the source of the sound. He couldn't see anything. He'd heard something falling down the stairs, something large he was certain, but the upstairs hallway and foyer were empty. It didn't make any sense. Only dust motes played in the air as if they'd been disturbed. But by what?

"Go back to bed," he instructed Anita, once he realised she'd followed him. As he turned to usher the girl back to her room there was a hammering on the front door. The booming echoed through the house and in the absence of anyone else running to open it, Callaghan strode down himself, casting his eye around for any evidence of something at the bottom of the stairs.

He pulled the door open revealing a weatherbeaten old man, the epitome of country farmer, in boots and an overcoat, with heavy work-worn hands, and a squint from too many years working outside. He wasn't dressed like a lawyer. The whereabouts of Anita's lawyer niggled away at him. He didn't want to give in to the suspicion that Anita was playing them all. But it was a bit hard to keep coming to her defence, the longer the mythical lawyer never showed up.

"Yes?"

The farmer narrowed his eyes at the sight of Callaghan as if he'd expected someone else at the door.

"Found these down by the water, looked like someone had been in the water. Thought I'd check and see things were all okay up here." A pair of waterlogged men's suede shoes in his hands; good only for the trash heap now, but Callaghan recognised them immediately. They'd been the source of many hours of amusement on the drive here; Scott's expensive Nordstrom shoes, shoes he'd taken great pride in keeping pristine to the point of teetering on the cusp of being too pedantic about them. After all, they were just shoes.

Callaghan took them from the other man's hands. He had a hundred questions, but didn't want to know the answer to any of them.

"You all right missy?" the farmer called up to Anita, who stood unsteadily at the top of the stairs.

She nodded.

"She's fine. She's hurt her foot but we're fine."

The old man's brow creased but he nodded.

Callaghan watched him clear his throat, as if there were something else he wanted to say, but he snapped it shut and turned away.

Anita called out but the barking of a dog drowned out any sound he would've heard. Callaghan slammed the door shut and wheeled away, bellowing out Scott's name, discarding the sopping wet shoes on the tiles. "Scott, you come down here now. Scott?"

No answer.

"What's happened to Scott?" Anita called out.

No answer.

Like a madman Callaghan crashed open doors, his voice hoarse as he yelled for Scott, his anger level rising. Taking the stairs two at a time, he dodged Anita shivering at the top and carried on with his destructive rampage; plant stands and hall tables swept from his path.

On the stairs, Anita flinched at an urn smashing on the floor but even that didn't put a halt to the increasing volume of Callaghan's cries. The sound of his body hitting an immoveable object did.

He collapsed at the base of the turret door, groaning.

"Callaghan, what's going on?"

Pushing himself to his knees, he stood up, trying to rotate his arm. Pain twisting knife-like in his shoulder socket. He'd dislocated it. He let his useless arm hang by his side, using his other hand to wrench at the door. It wouldn't open.

"Open up you bastard." Kicking the door, he rattled the knob as if his life depended on it. "Scott, open the bloody door. You've had your fun." One final boot into the bottom of the door, and he stomped back to Anita, who shrank back from the anger radiating from him.

"What happened?"

Callaghan grimaced, eyes closed, he was a picture of pain, "Dislocated my shoulder."

"What about Scott?"

"He's locked himself up there." It was then he noticed the sheen of sweat on Anita's face, her eyes tiny pinpricks and her teeth chattering as she wrapped her arms around herself.

"Why did he have Scott's shoes?"

Anita was in no fit condition to question Callaghan any further. It was obvious she wasn't fit for anything. A shame that, he thought, ushering her back to her room. She complied with minimal fuss as he put her back to bed. Brushing his good hand against her forehead he pulled back, the heat from her brow burning. His medical training went as far as the required workplace first aid certificate they sat every two years. But he wasn't equipped to deal with a blood infection.

His concerns over Scott's behaviour roiled about in his stomach. What the hell had Scott been doing outside? What was he playing at? It had dawned on him that out of all the rooms he'd searched, Yvonne hadn't been in any of them. Were they both upstairs having a right royal laugh at him? His fists clenched. He thought he'd left that behaviour at school. It surprised him when adults stooped to playground bullying when things didn't go their way. It wasn't his style to comment but so help him God, if those two didn't show their faces in the next hour, he'd drive Anita to the nearest doctor's surgery himself. And they could bloody well fend for themselves.

Anita had slipped into a fevered sleep so she'd be no use helping fix his shoulder. He'd not be able to fix it in here, he couldn't be certain he wouldn't scream. It'd been several years since he'd last dislocated it at college but he well remembered the pain.

Closing Anita's door, he made his way downstairs. Every tread sending shards of glass through his empty socket. Making it to the drawing room, he collapsed onto the couch and prepared himself for what was coming next.

Salvation beckoned to him in the form of a decanter in the liquor cabinet. The amber liquid's golden glow a promised balm to the exquisite pain in his shoulder. The smokey peat spilled up from the tumbler as the whisky hit the crystal. It didn't last long. Callaghan tipped the whole thing down his throat. The burning sensation a thousand times less unpleasant than the pain he was in.

He poured himself another drink, a modicum of guilt came over him; this was stealing although no one would begrudge him the alcohol given what he was planning to do. He'd planned to sip this one, but even lifting the glass to his lips was agony. Eyes shut, he knocked back the second glass which sent fingers of fire to the edge of his extremities. The liquor had anaesthetised the pain sufficiently for him to do what he needed to do.

Leaning against the doorframe, he took a deep breath, turned, and slammed his unaligned shoulder back into place.

The alcohol had done nothing to mask the pain of hitting the doorframe at the wrong angle; Callaghan screamed — a guttural primordial scream from deep within. Eyes glassy, sweat coursing down his face, he lined up for a second time. The second attempt left him on the floor, silent tears on his cheeks but his shoulder was back in its rightful joint.

CHAPTER 39

Anita fluttered between awake and asleep. The clicking a regular cadence in her ear, too hard to pinpoint in her fevered state. It reminded her of the clicking beetles which sometimes made their way inside in the summer months. The sheets clung to her like an old lover's embrace at the end of a relationship; familiar but unwelcome.

Click. Click. Click

The clicking mirroring her heartbeat.

Opening her eyes confused her. She wasn't at home; she wasn't sure where she was. Adrenaline flooded her body. Was he here? Paralysed, just like the night of her rape. Too afraid to fight, too weak to resist. The foul taste of fear filled her mouth. She wanted to sit up but was too terrified that even that infinitesimal movement would attract the attention of… who, exactly?

Her cloudy mind clicked in time with the clicking in her room. Her room in the house. The house with the portraits. That's when the terror dissipated like the fog in the morning. Someone must have put her back to bed because she didn't remember putting herself here. Flames flew up her leg when she moved as if there was a shackle around her ankle. The clicking continued.

The room had sunk into dusky greys, where even the brightest of colours morphed into a tonal grey, blending into everything else. Where the edges of the rug reached up into the wardrobe and neither object had a beginning nor an end. The walls transformed into window frames and the curtains became an extension of the chair — a hybrid installation more at home in the Museum of Modern Art than a bedroom. An optical illusion, but to Anita's fevered eyes, it was as if Salvador Dali himself had decorated the room while she slept. Where was that clicking coming from?

Slipping out of bed, Anita limped to the light switch, and flooded the room with reassuring light. The wardrobe stood ajar, the white dresses pushed to one side, a void in the middle. A hidey-hole, for someone small.

The remnants of the gilt frame lay charred amidst the motionless ravens. Anita skirted the hearth. She couldn't sleep with the wardrobe open. The idea, the possibility, that someone was hiding inside, haunted her at night. Closing wardrobe doors an obsessive compulsion; regardless of her location, the wardrobe door must be shut.

Before she reached the door, a scrap of paper at the edge of the hearth fluttered in the breeze she'd created. Barely more than a quiver but enough to catch her attention. Her fingers slid the newsprint from its resting place, the inky smell so reminiscent of a childhood spent pouring over the comic strips in the weekend newspaper. Of her father pontificating as he read the world news section. The newsprint's scent as identifiable as cotton candy or buttered popcorn at the summer fair.

Her mind wasn't playing fair. The words swam about, crashing across the narrow column with wavelike undulations. She couldn't focus. A missing woman? Over the cliffs? A smudge of a photo accompanied the brief article — a man and a woman, arms around each other, standing on the front steps of this house. Regardless of the size and graininess of the printing, the woman was the woman from the portrait — the portrait now reduced to colourless ash in her fireplace.

Click. Click. Click

Anita slammed the wardrobe door shut. The clicking stopped. Beetles must be a problem in an old house like this. The flames started up her leg again and the room dimmed as her blood pressure plummeted. She made it to the bed before she blacked out, the newspaper article crumpling under her hand. A moment before she lost consciousness, her befuddled mind heard a voice, a child's voice, a happy voice singing, *"You're next, you're next, you're next."*

CHAPTER 40

Callaghan rotated his shoulder. It was relatively pain free, aside from a dull ache which you'd expect after dislocating it and shunting it back into place. The numbing effects of the whisky had worn off and he needed more. This third glass he sipped at a more sedate pace. Standing at the window where only the night before they'd all enjoyed a post dinner drink, he felt a creeping sense of dread. The house was too quiet. Discounting Anita asleep upstairs, he hadn't heard a toilet flush or the kettle whistle or the easy banter between Yvonne and Scott.

Carrying his drink out to the foyer, he listened. There was nothing. Scott's ruined shoes lay on the tiles, damp mud leaking from the soles like a pool of blood congealing around a body. Stooping to pick them up, his fingers knocked a creamy white pearl, almost invisible against the tiles. Like a prize competition marble, it rolled in a straight line until the muddy puddle ensnared it.

Instead of picking up the shoes to dry them in front of the fire, Callaghan picked up the tiny bauble. The pearlescent white a stark contrast against his dark skin. Rolling it around in his fingers he tried to understand the significance of what he was seeing. It was on the edge of his consciousness, hiding behind a lifetime of memories and half remembered lives.

He brought the pearl to his mouth, and bit down on the tiny ball. Gritty like sand meant it was genuine. If it was smooth, then it was fake. His mouth filled with the grainy memory of summers at the beach. A real pearl then. Its perfect symmetry made it a cultured pearl, marred only by a tiny pinprick on one side. The hole a jeweller made to set the pearl into a brooch, or a ring. A ring like the seventies monstrosity Yvonne wore.

Then the penny dropped.

"Yvonne?" he yelled. "Scott?"

He cast about for... what, he wasn't sure. His hands curled over the pearl, nails digging into his palm. There, another pearl, and another two. Each as symmetrical as the other, with the distinctive tiny holes for the posts. Mounting pearls was a tricky business, and in all honesty, it was only a matter of time before Yvonne's ring disintegrated. She had no respect for the style of the ring; knocking about as if they were steel ball-bearings. Still, he would've expected her to have gathered them up for remounting.

"Yvonne?" he called out again. This wasn't good. Had the two of them driven off? Reassured by the sight of three cars outside, two still blanketed with snow. One set of footprints led to the house, and away from it again. The old man's footprints. He checked his cellphone. It was an old school model — phone calls and text messages. Didn't even have a camera. He didn't need to be distracted by social media or emails when he was working. That's what his work computer was for. A phone was a communication tool — nothing more, nothing less. No signal. He closed the dimming world outside behind him and with the pearls in one hand, his whisky in the other, he walked upstairs, forcing each foot up behind the other. Counting the pearls in his palm as he mounted each step — like a ritual — one, two, three, four. One, two, three, four. One, two, three, four. At the top of the staircase he paused. Nothing.

Lifting the glass to his lips, he recoiled. The warm peat scent replaced with something unidentifiable, but vile. Old vinegar was the closest approximation. He tipped the remnants into the nearest houseplant, a lush fairy fern, although he suspected this would kill it, and checked for a phone signal. No connection. He lifted his eyes in time to see the turret door swing open a few inches. It shuddered on its hinges as if it hadn't decided whether staying open was an option.

Callaghan wasn't sure if Scott was playing silly buggers now. He wasn't sure of anything, so his walk towards the turret was as if each footfall was deliberate and considered. "Hey Scott," he called out, volume turned halfway down. No need to wake Anita. The door swayed in an unseen breeze, hinges complaining at the movement. "Scott? Are you up there?"

Pushing the door all the way open, he placed one foot on the bottom step. His foot longer than the tread of the stairs. Midway to the second step he froze; bouncing down the stairs above him, almost in slow motion, were two more pearls. Like friendly competitors they crossed in front of each other, bouncing off the edges before chasing each other along the hall, rolling to a rest, their momentum spent.

He counted his pearls, one, two, three, four, and then there were the two on the floor. In his mind he conjured up an image of Yvonne's ring. Six spherical balls, balanced precariously on and around each other. The most unwieldy ring ever designed. And Yvonne was somewhere without the pearls of which she was so fond.

Callaghan called out her name, but deep within himself,

he knew she wouldn't answer. Just like he knew Scott wouldn't be upstairs, either. Thrusting the pearls into his pocket, and taking a deep breath, he climbed the stairs.

The turret was vacant. An empty coffee cup stood sentinel across the darkening landscape, accompanied by an artist's easel and a stool. The room reeked of old oil paint and mineral turpentine as if the wood had absorbed the scents of every brush stroke ever applied. A wooden palette propped against the easel tipped forward as Callaghan's tread made it past the top step. Within the confined space, the sound of the palette slapping the wooden floorboards reverberated like the ripples in a pond. Without thinking, Callaghan bent to return it to its original position. His fingers came away tacky with wet paint. In the twilight the colours were indiscernible, indistinct, a hundred different greys. Of course the palette would be wet. Hadn't Anita claimed the portrait Yvonne had found in the study was of the lawyer? Where were the paints? The jumbled mess of metallic tubes, the pale cakes of watercolours?

He was loath to wipe his hands on his pants but his only alternative were the cushions on the window seats. Rubbing his hands smeared the sticky colour over both palms and he tried to wipe them on the thick wooden planes of the easel.

Twilight is the master of disguise. The champion of falsehoods and fiction. The eye wasn't designed for twilight. At this time of last light and almost night, mankind should be settling down for the night, not stalking about badly lit houses where predators masquerade as shadows. Twilight distorts, and Callaghan held tight to that thought as the painting on the easel broke through his consciousness.

Yvonne's face, in all its glory looked back at him. A face too used to wearing makeup, her well plucked eyebrows defining her face like a fingerprint. Even in mottled grey, the hair was Yvonne's - a cotton candy cloud of twice dyed blonde. A dozen strings of pearls wrapped around her throat, their luminosity lost. No gentle wear could imbue these baubles with the glorious hue from being worn against skin.

Callaghan tested the paint. Wet. His touch left a dark stain on the image, fading to black as the twilight changed to night.

The chirping of a cellphone interrupted the stark silence. He'd all but forgotten about it, its digital screen illuminated the room, throwing light into corners where there wasn't meant to be any and giving colour to things better off hidden by the night.

Callaghan's hands stained red. His fingers had left crimson stains on the portrait on the easel. A portrait of Yvonne, eyes frozen, beseeching him to help. Pearl garlands tight around her papery neck.

His stomach turned. Bile thrusting its way up his throat. Callaghan tried to swallow, the bile chased by a primordial fear purging the acid from his stomach. He retched again and again. Sweat plastering his brow. His convulsing stomach had a life of its own, and he sunk to his knees. He could not tear his eyes away from those of his friend. As the glow of his cellphone dimmed, then disappeared, the image of Yvonne's face tattooed on his mind.

The convulsions eased off as logic took over. He stood up, legs like a newborn colt, and wiped his mouth on his sleeve. He grabbed the portrait and stumbled down the stairs. He didn't look back. If he'd looked back, he would have seen an unfinished painting still nestled on the wooden struts of the easel. A younger woman, another woman he knew.

CHAPTER 41

Emerging into the illuminated hallway, Callaghan stumbled like a drunk, the canvas clasped awkwardly in his good hand. His shoulder hurt, his stomach was spasming, and his throat burned. And his friend… he didn't want to think about what had happened to her. He couldn't. What he believed couldn't be possible. Logic told him someone was playing them and for whatever reason that someone didn't want them there.

Halfway down the hall he paused. Downstairs there was a thumping sound. Little sounds, but sounds which carried upstairs like debris on a wave. Lowering the canvas to the floor, he hugged the wall as he crept along the passage. Thump, thump, thump. The sound continuous, the spacing between each bang was consistent with the beating of his heart. Thump, thump, thump. Reaching the top of the staircase, Callaghan peered over the balustrade. The thumping stopped. There was no one there but paintings littered the floor. Knocked over, sharp corners piercing old canvases, the splintered wooden frames causing even more damage to the others they'd fallen on. Bodies lay upon bodies — a massacre of art.

Callaghan stood speechless at the carnage below him. Descending the stairs in a bewildered trance as he considered the cost of the damage. Depending on Anita's appraisal, the visible damage alone would amount to tens of thousands of dollars. This was not good, not good at all. He picked up the first few pieces on the off chance that they were the only ones damaged. But no, whoever had done this had gone to town and every painting in every stack was ruined. It was as if each painting had been thrown down with vicious force and then stood on — as if they were part of a giant game of hopscotch. Callaghan was a large man. He'd never had much cause for worrying about his own physical safety, but now he turned around, taking in the dark corners, the unlit rooms, and the unnatural stillness of the house. Ignoring the damaged art, he backed up till his heel hit the bottom step, then spun around and ran up the stairs.

At Anita's door, he didn't pause; he flung open her door. Anita's eyes opened and she screamed. Pure terror spewed from her mouth as she shot to the top of the bed, cowering in the corner, hair plastered to her forehead, sweat patches blooming under her arms and down her chest.

"Anita, stop it, it's me, Callaghan," he stepped up to the bed, his bulk looming over Anita. Her eyes wild, her screaming silent. He couldn't be sure she could see him. He reached out to placate her, to reassure her it was okay. She bolted.

CHAPTER 42

He was back, to rape her again, to silence her, to stop her from ever being able to identify him. She had to run. She would escape.

Anita bit the hand grasping for her. The thick taste of blood in her mouth oh so familiar, except this time it wasn't her blood, it was his. She pushed him away using a strength she didn't know she had. She saw him wheel backwards. He tripped on the carpet and his bulk spilled onto the floor. She heard, rather than saw, his head hit the hearth. A crunch of skull against tiles gave her legs flight, and she tumbled from bed on legs weak from the fever ravaging her.

As if she were being pursued by wolves, she fled the room. She had no plan but her legs drove her down the stairs. She didn't notice her precious artwork strewn across the floor, there was only one thought in her mind, and that was of escape.

Tripping, she landed on her knees. Somewhere above her someone was calling her name. How did he know her name? She ran on, oblivious to her whereabouts, she sought somewhere safe and familiar. She ducked into the nearest room.

Shutting the door softly behind her, she felt for a lock and found the satisfying shape of a key. She turned it and the lock fell into its chamber. She could breathe again, more afraid of the monster outside than she was of the dark pressing in around her. Sinking to the floor, she shoved her fist in her mouth to hide the scream threatening to erupt. The only sound in the room, the now familiar clicking. She didn't have time to worry about those beetles.

On hands and knees she blundered across to a rectangle of light on the other side of the room, escape still uppermost in her mind. She could climb out the window, run to the farmer, plead for help.

Click, click, click

The satin curtains pooled on the ground, the silken threads caressing Anita as she tried to find the opening. Thrashing against the fabric, it billowed around her. Fingers of icy air released from behind the luxurious folds stabbed at her, until she wrenched at the fabric, ripping it away from the clacking wooden curtain rings.

An avalanche of heavy satin fell onto Anita's head and knocked over a chair standing at the side of the window. The chair crashed to the ground, the sound interminably loud. Anita clawed at the window, sure her attacker would have heard the chair falling. The stunted *plink* of metal against floorboards was lost in the crashing of the chair. A tiny diamond earring lay unnoticed on the floor.

Fingers numb, the old fashioned latch refused to budge. She hit it over and over with the heel of her palm, the sharp edge slicing through her pink skin.

In the thinly veiled dark, Anita cast about for anything to force the window. With the curtains in a pool on the floor, the moonlight leaked into the room, its pale light couldn't

penetrate the far corners or the wasteland in the middle of
the room. It illuminated a hoard of tea chests stacked against
the wall.

Pawing through the first chest like a child under the tree
on Christmas Day, Anita seized upon the first item small
enough and heavy enough to do what she needed. She
bashed the small bronze sculpture against the metal latch. It
sprung free, and she heaved the window open, ignorant of
the cold swamping the room, swirling around her, darting
towards her naked limbs. She had to get out.

She slid over the window ledge, pausing for the briefest
of moments as she caught what she thought was a glimpse of
a face just as she launched herself from the window into the
snow fall. There'd been no one in the room with her, she'd
locked it. It was just a storeroom — a repository for
unwanted possessions. If only there were a place for
undesirable memories. She'd been mad to agree to come
here. She should have stayed at home, safe with her family.
Safe in her daily ritual of commuting to work and from work
on the bus; of smiling at the same familiar strangers, safe in
her thrice weekly gym sessions — greeting the usual girl on
reception, safe in the routine of simple hellos to other
women in her exercise class. Strangers she neither sought
out for friendship, nor did she encourage. Head down, work
hard, go home. She should have been satisfied with that. She
had everything in her life she needed, so didn't need more
responsibility. She didn't need glory in the workplace. What
had she been thinking?

Her fevered mind took over the thinking, and the
running. Anita had no idea where her bare feet were taking
her, it was enough they were taking her away, away from
him. She was headed pell-mell towards the pond, to the
chilling depths which hid so many secrets.

Flailing through the shrubs, she slowed, cocking her head

to one side. Someone was calling her. She stumbled to a stop. The moon couldn't pass through the canopy of tangled vines above her, but sound traveled, and she'd heard her name.

Hair wild, she blended into the undergrowth. The nicks and tears on her skin sending threads of dark blood down her arms and legs, which served as camouflage amongst the trees. Could it be him, or maybe it was Scott or Callaghan? Where had they been when her attacker entered her room? Had he done something to them? She didn't know what to do.

The fast running clouds obscured the light of the moon, and even to herself, she faded into nothing. Maybe she was nothing? By leaving her window ajar that summer, she'd all but left out a welcome mat for her attacker. It was her fault. It was nothing more than she deserved. She turned back, the decision made to check on her friends, on Yvonne. What if he attacked Yvonne? Her sense of direction was off and she'd turned herself around half a dozen times so whichever fevered direction she took now would be the wrong one.

One hesitant step taken, followed by a second, and another, as she probed her way back to the house, clinging to the shapeless shadows. An explosion from the undergrowth floored her, throwing her into the brambles. Anita threw her arms over her face, trying to fend off the monster laying into her. With no strength for a breath or for anything more than protecting her face, she curled into a ball and waited to die. Apologising over and over to her mother, for not listening to her advice, for not ringing, for not saying I love you often enough. Until finally she wept, calling out for her mother to save her.

CHAPTER 43

Head bent over the tractor's engine, he didn't hear the dog's muffled whining, a mumble over the coughing engine.

"Stupid thing. Come on, take," the farmer cajoled the engine. Damn thing kept cutting out. It'd turn over okay, idle a moment, then cut out. Happened every year round this time, it was the cold. Every year he promised he'd put money aside over the summer to buy a new one, a secondhand one. There was never enough money round to splurge on a new one. Still, it had to get him through the rest of the winter, being swiped off the road hadn't helped the old thing.

Hands covered with grease, the wrench slipped from his hands just as the engine died a third time. Clanging against the chassis, the wrench fell into the wintery grass, the dull metal camouflaged by the filthy snow and the morass of weeds. Now the dog's whines were as clear as a bell.

"What is it, boy?"

The dog took off across the field, barking frenetically. Birds took flight in front of him; panicking they shot off in every direction, wings beating against the still sky, their own cries in chorus with the dappled dog.

The farmer wiped his hands on a cloth, the smears of grease adding to a decade of stains already there. A dozen seasons of berries, eons of oil leaks and rain-covered seats. He whistled after him, the piercing sound flying through the air. It made no difference to the dog who barrelled into the undergrowth as if it were a pall of smoke wafting across the countryside.

He dropped the cloth on the overheated bonnet and strode after the wayward animal.

It wasn't hard to track him down. His whines cut through the brush like a knife through butter. At first he thought Ace had been injured but his whines were more concerned than hurt. An animal in the bush? He couldn't think what else could be out here.

"Come away Ace, leave it," he called out. Last thing he needed was for Ace to take a bite out of a rabid animal. He shone a powerful torch into the bushes until he spotted what his wayward dog had run off after.

"Heel Ace, heel. Leave it," slapping his hand against his grubby corduroy thigh, he summoned the dog. Shock flushed his face when he peered into the undergrowth, and found the woman from the house on the ground, half obscured by the remnants of autumn's leaves. The shock shouldn't have been a surprise — the house had a reputation. She wouldn't be the first person to stay in the house before melancholy took over. Most threw themselves off the cliff and were swallowed by the sea. One more funeral without a body. He'd warned them. He'd warned them all. That house did funny things to people. Poor girl, she'd seemed nice and well balanced when he'd last rescued her. Still, some people were most susceptible to their environment. She needed to get away from this place before it drove her too far towards madness.

Anita was too far gone to notice the light from the torch

or the soothing words he muttered in her direction. There was no recognition. He gathered up the cowering woman, careful of her cuts and scrapes. Hefting her into his arms, he stood up.

She struggled, thrashing like a cornered calf. The scent of oil on his hands penetrating her subconscious and tapping into her deepest fear. But he didn't know and clasped her closer. She pummelled at him, screaming. Her fists beating against his chest, useless against the larger man. She bucked in his arms, her incoherent screams ragged in his ears.

Ignoring her, he turned towards the house. Kubin's place was closer than his own but if she'd run from it, should he take her back? He clasped her tighter. He needed to get her inside and the artist's house was closest. She had friends there to care for her. How she came to be out here wasn't his business. They'd ignored his warnings, so he'd have to tell them again — they should leave, before it was too late.

Shifting the weight in his arms, he staggered towards the house, the dog by his side whimpering, the sounds from the girl worrying the dog.

"Quiet now, quiet. You're okay," he said, trying to calm her. She was in her own world. His words making no impact. Her struggles were slowing, more from tiredness he suspected than from his ineffectual words.

Halfway back, he saw one of the city boys scrambling down the hill. His eyes full of concern, not like Gates Junior when he'd pulled the girl from the pond. Gates had only been concerned about himself.

He called out to the man and the girl threw herself against him. He stumbled and dropped her as he tripped over. There was a sickening thump as her head struck the frozen ground. The farmer lay dazed himself on the ground. The dog nuzzled at his master, whining until the farmer shook himself. He took hold of the proffered hand from the other man, and pulled himself up, dizzy from the sudden movement.

The girl's body was limp but she was breathing. He tried to pick her up but the pain from his fall was too intense and he stepped back, swallowing a guttural grunt of pain. Cursed with age, he was grateful when the other man picked her up with an ease only the young have. The physical relief immediate, but mentally he was still worried, as was the dog. Ace alternated between whimpering and a low growl as if he knew something was off. Stupid animal, what did he know? He was just a dog. Still, the dog's whimpers forced deep lines up his forehead.

"Stop it. Leave it now, Ace."

Despite his concern he didn't waste time with polite conversation. She needed to get inside as soon as possible.

"You get her inside. Get her warm, then leave, all of you. Preferably tonight if you can." He was a man of few words, but he tried to tell him. To warn him.

The man looked back at him and nodded, an odd look on his face, but he'd gone before the farmer could analyse it. He watched as the city boy carried her back to the darkened house.

He lost sight of them in the evening gloom. A single light shone up in the turret where it always had when old Kubin was alive. He could only just make out the sight of someone sitting at the easel, a canvas in front of them. They were playing with fire up there. Something wasn't right about the house. He knew it and so did his father. The painting hanging over his fireplace at home all he had left of his mother after the same despondency had struck her after she'd sat for her portrait. He couldn't blame Leo. It'd been another artist who'd painted her, Leo's father, George

Laurence Kubin. His father never forgave the artist for sending his wife into a spiral of depression, forcing her brooding body over the cliffs, leaving behind a baby, a broken-hearted husband and an empty coffin.

CHAPTER 44

Callaghan swore under his breath. He'd just got Anita over the threshold before she slipped from his grasp. He caught her awkwardly before she hit the tiles.

Half carrying, half dragging, he got her into the drawing room and onto the couch. She hadn't woken, and lay with her fists clenched, covered with scrapes and congealed blood. He wasn't squeamish, but dealing with someone else's blood... he couldn't clean her up, Yvonne would have to do that, or someone else. Still, tracing her body with his eyes was an enjoyable moment, she was a pretty girl.

Annoyed the farmer hadn't followed them to the house to help, he didn't want to be in this house any longer himself. Now he was stuck here till Anita woke up. The lights flickered and Callaghan looked up, the electricity failing was the last thing they needed. The flickering steadied; he carried on breathing. His breath hanging in the air a sign of how cold the room was as if winter herself had taken up residence inside. It made no sense for it to be colder inside than out. Being torn down the best thing for it, the old house was probably crawling with termites or other vermin. He shuddered, his fastidiousness insulted by the thought, and by the cold.

Crouching in front of the fireplace he lit a match to the half-charred pine cones in the grate. The match burnt down to his fingers without touching the brittle cones. He lit another one and cast around for some paper to use as kindling. Nothing. Again the match stung his fingers and he dropped it, sucking on his burnt fingers. He remembered the paper in the old nursery. Perfect.

Looking towards Anita he shrugged off the feelings of unease creeping up, casting its fingers into his spine, massaging fear into his cerebral cortex. He needed paper for the fire, that's all. He'd get the girl warm, awake, then he'd put her in the car and drive somewhere, anywhere but here. As for Scott and Yvonne, he couldn't think of them, especially not the portrait of Yvonne upstairs. His skin crawled, he'd think of them later. Being alone with Anita had its appeal.

Leaving the drawing room, he paused outside the nursery door. He wasn't scared of much but every step he'd taken down the hall was shot with inexplicable dread. He needed paper and there was plenty in the waste paper basket.

The door opened and flicking the bakelite switch filled the room with light. It looked as it had earlier today. Was that only today? It felt like a lifetime ago. His stomach rumbled, reminding him how long ago it had been when they'd eaten together as a cohesive unit. The room was identical, the same spider feasting on the moth in the corner, spinning a silvery cocoon around the moth's carcass. He felt sorry for the moth, helpless in a web not of its own making. He felt the same way — stuck in a life he didn't want. He wasn't the man people thought him.

Shaking off the melancholy, he twisted handfuls of paper into tapers for the fire. Oblivious to the words on the pages;

ignorant of the images roughly sketched on the pages —
images of people long gone. No longer loved nor
remembered by anyone left living. In his haste, he didn't
register the *click, click, click* of a pen in the shadows.

Back in the drawing room, he shoved the papers into the
fireplace. After striking another match, the paper caught, and
the fire flared, spreading with ease to the pine cones and the
kindling. The house filled with a deep baritone cry.
Callaghan ignored it, it was the sound of the fire raging
through the sap and the damp wood; it was nothing he
hadn't heard before.

He moved the hair stuck to Anita's brow, his fingers
lingering on her forehead, enjoying the feel of her skin under
his skin. He pressed a fraction harder. She mumbled but
didn't wake.

"Anita, wake up, come on now."

There was no change.

"Come on Anita, wake up, it's just us here," Callaghan
said.

The girl moaned on the couch, her forehead as hot as the
fire in the hearth. He tucked a blanket around her. She
flinched before settling again. Callaghan sat on his ankles,
looking around the room, the flickering fire casting obscene
shadows which made the *netsukes* writhe grotesquely in the
fire's reflection. The ravens on the hearth tiles darted to and
fro, looking for something that wasn't there.

He needed a drink; not something alcoholic: he needed
water. Flicking switches as he went, he walked into the
kitchen and reached for the tap. His hand froze. Scott's face
was behind him, reflected in the window. Only it wasn't
Scott.

Callaghan turned, his mouth dry. Scott was hanging on
the wall. Mouth open, eyes wide, his shirt awry on his
shoulders, smudges of grey along the collar. Motionless,

within a gilded frame upon the wall. He couldn't pull his eyes away.

He lunged at it, ripping it from the wall. Whether he noticed that the paint was still wet, he couldn't have said, but he threw the painting onto the table. He grabbed a black-handled knife from the cutlery drawer, the sort used for deboning fish, and slashed at the canvas. A violent strike across the centre of the face, the two sides peeling back like petals.

"That's what I think of your sick joke," he yelled at nothing, brandishing the weapon. Red paint clung to the serrated edges of the knife.

He needed more than water now. Even if he emptied the whisky decanter, it wouldn't be enough. Leaving the scarred portrait on the table he stumbled towards the hallway, knife still in his hand, a great thirst consuming him.

The fat decanter sat where he'd left it, brooding with its amber belly, enticing him to drown his sorrows within its crystal arms. He sloshed a fair sized portion into his glass. Laughing as he tossed the drink back, at how much Scott would hate that portrait. The artist hadn't captured him at his debonair best so he'd done Scott a favour by destroying it. He couldn't wait for his friend to see it, knowing they'd laugh over it together. But deep in his subconscious, he knew Scott would never see it. A ludicrous thought, madness, much like Yvonne's painting upstairs. Scott and Yvonne. Would he be next? Fear joined the whisky burning his throat.

The knife lay next to his hand on the cabinet. The black handle obscene against the warmth of the walnut veneer. Callaghan pushed it with his finger, the weighted handle spun in a perfect arc, the blade flashing towards him and then away. Like a lethal game of spin the bottle. The girl on the couch murmured. He spun the knife a second time, a little harder. This time the knife over rotated, falling to the floor, missing his foot by less than an inch. So anaesthetised he didn't flinch. Scooping up the knife, he slammed it into the veneer. Crystal glasses rattled against the tray and the girl stirred.

Callaghan poured another drink, his stained fingers filthy against the faceted glass. The decanter almost empty, he ran his fingers along the diamond pattern of the crystal bottle. Solid, heavy, lead based, the most perfect receptacle for whisky ever designed. He had a small collection at home, broad based Baccarat and delicate Tiffany decanters. This would fit his collection.

Head fuzzy with alcohol and lack of food, he couldn't follow any coherent thought and slumped onto the couch, spilling the strong smelling liquor. What a waste. He wiped it with his free hand. He flexed his fingers; the knuckles cracking. They'd always done that. Drove his mother insane. The doctors put it down to too much exercise when he was young. Seemed you couldn't win these days. You either didn't exercise and got fat and lazy in front of a screen, or you exercised too much and wrecked yourself. His joints had never bothered him. It'd been a party trick when he was a teenager, clicking first his ankles, his wrists, and then his fingers. On a good day his neck would crack both ways, and his elbows. He'd never been able to sneak out, his ankles creaking every time he inched down the family staircase and his mother had hearing like a hawk.

Where were these thoughts coming from? Flexing his fingers again, he swapped his glass to the other hand. His knuckles, discoloured by decades of furniture oils and stains, clicked again, the noise echoing through the house. Which was odd because it really was such a little sound.

Anita stirred again, her hands coming up to her head.

"Hey," he said.

Anita tried opening her eyes. One eye opened, the other

swollen like a ripe peach, whipped by a branch, it wouldn't open more than halfway. Funny he hadn't noticed before. Shocked into sobriety now he was properly looking, he saw she was covered with scratches and streaks of congealed blood, her feet encased in dried filth.

With a start he remembered the infection in her foot. He hadn't thought to clean it. For someone who'd been thrashing like a lion in a circus cage only an hour earlier, she was oddly still... was it only an hour, he couldn't be sure. The clock on the mantel had stopped, and he didn't wear a watch. Some people did. Scott did, but he hadn't worn one for years, stupid things got in the way.

"How are you feeling?"

Weird how she lay there, staring at him. He waved a hand in front of her face, his fingers clicked, and then his wrist. She blinked and tried to talk, but seemed to have trouble. He held his whisky up to her lips, and her good eye screwed up in response.

"Water," she whispered.

Wrestling with himself, his public persona emerged. He'd get her a drink, to show she needed him. It was always good to be needed, it made it easier down the track, normally.

"Thirsty," Anita said.

"Of course," Callaghan said, smiling. Water, some food, and then they'd leave. The devil could take Yvonne and Scott for all he cared. Maybe the two of them were off on some lovers tryst somewhere, with Anita's elusive lawyer? He didn't care if all three of them were shacked up in some outhouse. He needed to leave, soon. He had an important date with the lovely Anita that he'd been thinking about for a long time.

CHAPTER 45

The raven perched on the edge of the gable. Ruffling its feathers, its beak opening and closing as if it were holding an unseen conversation with the world. It could have been sharing a warning about what it had seen through the windows of Kubin's not-so-empty house. A home is a receptacle to hold a family together — the photos on the walls the bruises of childhood, the crockery in the cupboards the eclectic memories of meals past. The empty clothes left hanging in the wardrobes mere shadows left behind, waiting to be sewn back on... this was no home.

The little girl wanted the pearls. She wanted to play with those pearly white balls and it wasn't fair she wasn't allowed to have them. George would've let her have them. He always gave her what she wanted. She always got what she wanted.

She liked collecting things. So far she had a pretty watch, and a shiny pen, and a mountain of other trinkets she'd squirrelled away from people who'd stayed at the house. Things they'd never miss, or need again, like Mummy's beautiful star-shaped brooch. But now Daddy had taken that away and he wouldn't let her play with the pearls the lady let roll down the stairs. She wasn't happy; it reminded her too much of that last summer with Mummy.

They'd been happy that summer. Mummy announced a new baby would come and Daddy gave her a pretty brooch to celebrate. For a while it was the happiest they'd been - Mummy, Daddy, all of them. But then one of Daddy's friends, the young artist with the clever fingers, whispered something into Daddy's ear which changed everything. The rest of the summer became colder than the long winters when she and her sister snuggled in bed together to keep warm. By the end of the summer, the adults flung vile words about the house with no thought where they'd land. Her parent's arguments more violent than the waves in the ocean beyond the cliffs. That was when mother said the baby wasn't his. His reply would haunt her forever — he replied he already knew, and that he'd considered it an act of charity to allow her to stay under his roof. The argument continued with her father suggesting that perhaps the new babe wasn't the only child which he hadn't fathered. It hadn't been hard to figure out who he meant.

The artist found her crying by the pond. Her imperfect face streaked with tears. Hers the only head in the family covered with mousey brown hair and eyes the colour of the earth staining her knees. He promised he'd fix her family. And she believed him.

Snapping out of her reverie, head in her hands, she waited for the artist to wake. Why did his fingers get so pained? He'd been able to paint like lightning before, fast and furious. It was frustrating having these people in her house, destroying their carefully constructed life. She drummed her fingers against the window, enjoying the sound it made, almost like the grasping fumbling noises that woman had made on the stairs before the artist finished her portrait.

She was tired of being alone, her memories of the other children tainted by her false father's words but still, she missed them a little. Their portraits ruined now, faces smeared, and burnt, and cut. There would be no return to those halcyon summers of swimming in the pond and playing games on the lawn. She didn't miss them, truly she didn't. They weren't her brothers and sister and the artist had been more than happy to paint their portraits when she'd asked. Her foolish mother had been happy too. She didn't understand what would happen.

Her nose flared when she thought of Mother — such a boring woman, it still surprised her Mother had been bold enough to dally with the artist, the one Father invited to join the family every summer. Such a silly thing to do, to invite so many strangers to summer at your house with your family there.

How she'd laughed when her brothers and sister disappeared — three blue-eyed, blonde haired children, angelic in every way, and so different from her own brown-eyed mousey self. They'd found her by the pond, laughing at the water's edge. If they'd arrived moments earlier, they would have seen her systematically stomping in the muddy shallows, in three different pairs of shoes, before hurling them all as far out into the pond as she could. They'd gone for a swim she'd said, in their clothes she said, but hadn't surfaced she'd said. Childish laughter bubbled from her lips. They said she was in shock. She wasn't in shock. She had her parents all to herself, which would make Father love her now.

The memory forcing a smile from her lips.

CHAPTER 46

Callaghan had piled an assortment of food onto a tray —
tomatoes, slices of cheese, the last of the loaf, some relish
he'd found in the fridge and a limp carrot — peeled and
sliced to make it more appealing. Walking into the lounge, he
lowered the tray and picked up a tomato, biting into it like an
apple, the flesh parting between his teeth.

"Have some of this," Callaghan suggested, a tiny pip
caught in the corner of his mouth. He wiped it away with his
stained hand before taking a second bite, juice dribbling
down his unshaven chin. He seemed to morph into someone
she didn't know.

Anita's stomach heaved at the sight of the tomato juice.
She couldn't watch, it wasn't normal to eat a tomato that
way. Shaking her head, she turned away from her colleague,
focusing instead on the glass of water he'd handed her.
Sapped by events she only had a shadowy recollection of, she
could see nothing beyond the windows, it were as if a black
cloth enveloped the house; smothering her with a force she
had no control over. There was no logical explanation for
why she felt that way, but the sense of being trapped kept her

cowering on the couch, avoiding Callaghan's appraising gaze.

"Where are the others?" she asked.

"They've gone to town for provisions. I think they found a jeep in a shed. None of our cars would make it into town. That's where they are, in town," he said, as if it were the truth.

Anita wasn't sure she believed him. He'd looked away when he'd answered, eyes flicking over everything in the lounge except her. She sipped the water, the liquid barely touching her parched mouth, but the vile taste of tomatoes had tainted the water. She gagged, doubling over as coughing racked her body.

Callaghan leaned forward and slapped her back. The heady scent of overripe tomatoes filled her nostrils, she flinched. His large hands felt like rocks pinning her down. The ingrained oils on his hands mixed with the earthy scent of the tomato gushing from his mouth, formed a familiar scent, one which visited her in never-ending looped nightmares where her attacker smothered her again and again, his hand covering her mouth, the other between her legs. A hand reeking of motor oil and tomatoes. No, not motor oil. Had it ever been motor oil? Or was it the heady smell of furniture stain, that peculiar marriage between linseed oil and mineral spirits.

She looked at Callaghan with new eyes. He'd stepped back, eyes blank again. There was nothing concerning about him, a coworker. Her mind focused on him — the curve of his shoulders, his height, the inclination of his head. They'd worked together for over two years. Not side by side, but in the same office, doing the same things, attending the same meetings. He'd smiled, said good morning, all normal coworker type things, never inappropriate. He'd even dropped a group of them home once after an evening auction; he'd dropped four of them off, one by one, like a school bus service. There'd been plenty of laughter, and it'd felt natural sitting in his car. He hadn't asked to come in and she hadn't asked him to. That had been at the start of the summer, the summer of the attack. No, she told herself. Stop it.

"When are they coming back?" she said, watching the back of his head.

"No idea," he turned to face her. "The packers will be here tomorrow," he added.

Anita frowned. She was so confused. She'd been upstairs, Yvonne too, but then she wasn't. The picture fell into the fire, or the ravens pushed it in, but from here her mind grew fuzzy. She'd been in bed, there were no ravens inside, they were pictures on tiles. Her stomach turned queasy.

"And Alan, has he shown up yet? Did you ask the farmer?"

Anger crossed Callaghan's face like a shadow. "There's no sign of him, other than his car. I didn't ask the farmer. Is that who the old man is?"

Anita struggled up, trying to ignore the flash of anger across the other man's face, realising she'd feel safer in the company of the old man than with Callaghan. A disturbing thought.

"Is he here now?"

"Who, the old man?"

Anita nodded.

"No, his dog found you outside, and I got to you before the old man did." He smiled. "Isn't it amazing how bodies react to stress?" The smile absent from his eyes.

"I don't understand?"

"You climbed out a window. The infection in your foot sent you off on a wild adventure. It's amazing you're functioning at all."

Anita sank back into the folds of the couch, fragments of

film running through her head — windows, people calling her, terror, children and ravens. Mostly ravens, flinging themselves at her head, her arms, her eyes, squabbling over rotting tomatoes, their murderous cries as their clumsy feet knocked over tins of furniture stain. Stain which morphed into crimson rivulets dripping from a scarred wooden bench. The steady drip so loud it could have been in the room with her.

"What's that noise?" Callaghan asked, jolting her from the dark place she'd descended into.

"What noise?"

"That dripping noise," Callaghan said. For the first time his eyes took on a hint of interest. "Has someone left the bath running?"

Anita shrugged, looking towards the ceiling for any sign of a leak. In the deepest recesses of her mind she wondered if the dripping was bath water left running, or the dripping of something else. "Should you go look?"

Callaghan nodded, wiping his mouth with the back of his hand and abandoned the slice of loaf he'd topped with thick cheese and a smear of red relish.

The relief of seeing Callaghan leave the room tempered with unease from the steady dripping sound.

Drip, Drip, Drip

Callaghan had a mediocre fire going in the grate, and she moved closer, conscious now her clothes were damp. *She'd climbed out a window?* She had no recollection of that. In the fire's glow, her hands looked more like those of a woman who'd spent the week gardening and not appraising art.

The tray with the remains of Callaghan's tomatoes lay next to her, complete with crumbs from the loaf and a sheen from the fire on the slices of cheese left for her to eat. Very Daliesque. She reached for a tomato, its flesh too pliable as if everything underneath the skin had turned to liquid. Much like she felt. The green stalk was dry and brittle and reeked of the plant it had been torn from. Out of season, stored in a blast chiller. Ludicrous to be eating tomatoes in winter. She brought the red fruit to her lips. Both were cold to the touch, the fire the only point of heat in the room.

Mesmerised by the fire, she let it flood her and it filled the voids of her mind, coaxing out memories she'd repressed. Why wouldn't she eat a tomato? She remembered eating them as a child. Thick slabs coated with dark pepper. Sometimes her mother would grill them — she'd cover them with cheese and slide them under the grill. She'd peer in and watch the cheese bubble up and the bright red edges blacken before pulling the tray out.

She slipped one hand into her pocket, the other still gripping the plump fruit. Her thawing fingers flexed, entangled within the confines of the denim pocket. She yanked her hand free, bringing with it the wispy threads capturing her fingers. A lock of long blonde hair loosed from its unspooled ribbon. Gazing at the hair, she fought for a memory — the lock of hair from the frame she'd dropped. Letting the ancient strands fall through her fingers, they floated towards the hearth. A breath of wind nudged them into the flames, ensnaring the fine filaments. The hair shrivelled up in less time than it took Anita to take a breath. As the hair disappeared, she registered a childlike crying coming from somewhere in the house. A crying cut off as if a closing door sealed the sound away.

The crying released her memories and she dropped the tomato, its overripe flesh splitting on the tiles, pulp oozing out. Juice sizzled on the grate, competing with the dripping sound reverberating around the room, and with the sobs emanating from Anita.

CHAPTER 47

A bird circling aloft would see the shattered ruins of the garden, concrete bones adorning the graveyard, a misshapen pond creeping towards the overgrown pathways. From above, the house looked like a child's sandcastle, angles jutting out without sense. A turret plonked atop of the crooked gothic architecture. A film set laid out by workers from a dozen different cultures. No rhyme nor reason to the form. An estate designed by committee.

The hound sniffled in the shrubs, his nose buried in the decaying leaf rot. Centipedes and other dark-bodied beetles scurried from the intrusion. The dog's long claws raked at the damp earth. Sprays of soil exploded behind the dog coating the glossy holly leaves. Pausing, he inspected the cavity, paying no attention to the other creatures around him. There'd been a scent here, an exciting one, and he'd tracked it from across the snowy fields to this forgotten corner where stone memorials stood sentinel. No one remembered them but their scents remained, drawing him to this disturbed mound where nothing grew.

His ears twitched back — he'd heard a cry, calling his name. There was no urgency to the cry. He dug deeper, pawing at the earth. A yelp; he skittered backwards, baring his teeth, growling at the hole. Sinking to his stomach, he whimpered, licking at the pad of his paw. He didn't understand why licking his paw made the pain worse. He tried standing but his fleshy pad was unable to bear any weight. The scent was still there but he couldn't dig any further. The filtered moonlight half exposed a glassy eye, a lock of hair, and a sliver of cheek. He whimpered. The scent increased, and he was desperate to dig it up, but the pain.

His ears swivelled. He was being called again. Torn, he focused on the hole, and inched closer till he could stretch out and nudge the earth, one last effort to uncover the source of the scent. A tiny hand appeared. Five perfect fingers frozen in time. He seized the hand in his mouth and shuffled backwards, pulling the broken thing from the earth. A filthy ribbon trailing behind as he limped back through the bushes. The man calling his name more insistent, his calls more strident. Another whimper escaped from the back of his throat.

"Ace, here boy, come here. Where are you, you damn dog?" The farmer stomped through the overgrown gardens. He'd done little about keeping the weeds back, didn't seem to be any point. Old Kubin never came down here, just threw him enough money every month to keep his drive clear and the worst of the shrubs away from the windows. That's what Kubin asked him to do and what he'd paid him for. Now he was dead, that extra income would dry up. Wouldn't make much difference to his life, except he wouldn't have to traipse over here every week. It'd give him more time to concentrate on his own farm.

What wild goose chase was that blasted animal on now? He'd never had this trouble with the dog before. Should've left the dog at home, knew it'd been a bad idea after what happened last time. But an inner fear forced his hand and so he'd come out with his dog, to check for wayward stock, positive he'd heard a wolf or a stray dog. And then the blasted animal had taken off towards Kubin's house again. Chasing rabbits, or something else. No point dwelling on what might be up at the house.

Crossing Kubin's gardens, he felt exposed. There were no lights at the windows, save for the one spilling from the turret. From this angle he couldn't see anyone up there, which was fine.

His rubber boots crunched through the crystalline garden, leaving giant footprints in his wake. He whistled, an ear-piercing shrillness which startled the sleeping ravens. They took to the air, their displeasure made obvious by their indignant cries. Stuff the buggers, the farmer thought, that was the only thing they were good for — home decor. He went to whistle again when the dog emerged from the undergrowth. The dog looked disfigured, misshapen in the twilight. With his uneven gait, he could have been a monster materialising from the bush. The farmer faltered, his hand coming up to massage the lump on his own head from where he'd fallen over carrying the girl. It was a passing moment. He wasn't concussed. The whimpering from the dog marked him as his own.

Kneeling on his arthritic knee beside the dog, he stroked the animal's damp coat. "What have you got, Ace?" he asked.

The dog dropped the dirt-encrusted thing and lay down, paw outstretched, whimpering, pleading with him to fix it. He cursed himself for forgetting a torch but he had a box of waterproof matches in the pocket of his old coat.

You never knew when you might need matches or a small knife.

The match flared, sulphur pungent in the nature-washed air. In illuminating the night, the match showed much more than nature intended. The farmer fell back, dropping the match, extinguishing the light. The image of what he'd seen could never be extinguished. Laying between the dog's paws, perfect in so many ways but brutally damaged in others, was a baby.

He turned and vomited, heaving until there was nothing left to expel. He wiped his mouth on his sleeve. Filled with revulsion, but doubting his own mind, he needed another look. He struck a second match, his hands trembling so much that the match snapped in half. A third match suffered the same fate. By the fourth match, with the painful whimpers of the dog increasing, he forced his old hands to steady. The match lit and he lowered it towards the baby. Two perfect hands and perfect feet, one still clad in a black leather shoe. Moving the match he found the face, or what was left of her face. For it had been a girl, with a head of curly blonde hair. The whole side caved in now, a jagged edge left where her cheek, nose and chin would have been. The match spluttered and died as he reached out to touch the thing, the baby.

As he touched the porcelain white edge of the girl's face, realisation dawned that this thing wasn't a real baby, but a doll, the twilight lending a realism he'd misinterpreted. What a fool. The dog whimpered again, pushing its hot nose into his hand.

"Hey boy, I'm all yours now, what have you done?" He struck another match to check the dog's proffered paw. Embedded deep in the pad was a shard of porcelain. He let the match burn down, and by feel only, he tugged it from the sandpaper-rough pad. "There you go, boy," he said. The dog licked his paw, his tail thumping on the ground.

"Come on now," he said, standing. He slapped his thigh, but the dog made no move to join him. "Come on," he cajoled. The animal looked up at him but continued with his ministrations after barely a glance.

"Ace," said the farmer, his voice rising with the command. He made to pick up the doll but a low growl from the dog stopped him. "Cut that out, come on." The farmer pulled the doll away by her porcelain ankle.

Ace snapped at the man's hand, his growling taking on a deeper menace.

The farmer stepped back, changing his grip on the doll, holding it now around its naked stomach.

The dog stood up, hackles raised, his exposed canine teeth glinting in the moonlight.

The farmer had lived with dogs all his life, farm dogs and family dogs. Now and then you got one who snapped; one minute they were your best friend, but the next minute nature stepped in, or evolution, and the animal turned unpredictable and dangerous. He never expected it to happen to Ace. Softening his voice, he talked quietly to the dog. Eight years they'd been together, a long time for any friendship, and although it was too dark to see Ace's eyes, he could hear the threat in the dog's growls. All over a doll? The dog could have it if he wanted. He didn't want the damn dog to injure himself again, that was his only concern.

"You want this then?" he asked, laying the doll on the frozen ground. The growling stopped, and the dog nuzzled the doll, licking at the delicate china hands. A howling down by the pond startled them both. There were no other dogs in this area, not close enough for them to hear, anyway. The farmer slapped his thigh, distracting Ace from the of sound of the other animal.

The dog considered him before picking up the doll in his mouth and limping towards the old man. The farmer reached out, as if to pat his friend, but there was something about the way the dog held his head which made him pull back with confusion. Now wasn't the time to think about the strangeness of the dog. This place made everyone a little mad, always had, always would. The sooner they got home, the better.

"Come on then, Ace," he said. Off they walked, both man and dog limping. Behind them the howling started up again. The dog turned to look back, the doll hanging obscenely from his jaws. "Come on, boy." Reluctantly the dog followed behind the longer-limbed man, towards the shrouded house.

The farmer strode towards Kubin's house. In the distance he could see the outlines of the barren trees lining the driveway, leaning away from the house, pushed that way by the strong sea breezes. To him they'd always looked like they were trying to escape the pull of the house. He didn't want to be anywhere near the place either, so understood their reluctance to be any closer than necessary.

Unease caressed his shoulders. It wasn't just the thing with the dog and the shoes by the pond. Individually those things were curious but were probably nothing. A feeling of indecipherable dread descended, stemming more from when he'd walked away from the girl. Leaving her to the other man. He shouldn't have. There was something about how her colleague had looked at her; he'd looked at her the way a cat looks at a sparrow it has caught in the garden, toying with it at leisure, allowing it to hop away before pouncing again, enjoying the sport more than the meal. That was how the other man had looked at her.

Mounting the steps he hammered at the door, tapping clods of earth from his boots. This time he meant to go inside. Silence greeted his knocking. At least five people were in that house, someone should have come to the door.

The dog sat on its haunches watching, before lowering the doll to the front stoop — an offering.

CHAPTER 48

Callaghan wandered the halls, his ears leading the way. The dripping sound shifted around, teasing him with its invisibility. Head fuzzy from alcohol, he wanted nothing more than to go back to Anita, her vulnerability so appealing. But the dripping sounded like insects in his brain and he couldn't concentrate on anything else.

He fancied the closer he got to the kitchen, the louder the dripping was. Straightening he barged into the room, an unbreakable force, making a beeline for the taps. Without hesitating he twisted both taps, the metal like ice under his hands. They didn't budge. They were already off. Puzzled, he stared at the taps, as if expecting them to be the source of the sound. The dripping came from behind him.

He turned.

Scott's ruined portrait lay on the table, the slashed canvas as Callaghan had left it. Scott's beloved watch lay underneath the shattered paint. Callaghan took a step forward. He hadn't seen that there before. He took another step and reached for the wristwatch. His foot skidded in a dark patch blossoming on the floor.

He stepped back, the print on the ground a facsimile of his own shoe, cast in red... *paint?*

The sound of another drop of liquid joining the pool echoed round the kitchen. Callaghan peered at the puddle, his foot now rooted to the floor. Looking upwards, he could find no source for the sound. He looked again at the table, at the distasteful portrait he'd abandoned there. He blinked. Another drip. This time, in the fraction of the second he opened his eyes, he saw a red droplet form on the edge of the frame. It wobbled, like a raindrop on a leaf, before quivering once more and plummeting to the floor.

Drip

Callaghan bucked as if he'd been shot in the back, and bolted from the room, Scott's watch clasped in his hand, pulse racing. He gave no logical thought to what he'd seen, there was no explanation. Behind him red footprints marked his flight, each one more faded than its predecessor, like his sanity — diminishing faster than his footfalls.

"Get up, get up," he yelled at Anita, not even registering that she was up, his wild eyes caught by the red mess on the hearth. He stopped, his body freezing in mid-motion. *It can't be in here too.* He backed out of the lounge, thrusting the watch into his pocket, where it clunked against the forgotten jade *netsuke.* His eyes focused on the tomato, focused but his brain disengaged, translating the tomato as bloodied paint.

Reaching the foyer, he spun round, portrait after portrait stacked against the walls, mocking him, teasing him. Most facing inwards, stacked that way to avoid damage. *Were they laughing at him, those unseen faces?* He tripped over his own feet, the sudden jolt reengaging rational thought. There was no dripping blood out here, only frames, wooden frames. A trick, a stupid trick.

He seized the nearest frame, and hurled it across the foyer, followed by another and another. The wooden frames shattering upon impact. The sound drowning out that of the dripping paint. He wasn't a fool.

The shadow of the girl stood in the doorway. Rage fuelled him. He spent so much energy controlling his dark rage, that when he released it, he felt at peace. Free to be himself. Years ago, when it first happened, it had frightened him, now he savoured the moments when they came, enjoying the fruits they delivered. He'd tamed himself over the years, refusing to give in to his desires, knowing he had to be careful, although sometimes in moments of weakness, he caved.

The darkness was building, he should stop it. They might catch him. But no, no they wouldn't. Scott was gone, Yvonne too. The lawyer a figment of the girl's imagination, unless he'd gone the same way as the others. No, now was a perfect time. The location wasn't perfect but he had all night with her.

He let the feelings overcome him, and like a wave, they washed away his humanity. He turned towards Anita. It had been a long time since he'd had such an opportunity and he would not waste it. The best thing was, he could see in her eyes that she knew. She knew who he was and what was about to happen.

The darkness within him so all-consuming, the real terrors in the house faded away.

CHAPTER 49

The little girl was angry now. That watch was part of her collection. It was hers now. That bad man had no right to take it from the frame. It was hers.

She stomped upstairs and shook the artist awake.

"Make him go now," she said.

"Before the girl?" the artist asked, unfurling his fingers and gesturing towards the piece of unfinished art on the easel.

The girl stomped again, indecision rifling through her mind. She wanted the girl gone but the man had taken her watch. She hated anyone touching her special things. When Mother found her wearing her special brooch she'd got such a smack, and sent to bed with no supper. What a wicked woman. It hadn't been hard to steal the brooch back, especially after Mother had gone away. And now she'd never, ever, be coming back. She giggled.

"Well?" asked the painter, dipping a brush into a fresh coil of paint.

"The girl! Yes, the girl first, finish her. But let me run to her room first, before you finish. I have nothing of hers yet for my collection."

"You'll need something of the man's too," the artist suggested, the words coming barely formed, as if he had no energy left to talk.

The girl hesitated. Something didn't feel right. She watched his eyes, the way they flicked from her to the art and away again. She hated it when adults kept secrets. She really did. Decision made, she fled from the turret, leaving the artist in peace.

His brush heavy, weighed down by souls of so many. He'd thought this had all come to an end but Ruth was insatiable. Leonard had stopped it, his own brush as talented as his father's. But now it had begun again, his old hand forced to capture the souls of those in the house. It'd been fun all those years ago, fun and games. It's always fun until someone gets hurt.

Leonard wasn't his only talented child. Ruth had proven herself more than adept with a pencil. Those hours of lessons unwasted. It'd been too late for him to stop what happened next, but he had no will power against her. He couldn't say no but he could stretch out the time he took to complete the portrait. Surely the visitors in the house had to leave soon?

Dabbing at the canvas, a creamy scar across a jawline. Changing brushes, rubbing the fibres between his rusty fingers to loosen the bristles, every movement like wading through water. He couldn't understand why and rotated his neck to move the weariness settling there. He wanted to say no to Ruth, truly he did, but she was his special treasure and he couldn't say no.

CHAPTER 50

Ruth moved wraith-like through the house, shaking with anticipation. Soon she'd add to her collection, a collection she was immensely proud of. Other girls her age collected shells and inky black raven feathers, or tiny china animals or pieces for their doll houses, she collected far more valuable things, treasures belonging to other people.

Slipping into Anita's room, she blanched at the sight of the bare space on the walls, the space where she and her siblings had so recently hung. The lady with the sore foot had taken them down, that was obvious given she was now standing in her old room instead of hanging on the wall, but the wall looked so different without the others up there. Mother and Father thought it might cheer her up, having them hanging there. But instead she hated the sight of them; sad, sappy eyes begging for release.

She crept into the hollow in the wardrobe, absorbing the scents of her childhood, of her sister, long gone now. Only a tiny piece of Tabby, Tabitha, remained. Her scent woven into the cotton fibres of the dresses left hanging. Tabby should've let her play with the china-faced doll. Tabby got all the good presents. She only got the hand-me-downs. Last birthday they'd given Tabby a new dress, the doll and a silver locket. She'd never been given any jewellery. Daddy had been so cross when Tabby told him the locket was lost after only one day. The look of sadness on Daddy's face was worth it. She was still so very cross at Tabby; they could have played with the doll together. If only Tabby hadn't been so selfish, then maybe Tabby wouldn't be in a painting.

Ruth wondered if Tabitha's locket was still where she'd left it. The lady could've found it after she'd taken the pictures off the walls but she hadn't said anything. The artist had helped her hide the locket in the back; he was better at hiding things than she was.

There were no arguments in the wardrobe, closing the door felt like being inside a muffled world, safe and silent. Reaching into the back of the wardrobe, her fingers curled around a felt bag tucked into a depression in the base. Tipping the contents out in the semi darkness, she picked over the treasures she'd never got to use. Things belonging to people who'd left before she'd given the treasures to the artist — an onyx tie pin, a diamond stud, a jumble of keys, a tarnished lipstick holder. She couldn't remember now who they'd all belonged to, or why she'd collected them, but she still liked holding them, counting them. The pearls would've looked perfect among these treasures. It was wrong that she wasn't allowed to have them. The lady didn't need them anymore.

Poking the assortment back into the drawstring bag, she was dismayed to see the bag peppered with tiny holes, there shouldn't be moths in her wardrobe. Confusion fluttered across her face the way a moth flutters around a flame at night. Indignation overcame her, the staff should have seen to this. She'd have to talk to Father about this, it wouldn't do.

Her childish mind couldn't twist itself around the fact that the house was empty of staff; long gone now, many of them by Ruth's own hand.

Pushing her way from the wardrobe, she remembered her task. Something belonging to the lady. *What should it be?* It needed to be something special for her collection. Rifling through the dressing table, she couldn't find anything small enough. This lady must be very poor, there was no jewellery or pretty perfume bottles, or silver hair slides. Frustration built, there had to be something.

Pirouetting, she spied Anita's cellphone on the bedside table. The girl didn't know what it was, but it was shiny and small. Stroking the sleek lines, square like a book but with no pages, a paperweight? It felt right in her hand, and it was the perfect size, so now it was hers. Now she just needed something belonging to the man. Men were easy — cufflinks, tie pins, cigarette lighters.

She skipped down the hall, forgetting she was trying to avoid her father.

"Hello Ruth," a voice said, from the doorway to Callaghan's room.

Ruth stumbled, panic filling her eyes and turning her surly. Her good mood evaporating as quickly as she'd been skipping. Looking anywhere other than towards the black-coated man, she fidgeted with the hem of her dress.

"What have you done?" he asked, his face shadowed in the doorway.

She'd been so close and now he'd ruin it. She cast sly glances up at him, and past him, into the room.

"Nothing," she said, still avoiding eye contact. He wasn't even her father so she didn't have to answer. Her real father was upstairs finishing, so she needed to hurry or it would be too late — the paint would dry, and she couldn't let that happen.

"I'm just looking," she managed, looking up at the man from under her eyelashes, all sweetness and light now. She knew how to get what she wanted — sugar and spice and all things nice, that's what little girls were made of.

"Come now Ruth, we find ourselves here in this house, in a time not of our own? Are you being naughty? I think maybe yes?" Abraham said, his sad eyes probing her face.

Ruth shook her head, mouthing the word 'no'. She couldn't bring herself to say it aloud. Picking at the embroidery of her dress, she tried not to look towards the turret door, worrying about time in a way only a child can, with frantic panic.

The man held out his arms, inviting her into an embrace. Every part of Ruth yearned to fall into his arms. To be hugged as if she were the only person in the world who mattered. That was all she'd ever wanted, and which she'd never had. Joy infused her face as she took a hesitant step forward.

"What's that in your hand?" he asked instead, plucking Anita's cellphone from Ruth's outstretched arms.

The girl's face twisted as she tried to snatch the treasure back.

"It's mine, give it back," Ruth shrieked. She remembered the whispers, the giggles, the rumours. Remembering he wasn't her father, he was nobody, and now he'd taken her treasure away. He'd done that once before, and things hadn't ended well for him then either.

"Give it back," Ruth screamed, stomping her foot. "You can't have my treasure, you're not even my father."

The verbal slap had no effect. Abraham examined the treasure before slipping the silver cube into his pocket.

"No!" Ruth cried, beating at the man.

He tried grappling with her but Ruth slid from his grasp

like a feral cat. Darting down the stairs, leading him away from the artist. He couldn't know the artist was painting again. Checking behind to see if he'd followed, she flew through the house, the fairy ferns withering in her wake.

CHAPTER 51

"Hello Anita," Callaghan said, his mouth breaking into a rare smile. He straightened his collar, as he put himself back together, smoothing his trousers, tucking in his shirt. Taking a step closer, his body squared with a confidence Anita hadn't seen in him before.

Gripping the doorframe for security and stability, Anita remained rooted to the spot. Naked terror touched every nerve in her body. Looking at him with fresh eyes, she no longer saw the reserved but congenial coworker. In his place, she remembered a monster in a pair of chinos on a hot summer night. A monster who'd once stood in her doorway, eating a tomato like an apple. A doorway so like the one she was leaning into.

She jumped back, as if scalded by the wooden frame. A deluge of pennies dropped within her memory.

Callaghan was the monster from that night.

Wobbling in the dining room, her bare feet sinking into the thick rug, surrounded by the detritus of her work, she frantically considered her options as Callaghan advanced. She had to run but she couldn't get the signal from her head to her feet. Tree-like she froze. Callaghan was so close she could smell him — stale sweat and old aftershave. Madness too, if madness had a scent.

Callaghan put his hands in his pockets as if he didn't expect any fight from her. As if he expected her to roll over and play. It wasn't until he pulled them out that she realised he was emptying his pockets in readiness for what was coming next.

He tossed the things from his pockets onto the table where they clattered against her laptop. Unbuckling his belt, he pulled it through the loops of his trousers, teasing out the drama, enjoying the terror on Anita's face.

"We've been here once before, haven't we? Remember how delicious it was? Such a warm night too, not like here. We should move into the warmer room, you'd like that wouldn't you?"

He made to shoo her towards the drawing room, where the fire spluttered in the hearth, when the shrill sound of a child's voice distracted him.

"What the hell?" he said, turning towards the stairs.

Anita hurtled away from the distracted man. Her body a mess of bruises and sprains but none of them registered in her mind. She only had one thought. To escape.

Callaghan roared after her, knocking past the dining chairs she'd pulled behind her. Anita bashed her shoulder against the flimsy patio doors but they didn't move. Fumbling with the latch she tried again as Callaghan reached her. Ducking under his arms, she raced back through the dining room, momentarily considering the front door, but remembered how heavy it was — she'd needed two hands to swing it open. Changing direction towards the kitchen, had the corridor always been this long?

Throwing open the back door, she surged into the night. With Callaghan's cries assaulting her ears she didn't hear the knocking at the front door or the howling of a dog not so far away. Scrambling through the undergrowth, brambles ripping at her skin, her feet, her hair, terror had her in its talons. Mutely she ran from her aggressor, no spare energy left for screaming. With no jacket, her skin felt encased in ice.

"Ah-ni-taaa," Callaghan called out. His longer stride bringing him closer and closer. Outside, he was as blind as she was. She didn't stop. The blood pumping in her ears laced with adrenaline, fuelling her flight.

Stumbling, pain arced through her foot. Behind her Callaghan was cooing, the way you would settle a crying baby. She carried on, pushing the pain away, but tripped again, on a root? No, a gravestone. She'd run straight into the family graveyard. She slipped through the broken doorway into the darkened mausoleum, inching round the remains of the door. Her toe nudged the pile of gardening tools stacked against the wall. A clatter as the metal heads knocked against themselves. She stopped breathing, waiting for Callaghan to locate the noise and find her. He was crashing around outside, further away though, still calling for her.

As her eyes adjusted to the gloom, she reached for the nearest tool, a hand trowel. Holding it empowered her. She had no idea if the edge was sharp enough to stop him if he found her but the trowel gave her a sense of protection.

A light bloomed outside. Callaghan had found his cellphone and was using it to cast long sweeps through the gardens, calling her the whole time, "Anita, come out, come out, wherever you are…"

She shuffled deeper into the darkness, palms clammy, she wiped them on her jeans. The trowel slipped from her lap onto the tiled floor, the clattering horrendously loud in the small space.

"Ah, I've found you now my little cherub," Callaghan quipped, changing direction towards the mausoleum.

Pressing herself into the wall, Anita prepared to fight. Somewhere, outside, a dog howled.

Callaghan pushed his cellphone through the wrecked door, illuminating rows of marble plinths, the names of dead people recorded for eternity.

"Come now Anita, no more games, it's freezing out here."

Anita watched as puffs of icy breath followed every word, the cold holding her captive against the back wall. Callaghan wavered in the doorway as if stepping foot inside wasn't a prospect he felt comfortable with.

"Don't make me come in there and get you. We both know how that will end. Let's go back to the house now," he said, stomping his feet against the chill.

She pushed herself further into the wall, the hand shovel digging into her leg, the pain inconsequential to the fear enveloping her.

A howling permeated the tiny room. It wasn't so far away now. It was close, very close. Callaghan stepped back, the light from his phone swinging towards the sound, leaving Anita in the dark. His outline moving tentatively away from the safety of the doorway. She struggled with herself, trying to decide what to do. Should she run while he's distracted? Or stay and fight?

Closer now, the howling echoing inside, and Anita strained to see beyond the darkness. More scared of the man than the animal, she prayed that one would take care of the other. Callaghan was waving his phone around like a fiery torch, fending off rabid wolves. She couldn't see what he was looking at. Again she thought about making a run for it and she edged towards the doorway, trowel tight in her hand.

The light went out.

A hand seized her. Callaghan's fingers sinking into her

arm. Anita screamed. Callaghan grabbed the hand holding the trowel as she struggled to bring her arm up, to slash at the monster. He slapped her, an almighty crack across her cheek. Her head flew backwards with the force. Anita tried stabbing him with the trowel but Callaghan wrenched her wrist backwards, threatening to snap it. Screaming she dropped the weapon, naked under the control of the bigger man.

They'd forgotten about the dog. From the blackness of the night it hurled itself at Callaghan, a tangle of fur and claws and teeth. *Protecting her?* Anita scrambled away on hands and knees, the brutal fight between man and beast raging around her. The jumble of man and dog knocked her down again. The snapping of the dogs teeth and the grunting of Callaghan became one sound.

A yelp.

Anita didn't know what had happened to the dog but wasted no time scrambling to her feet. She flew back towards the house. Possessed with an unnatural evil, Callaghan wasn't prepared to let her escape and roared after her. The animal no longer a threat; incapacitated with a hefty blow to the head.

The lit turret guided their way.

CHAPTER 52

Abraham stood unmoving in the window. Bound in starched black mourning cloth, the way a grieving widower should, he looked mummified in the half light. Stopping his daughter was his priority. There was an evil within her, from where it came, he didn't know, but someone had to stop her. He'd been about to follow her when the commotion downstairs distracted him. It hadn't been Ruth this time. It was the others in the house — the young woman and the quiet man.

The woman had released him from his prison, and now the man was, what? Attacking her? Puzzling over the words, nothing made sense. Everything so vague, the outlines fuzzy and words muffled. But he'd discerned the gist of what was happening and he wouldn't allow that in his house.

He whistled. A flash of yellow outside, and the hound, his wife's dog, took off towards its unseen prey. The dog was all that remained of her now. He'd seen the remains of her portrait in the fire and grief overcame him a second time. Upon reflection it was better she'd gone, joining her children in heaven, three of her children. What Ruth had become would've broken her heart. Of the baby who'd joined their family at the end, he gave no thought.

The artist had corrupted them all. If only he'd known earlier. So much heartbreak could have been avoided. So much unnecessary loss and now he needed to stop him before this madness went any further. He didn't understand how it'd happened, or why, but too many lives had been ruined by the flick of the artist's brush or the stroke of his daughter's pencil. Instinctively he knew where Ruth was, she'd be drawing, in the nursery. Stopping Ruth, and protecting the stranger, almost the same thing.

Hand on the stair rail, he started his descent, the cuff of his sleeve peeping from the black cloth, gaping without its cufflink holding it closed. It seemed easier not to bother after his wife died, fiddly things. Grief still had him well within her clutches.

CHAPTER 53

Running in through the patio doors of the drawing room, barging past the glorious furniture, the crackling fire, the leftover lunch, ignoring the unfinished art on the table, her laptop still beaming it's brightly coloured screen saver, she skidded through the foyer, her feet slick with snow and decaying leaves. Flying up the stairs she tripped over the top step, landing on her knees. Another bruise, another pain. Prone on the floor for barely more than a second, she came face to face with Yvonne. With Yvonne's portrait; the pearl adorned portrait Callaghan had left in the hall. Yvonne's papery skin the colour of Egyptian alabaster, she looked more ephemeral on canvas than she'd ever looked in life.

Behind her came the calls of the man in pursuit of prey. One last look at Yvonne and Anita was up, racing into her room. She needed two things, her car keys and cellphone. Yanking open the dressing table drawer, she grabbed her keyring. A ring of odd sized keys, not much to show for her life so far — keys for her car, house, gym locker. She wouldn't have a life if she didn't move now.

Sprinting over to the bedside table, she reached for her

cellphone, for the cellphone she'd left there. Her hand faltered over the emptiness. Callaghan was calling out to her from downstairs, cooing to her like a dove to its mate in the dovecote. She checked under the folds of the cover and the tangled mess of the unmade sheets, and threw herself onto the floor. Rummaging around she found only dust.

Where was it? She knew she'd left it beside her bed; she knew. Creeping to the doorway, she could hear the monster downstairs singing in the foyer. Pressing into the wall, she crept along the hallway. Maybe she'd left her phone in the turret when she tried ringing her mother, it was the only other place it could be.

Inching her way, Yvonne's eyes followed her. Anita tried not to look but it was like watching the looped replay of a car crash on the news, her eyes drawn to the image. How had someone painted Yvonne's portrait so quickly and so well? She sent a silent plea to Yvonne and to Scott to come back from wherever they were although there was a part of her mind which knew they weren't returning. That Callaghan had ensured they were alone.

Reaching the turret door, every inch of her body ached. The stress so unbearable that the concept of giving up appealed to her fragile mind. Facing the prospect of being upstairs with no weapon was the worst idea she'd ever had. If she couldn't get to her car, she needed to call for help and then hide somewhere safe. Safe seemed like a place so very far away.

She splayed the keys from her keyring between her fingers and wiggled her way through the partially open door.

Tiptoeing up the stairs mouselike, she couldn't remember if the stairs creaked, so took every step as deliberately as the moves of a chess master. Heart in her mouth, terrified a creaking stair tread would give her away. Not that Callaghan had any cause to think she could escape from up here. He could wait at the bottom until hunger or thirst dictated she come down. Until she gave in.

Light dripped from an oil lamp hanging from a hook on the doorframe. The heady smell of kerosene and paint so prevalent it burnt the back of her throat. Lamplight wasn't the same as electric light — it wavered and glossed over everything it touched, causing shadows to dance and the windows to ripple like waves. No wonder the Renaissance delivered so many masterpieces. With no electricity casting its ugly countenance, only beauty remained, capturing the glow of an aura, or the highlights in the hair of a muse.

The lamp left shadows clinging to the seats, weird depressions and shapes seemingly born from the fabric. She groped for her cellphone, one ear aimed towards the doorway. The faint scent of a man lingered in the room, Scott's aftershave? Or Callaghan's? She retched. The memory of his stained hands and tomato-filled mouth, the nightmare refusing to end.

Lifting the lamp from the wall, the metal handle cutting into her hand; she lowered the light in one last effort to find her phone. Casting it back and forth, the light spread across the painting on the easel, across the unfinished portrait she'd seen only days ago — the painting of a woman. But now the face was done, the cheeks, the nose, the lift of the brow, the definition around the eyes, and the slope of the neck all beautifully detailed. Even the hair, tiny stroke after tiny stroke laid brown tresses on the canvas, with the flame picking out a subtle hint of red among the brown. A young woman, not so young she'd need identification at the liquor store, but still with youth on her side. Sad eyes. No, not sad, but unfinished, unfinished eyes. If eyes are the window to a man's soul, then what are they to a woman? Callaghan was all but forgotten downstairs.

Pushing the lantern closer, she knew who this was. It was

a portrait of her, almost complete. She knew the instant those eyes were finished, she would be too.

Touching the painting, her fingers came away wet. Someone was here, painting, moments before her. Who?

She touched her own eyes, to assure herself they were still there. Her body threatening to give way.

"Ah-ni-taa," she heard Callaghan calling, his voice so far away yet so close. Too close. She blinked. The portrait still there when she opened her eyes. What would happen if she smudged the paint? She looked at her fingers in horror, the brown paint from her hair drying on her fingertips. Remembering the portrait of Alan, her body shuddered. The lantern light flickered in response, her mirror image dancing on the canvas. Alan had been painted by the same artist who was in this house, now, somewhere. Yvonne too. Yvonne's portrait had been painted and she'd disappeared.

A sob escaped. She wanted to grab the canvas and set it alight. Destroy it before she herself was. But something stopped her.

She daren't turn her back, she didn't trust the light, or the room, or the artist, or her sanity. Lowering the lantern to the floor, she took the canvas in both hands, avoiding the wet paint, amazed at how light a canvas could be with no frame to bolt it to gravity. Looking into her own empty eyes, she felt herself sliding into the picture, imagining the view from within the paint. What would she see looking out at the world from inside the canvas?

A movement outside on the driveway caught her eye — the old man, in all his protective, elderly glory, walking away. Dropping the painting she waved the lantern, like a madwoman signalling him. The dog saw her, looking up towards her, pausing behind his master, before carrying on. She should scream or hammer on the glass, but then

Callaghan would know where she was. Torn between the here and now — between the canvas and the man outside, she chose the man, just as he and his dog disappeared in the dark.

She abandoned the lantern and grabbing her keys, she slipped down the turret stairs. She'd make a run for the door and scream for the farmer once she was outside. It was the only choice left. Then she'd jump in her car, lock herself in and drive to safety.

Callaghan has fallen silent. Was he laying in wait on the other side of the door? She held herself flat against the door, counting her breaths until her heartbeat slowed, listening for anyone doing the same. This a one time only chance. There was no sign of anyone through the gap but that didn't mean it was safe.

A deep breath, and keys in hand she edged out, probing the corridor. At least he couldn't sneak up behind her and the corridor was empty. Yvonne the only face she could see. Her poor friend but she couldn't think of her now, she had to think of herself, only herself.

Her heart breaking for Yvonne, she was oblivious to the man concealed in the doorway of Alan's room. A man reeking of whisky, wood stain and tomato, so gripped by a long nurtured psychosis, that his actions were normal to him. So much part of his day-to-day life, that grabbing Anita and throwing her against the wall until her head cracked on the old wooden wainscoting was no different to dropping a carton of eggs on the supermarket floor.

Anita screamed, twisting like a fish on a lure. Thrashing she stabbed at Callaghan with the keys, again and again, the two of them doing a macabre dance, the portraits on the walls watching their chemistry.

Down they went, the larger man pinning her to the floor. Eyes laughing, he grinned.

"Got you," he said, his grip tightening, fingers pressing into the soft flesh of her arms.

Anita screamed again and he slapped her, leaving red welts across her face. But in that one moment he'd released her arm, and with the keys still in between her fingers she slashed at his face. By some miracle the angle was right, and the keys sliced through his eye like a knife through butter. Callaghan bellowed, bucking away from the pain. Anita jumped up; running down the hall and then downstairs, taking them two and three at a time, every movement jarring her already incoherent thoughts. She made it to the front door.

Nothing had ever looked as formidable as this door; grasping the handle with both hands, Anita twisted and pulled. The heavy door gave way, opening onto the blackest of nights, lit by the coldest of moons.

With Callaghan leaping down the stairs behind her, she ran for her car. It was closer than the farmer who'd disappeared into the blackness. Praying she'd left it unlocked, she reached for the door handle. Caked in ice, her hand stuck to the cold metal. Panicking she pulled away before trying again. Her hand slipped off. The third time gave a satisfying click as the door swung open and she leapt into the icy car, slamming the door. She hit the lock as Callaghan reached her. A face of pure evil, with a bizarre smile stretching across his teeth, leered at her window. He didn't seem affected by the temperature or the snow as he walked around trying all the doors, his mangled eye made even more macabre by the smile on his face.

Anita swivelled around, the leather seat freezing cold beneath her. He couldn't get in, she'd locked the car. She checked her pockets for her keys. *Where the hell where her keys?* She searched again, thrusting her hands deep into her pockets, nothing. She plastered her face against the condensation on the windows, searching the driveway for her distinctive keyring. There was no sign of it amongst the messy snow and the scuffing of footprints. No point checking the glove box or behind the sun visor for a spare key, she wasn't that stupid. The car's only spare key hung on a hook in her mother's kitchen.

Callaghan paced around the car, grinning, darting towards her like a wound up Jack-in-the-box. She jumped back in fright, leading to hysterical laughter from the man outside. Surely the farmer must be able to hear this. She stared down the driveway and thumped uselessly on the horn. The car horn wouldn't work without the key.

She didn't have many choices left. She could unlock the car and make a run for it when Callaghan was on the other side of the car and scream for the farmer. But there was only a slight chance the old man would hear her or that he'd be of any help.

Emptying the glove box she hunted for anything she could use as a weapon. She found a pair of blunt nosed scissors in the first aid kit. Not the most lethal of weapons but they'd do. Anita held them in her fist and turned to check on Callaghan's location. He'd backed away from her car and was examining something in the snow. As she strained to see what he was picking up, her car beeped, and all four door locks popped up. Callaghan turned around smiling, dangling her car keys in front of him, like a pendulum. Anita dived across the car to wrench open the passenger door.

Click

The doors locked again.

As Callaghan slowly approached her, she could hear him whistling. Whistling and smiling.

CHAPTER 54

The artist returned to his easel, choosing a brush as natural as breathing. His fingers fumbled and the slender sable brush tumbled to the floor, the ping of wood against wood echoing in the turret. Bending to retrieve the brush was beyond him.

He massaged his useless paw. Every stroke was more painful than the last. His fingers refused to straighten now, leaving him with birdlike talons. His hands a ghost of their artistic tapered past. The girl forced him to paint but he'd lost the will. Today would be his last day. He missed the light. It was better painting in summer, when the weather was warmer, the sun bolder, filling the room with an abundance of light. Enough light to chase most shadows from the corners; there was never enough to chase them all away.

Stabbing his swollen finger into the puddle of paint on the palette, he raised his hand to the canvas, the shaking more noticeable now. How he missed his youth, if only he could paint that back. Catching his spotted wrist with his other hand, he guided this stranger's hand, pausing, as he struggled to remember what came next. Ruth should be here to tell him, like he'd been able to guide her back in those glorious summers they'd had together. Tutor and student. Master and prodigy.

He struggled with the colour. The hue too dark, it needed to be lightened; it needed a smudge of white. He squeezed the tube of paint and a coil of oily white manifested on the palette, silvery in the lamp light. Swirling it together with the dirty green, he lifted his paint soaked finger to the canvas, but it wasn't fine enough to convey the fear in her eyes. To capture her fear he needed the nimble hand of a child, and the thinnest of brushes.

Fear was the easiest emotion to paint but now fear had taken hold of him. If he couldn't paint, what use was he?

Ruth reappeared at the top of the stairs, a new treasure clasped in her hand — a diamond earring.

"This one... I can't finish. You must finish it for me."

Ruth picked up the paintbrush, checking for permission, before she rolled the bristles in the paint on the palette. The artist hadn't got the colour right for her eyes. She'd seen her, mucking around in her bedroom, silly woman, so remembered what colour her eyes were — a yucky green, not pretty at all. Squeezing out more brown, she mixed it carefully — you had to be careful otherwise everything ended up the colour of mud. The artist taught her well.

Art the one lesson she'd been happy to take. Not like practising her writing and reading, or playing the stupid piano. Those things bored her. Art was different. Mummy had been so happy when she'd told her she wanted to become an artist, so no one cared when she ran off to the playroom to draw, or went down to the pond to sketch. A shame they'd always been too busy to look at her drawings though.

Ruth giggled, imagining how the silly lady felt now. She tried to see out the window but was too short, so climbed up onto the seat to peer into the darkness. The lights of the car kept flashing as the big man pointed at it, some magic she didn't understand. Every time the lights flashed, the lights inside the car turned on and the lady's face lit up like a candle. She was too far away for Ruth to see her eyes properly but those little glances were enough to jolt her memory.

Memories of her sister's eyes slipped through. Tabitha had been mean, so mean, and deserved to disappear. Ruth stomped that memory away. She didn't think about her brothers, or Tabby, or her mother because she didn't need them, she had the artist. The artist didn't seem that old but his fingers did. They were all strange shapes, with knuckles bigger than plums. She wondered if they were squishy. She needed to touch them to check. They'd be good to paint. Chewing on the end of the paint brush she gave it some thought.

Jolted from her daydreams by the sound of a scream outside, she jumped back onto the seat, pushing her face against the glass. The lady had fallen out of the car and was trying to run down the driveway with the man chasing her. This was more exciting than when everyone was searching for her brothers and sister in the pond. She'd told them all they'd been swimming and that she'd wanted to draw so hadn't gone in. She'd been a bit vague about what happened next but no one minded that she didn't exactly know what had happened. Daddy and some of the others dived into the water but it was so murky and deep that they couldn't find Tabby, or Cole, or Saul. *She* knew where they were; they were in her sketch pad. And after they'd gone, she'd had Tabby's doll all to herself, and the *Meccano*, and the playroom, and Mummy and Daddy.

Now she only had her real father.

CHAPTER 55

Tumbling from the car, Anita sprinted away.

A yell behind her as Callaghan realised he'd left the door unlocked a fraction of a second too long.

Scissors in hand, she ran faster than she'd ever sprinted at school, faster than running for the bus when she was late for work, faster even than when the ice cream van turned into her quiet childhood street. Anita ran for her life.

She could hear him jogging behind her, the crunching of his feet against the snowy gravel. Pain shot through her fingers and toes. She dropped the scissors and skidded to a halt, wanting to pick them up. But he was too close, her fingers too sore. She took off again, slower this time, too hard to run, her legs were so sore. Pain came in waves up through her feet. Unbearable pain.

Crying and screaming and sobbing and running, the raw air stung like a thousand bees. She couldn't breathe. Callaghan was so close, she forced herself to go on, one foot in front of the other. Now he was whistling behind her, she chanced a glance backwards; he wasn't even running, just walking. How could she still be so close to the car? She thought she'd run all the way to the road. She couldn't still be in the driveway? The whistling pierced holes in her mind. Her vision narrowed, dark shadows pressing in on her from both sides.

"Help me," she screamed, or thought she'd screamed, but only whimpers fell from her mouth. Her mouth wouldn't form the words and she tried moistening her lips, but the signals from her brain weren't getting through. Like a main street mime she carried on running, in slow motion, as Callaghan's whistles came closer and closer.

Pain squeezed her ribs. Her cheekbones became razor blades. The darkness outside faded to a blacker black than the back of the deepest cupboard. Her legs gave way. Anita tumbled to the ground. And disappeared.

CHAPTER 56

The girl stepped back, smiling, a gap-toothed, full face kind of smile, the smile of childish innocence.

"What do you think?" she asked, the slender brush still in her hand.

The artist smiled at his student. A smile which twitched at the corners of his mouth, but got no further.

"You've captured her well," he said, acknowledging her skill, massaging his hands, barely able to flex his fingers now. Too tired to play these games, it had been going on so long that to stop required more energy than he had.

"Just the man left to finish," she said, hopping from one foot to the other, excitement all over her face.

"You'll need something for the frame," the artist said.

Ruth's face fell. He was right. They needed something of the man's for the frame. She hopped off the stool and took off down the stairs, like a rabbit let loose from a cage.

As she disappeared downstairs, the artist lowered himself onto the stool. Too long he'd been here but now he was too tired, his hands dysfunctional. Picking up a brush, he rolled it between his fingers. It felt clumsy in his hands, as if his fingers weren't even his own, making it difficult to control the brush.

Lifting the brush to the canvas, he sketched a loose outline of a face, smudging the paint on the chin, making it as broad as it had once been. A touch of vanity but all he had left. Pain marred his face with every stroke of the brush.

A dark figure appeared at his shoulder.

"Hello Abraham," the artist said, concentrating on the shape of the ears under his brush. No need to be perfect, he'd disguise any mistakes later when he added the hair.

"We need to talk about Ruth," Abraham said, looking at the face forming under the artist's brush.

"We do," the artist replied, squeezing more paint onto the palette using the stained palette brush to mix it.

"This has to stop," Abraham said.

The artist nodded.

"You have to stop her," Abraham said, his voice sounding hollow to the artist's ears.

The artist took a deep breath, requiring more energy than he'd expected to fill his lungs. He'd been here before, when the decision had been taken from his hands. This time no one would make the decision for him he'd chosen his own path.

Choosing a thicker brush, he shaded the hair, blending it with the edge of his thumb. He stopped, puzzled, looking at his thumb — he'd felt nothing. He rubbed it harder against the canvas, smearing dark paint down over the brow but felt nothing. Forehead furrowing, he turned his hands over, examining his palms. They existed but he felt nothing. Ruth must be in the nursery, they were too late.

Looking up at Abraham, the artist opened his palms. Fingers splayed wide, he looked at Abraham, beseechingly.

"You'll be next," the artist said.

"But you'll be first," Abraham replied, appearing unmoved by the man's plea for help.

"She'll be downstairs, in the nursery, your daughter," the artist said.

"Not my daughter," Abraham replied.

"Ruth was always your daughter. Never mine," the artist said.

Abraham blinked, hands fluttering at his side.

"The baby was mine, the boy, but never Ruth. Oh I wished she were mine. So alike we were, but…"

"You made me think she was yours. You made us all believe," said Abraham.

The artist shrugged. "Only the boy was mine. Only Leo. And he stopped all this when he was old enough, he did what he had to. But Ruth, Ruth will carry on exactly where she left off."

Abraham turned towards the door.

"Ruth can't be stopped, Abraham."

Abraham paused in the doorframe and pulled a star-shaped brooch from his pocket and slipped it into the artist's palm.

"You can stop her, George," Abraham said, before he too disappeared down the stairs.

The artist sat there, weighing up his choices, turning the brooch over in his hands. He remembered when Abraham had given her this piece, even though he must have suspected he wasn't the father of the babe. She'd been happy with the deception, it kept her family life perfect, kept everything the way it should be. It wasn't perfect for him though. It was his babe in her belly, his Leo. Things should have changed.

Helping Ruth tidy away the people obstructing his own

happiness had been easy. He had no love for the other children, so they were first. After the baby came, she'd shown him less affection than the household staff, pretending that nothing had happened, playing at happy families. And that was unforgivable.

Before she vanished, she'd named the baby Leonard, the closest name to Lawrence she'd dared. Maybe that's when Abraham suspected the boy wasn't his? He'd been bereft when she'd disappeared, when they all thought she'd thrown herself off the cliffs, spiralling into depression after losing her children and the birth of the new babe. Painting her portrait had torn his heart in two, but she had wronged him, and needed punishing. He'd intended to restore her to his side but that never happened. Ruth happened. And Ruth always got what she wanted. It was only when Leonard returned as an adult that Ruth was put in her place, up on the wall with the others.

Leonard had done so well with his art lessons, captivating the world with his exquisite portraiture. He'd come back to the house when he'd asked him, like a good son, although he couldn't trust him any more than he could Ruth. But Leonard had been careful, as only an adult can be, and George was proud of his son. And now he would join him.

Let Abraham deal with his daughter.

The artist pinned the star brooch to his chest, over his heart. A heart forever lost to a woman he'd destroyed. He'd had the talent to create beauty and the power to destroy it. Hindsight is a terrible gift when you realise you've destroyed more beauty than you created.

Returning to his first brush, he flew across the canvas finishing the brow, the jaw, the cheeks of the man appearing before him. With one pained hand, he stroked the unshaved planes of his own face, adding a darkening shadow along the jaw line. Until that moment, he'd persuaded himself he'd been painting the man downstairs, or Abraham. Either would have suited him but his time was over. He was done.

His son Leonard's legacy would live on; his art had reached the lofty heights of being collectible, desirable, because of his reclusiveness. Would they be so quick to hang the art in their homes if they realised how wicked Leo had been? How wicked he'd been himself all those years before? He'd stopped signing his own art long ago. *G.L.K.*, the kiss of death.

George Kubin picked a clean brush and dipped it in a delicate eggshell white, which had the hint of a glaze. Dabbing the canvas, he sketched the outline of a star to the man's shirt — eight points, with delicate gems positioned along each arm of the star. Using a thinner brush, he added radiating prisms of light from each of the refracted surfaces — the perfect rendering of a diamond brooch.

Leaving only the old eyes, which had seen people come and people go. Their loss neither disturbed him nor invigorated him, they were art. Like all art, some pieces were more entertaining and memorable than others. Uncertain whether he'd feel anything when he finished, the crippling pain in his hands taking him beyond caring. The portrait in front of him was no masterpiece, a rough likeness, no more or less. This would be his last piece. Let Abraham deal with his daughter. He wanted to be with his son now.

George Laurence Kubin picked up another brush, swirling the sparse bristles in a dollop of black oil paint. Guiding his painting hand with his other, his fingers on the surface of the canvas, he painted in his eyes. The light in his eyes dimming with every stroke until the only sound in the turret was that of an unheld brush falling to the floor. And the artist was gone.

CHAPTER 57

Callaghan slammed shut the car door, locking it once more. She wouldn't be using it again. He ran back towards the house, car keys clutched in his hand. He slowed at the top of the front steps, fear pouring off him. *What the hell?* Someone had left a baby doll at the door. A sick joke. He kicked it away and the doll thumped into the wall of the house.

Callaghan's smug smile was replaced with naked terror. It was a hallucination; he was hallucinating, she can't have disappeared; she must have run into shadow. The stupid girl had taken off down the driveway and was probably crying on the shoulder of that damn farmer.

He needed to pack up his things and get out of here, then he'd deal with Anita, that was a priority. Back inside he faced the portraits Anita had stacked in piles on the floor, now lying in jumbled heaps, all face down. It was better that way. He liked no one watching him do the things he did. It was easier to do things unseen. The dead-eyed portraits watching him made him feel uncomfortable.

His neck prickled and he spun around. *Were the others*

back? No, it was nothing other the groans of an old house settling around him, the clicking of pipes or insects.

Taking the stairs two at a time, it took less than a minute to pack his bag. Leaving his bedroom, he shivered. The frigid breeze followed him upstairs and in the darkened corridor he saw Yvonne's portrait on the floor and skirted it as if it were a somnambulant snake.

Throwing his bag towards the front door, he ducked back into the drawing room to collect his laptop and the rest of his things. Snapping the computer shut, he froze at the unmistakable crunch of footsteps behind him.

Straightening up from the coffee table, he squared his shoulders and turned around.

There was nothing there. No one, nothing.

He turned back and there was Anita, her large eyes wide, plump lips open in an approximation of a grimace. Fear emanated from her in waves. Callaghan's breathing restarted. A painting, not Anita. *Where the hell had that come from?* It was a sick joke, this whole thing. And whoever the joker was would be coming after him next.

Grabbing the portrait of Anita he didn't notice the wetness of the paint, or smell the oil paint. He wanted to pack his car and get the hell out. Someone was picking them off one by one, like a sniper from a rooftop. *Was it the farmer?* Christ, he was lucky he was still alive. That's what he'd tell the police anyway, if he had to. He didn't have a plan other than to get away from here as fast as possible, drive home, and then what? Go back to work like nothing had happened? Hypocritically, he didn't want to think about what the farmer was doing to Anita. Callaghan deliberated about whether there was anything of value inside he could take, which would help make his life a little easier. Preferably something easy to dispose of. If he thought too long about it, he'd be next. *Stuff it*, he thought and sprinted down the front steps, his long legs making quick work of the distance between the house and Anita's car.

Shoving the painting into the back seat of Anita's car, he flung his bag in after it. There was no time to find the keys for the car he'd arrived in, Anita's car would do. He'd leave it outside her place, although now he remembered hearing she'd moved home so wasn't entirely sure where her home was. No worries, he'd leave the car down the road from work and that way it would look like she'd driven back and had gone missing from there. Someone would find it. If anyone asked him about it, he'd say he'd driven his own car there and back. Easy. Plausible. Doable.

A peculiar sense of being watched washed over him and he scanned the empty night. There were no odd sounds or twitching bushes he could see. Still, the unease wrapped itself around him. He'd have one last scout around the house, a quick one, then he'd go. He wouldn't give the farmer the satisfaction of getting him as well and he wouldn't be as easy to overpower as Anita, that was certain.

The dining room had nothing of value other than more stacks of artwork Anita had been working on. Two paintings caught his eye; one a delicately rendered painting, devoid of people, a study of a stool by a fireplace, dark and brooding. The perfect thing for a gentleman's study or office. The other painting was a landscape with a pebbled beach as a backdrop. The upturned hull of a boat dominated the foreground. The landscape brought back fond memories of a childhood spent racing at the local yacht club. Yes, he'd have that one too. He moved them both to the doorway and as he dumped them on the floor, he spied a gold cufflink. Somehow the cufflink had become caught in the gilt fretwork of the frame with the name *Abraham* scrawled on the reverse. He slid it into his pocket and a fleeting smile dashed across his face.

Through to the drawing room, his eyes lingered on the

netsukes he'd admired only the day before. He patted his pocket before realising the broken jade head was no longer there. What had he done with it? It didn't matter; it was worthless anyway, nothing more than a trinket. Selecting two more at random, he shoved them deep into his pocket.

To the kitchen now, Yvonne had been cataloguing jewellery there. Although he couldn't remember her finding anything valuable, it never hurt to have a few small pieces of gold tucked away for a rainy day. Gold was such a portable commodity, no one ever questioned the provenance of an old wedding band or an odd cufflink, the usual detritus of a house move or the death of a relative. It wasn't as if he was hocking off one carat diamond rings regularly.

Scooping up a handful of jewellery, he let the pieces slide through his fingers until he snagged a gate link bracelet with a broken security chain and a gold tie clip. They joined the *netsukes* in his pocket. A last look in the study and then upstairs to double check Anita wasn't hiding in her room or in any of the others.

There was nothing of any obvious value in the study and he had no desire to spend the time it would take sorting through hordes of books on the off chance any of them were valuable. He had to get out of this place before the farmer found him.

Striding upstairs, he barged into Anita's room. It was as he'd left it; the half-charred portrait hanging out of the fireplace, clothes strewn around the floor. Realisation dawned that there was a flaw in his plan so he shovelled Anita's things into her bag. Damn he was lucky he'd come upstairs. Checking the open wardrobe he batted at the clothes, pawing them to check if Anita had hung anything up. The ancient dust swirled around him, castigating him for disturbing the history hanging on its rails. A violent sneeze wrenched his neck and a shot of pain flew up one side.

Bending to stretch out the pain, he caught sight of something at the back of cupboard. He pulled out a velvet drawstring bag, with enough heft to it to excite him. Hidden treasure. Without checking its contents he added it to his pocket, which now bulged cartoon-like at the front of his pants.

He hurried to check the drawers of the dressing table, the pain in his neck indescribable. The clothes all looked like clothes anyone could own. He had no clue if they belonged to Anita or not. Slamming the drawer shut, he decided it didn't matter. He'd packed everything which looked modern so now it looked like someone had rifled through it on a baggage carousel, but he could close the zip and that's all that mattered.

The other rooms contained nothing of value. Callaghan had only half looked, more focused on listening for... the others, the farmer. He didn't want to be surprised. He knew the value of surprise; that sense of titillation when someone didn't know you were behind them, watching them. That moment he'd watched Anita sleeping had been exquisite. The waking of her, even more so.

He flinched. What was that? The rustle of paper? Creeping to the edge of the stairs, the front door stood wide, opening to a dark beyond. The patio doors were still open, causing the cold to flood every room. Between them the open doors created a torrential draught. His fingers tingled. The cold. The wind must be playing with some papers somewhere in the house. He persuaded himself to ignore the sound. He'd check upstairs, giving him to chance to see if there was any sign of life on the long driveway and then he'd go. Unbidden, his body shuddered again.

The turret door lay open, sagging on its hinges, moving fractionally in the unseen breeze. Callaghan was no more afraid of going upstairs than he was of his own shadow, yet he still felt as though someone were watching him. That bloody portrait which looked like Yvonne. His mind had persuaded him it was a painting of her. Funny thing the mind, it had the power to delude you regardless of the evidence. He'd dispose of it as soon as he'd checked upstairs. No one would miss one shoddy painting. The painting of Anita though, that he'd keep.

The lantern cast its glow about the room, blinding him as he made it upstairs, rendering outside an impenetrable wall of black. The light illuminated another painting on the easel, the painting of a man he didn't recognise. Callaghan lifted the lantern off its hook to take a closer look and the light reflected off the paint. The shiny, wet, fresh paint.

Pinned to the chest of the man in the portrait was a diamond brooch, its facets gleaming in the light. The brooch Yvonne had obsessed over before she'd disappeared, before he'd found the painting which looked like her. And the painting of Scott. And Anita.

CHAPTER 58

Callaghan dropped the lantern and ran down the turret stairs, grabbing Anita's bag and the portrait of Yvonne as he went. On wings he didn't have he flew down the stairs, tripping over the bottom step. The bag, the painting, and Callaghan, crashed to the ground. Yvonne's portrait disintegrated — the suitcase pulverising the stretched canvas. Unseen, a silver ring rolled away from the frame and across the floor, spinning to a stop amongst the other damaged portraits. Yvonne's silver ring. There could be no salvation for Yvonne now.

Crying out as he landed, he glanced at the ruined portrait before pulling Anita's bag free from the canvas. His tumble making the strain in his neck ache even more but he didn't have time to worry about that now. He wished that the effects of the alcohol hadn't worn off so quickly. He could have done with being far less conscious of what was happening. He'd have a drink at home.

Grabbing the two paintings he'd left in the doorway, he limped to the front door.

"You're next."

He spun round but there was no one there. He frowned. He'd heard someone, he was sure. He struggled with the pain inching its way up into his temples. A flicker at the top of the stairs distracted him, the orange flicker of a flame leaking down the hallway. The wood panelling the perfect fuel for a hungry fire. It had been the sound of the flames he'd heard.

It was tempting to hurl Anita's bag into the fire, then they'd presume she'd died in the blaze. The perfect ending to a tragic tale. That story would be no good if she turned up, although he thought that unlikely. People might think him a monster but he'd never murdered anyone. That he'd thought about it was of no consequence. He wasn't going to be here when the farmer returned and a fire was just the sort of thing to bring him out from wherever his hellhole of a home was.

He struggled down the steps, into the night, as the fire leapt down the stairs and danced through the dining room into the drawing room, where the twisted faces of the *netsukes* darkened and cracked under the embrace of the flames.

En masse the ravens took to the sky, their screams reminiscent of a child screaming. Moths flocked towards the flames and Callaghan swatted them away as he limped to Anita's car, their velveteen bodies scorched by the heat they were so attracted to.

The birds were nowhere near him but their screams were killing him as they swooped on the moths. The pains in his joints crushing him.

He threw the paintings into the passenger seat and climbed in behind them. All care of the delicate gilded frames gone now. The screaming of the ravens so loud and so close. He thought he was dying, his neck pain joined by new aches in his arms and legs. He struggled to get the key into the ignition. After two attempts, a burst of music from the radio joined the screams of the ravens. He turned the key and the engine spluttered once and died. He tried again. On his third attempt, the engine took, the rumbling sound still not drowning out the cries of the filthy birds.

He slammed his door shut, cranking up the heat. Everything seemed harder to do, working the clutch and accelerator taking momentous concentration.

The house behind him curtained in flickering orange silk as the flames devoured the old wood. He didn't see the little girl standing in the doorway, a piece of drawing charcoal in her hand, as she feverishly tried to finish her portrait, her incandescent screams of rage at his escape joining those of the ravens.

He didn't see Abraham bending to pick up the broken doll. Examining it and realisation of what Ruth had done dawning on his face before he cradled it in his arms as if it were real. As if it were one of his own lost children.

Callaghan could barely focus on the driveway as he manoeuvred his way down the narrow gravel drive disguised by snow and night. Even with his headlights on high, his vision narrowed as though he were looking through a pinhole camera. Unaware as he drove away from the house with her empty frame in his car, that he was pulling Ruth with him; away from the only home she'd ever known and severing the power she possessed.

Callaghan didn't look back at the conflagration behind him. He was oblivious to the flames licking at the art paper and charcoal pencil Ruth held — the unfinished portrait of Callaghan turning to ash in her tiny hands. He didn't see the jade dog's head tumbling from her pocket and shattering in the heat.

But he felt the incredible release of pain, as if he'd been injected with morphine. As the pain disappeared, his vision returned and he pressed harder on the accelerator, all caution gone. He was going home.

Abraham stood next to Ruth. The memories of loss dredged up by the damaged doll, now lost to the flames.

"Daddy," Ruth cried, hands smeared with charcoal, eyes huge in her terrified face. The acceleration of Callaghan's car pulling her from her home. Pulling her away from the life she had created for herself and away from the lives she had destroyed for others.

Abraham abandoned the china-faced doll to the hungry fire and took his daughter into his arms. Forgiveness a release.

As Ruth crumpled into her father's embrace, they vanished. Obliterated by the monster in the car.

The End…

Leo Kubin isn't the only unusual character written by Kirsten McKenzie. May we introduce you to Doctor Perry, a man who prefers his patients elderly and alone. He inhabits the pages of the medical thriller, *Doctor Perry…*
[Click here to read Doctor Perry]

THE FORGER AND THE THIEF

Five strangers entangled in the forger's wicked web, each with a dangerous secret, and an apocalyptic flood threatening to reveal everything.

A **wife** on the run, a **student** searching for stolen art, a **cleaner** who has lined more than his pockets, a **policeman** whose career is almost over, and a **guest** who should never have received a wedding invite.

In a race against time, and desperate to save themselves and all they hold dear, will their secrets prove more treacherous than the ominous floodwaters swallowing the historic city of Florence?

Dive into a world of lies and deceit, where nothing is as it seems on the surface…

Read The Forger and the Thief now

REVIEW

Dear Reader,

If you enjoyed *Painted*, I would love it if you could please post a review on your favourite digital platform? You may also enjoy reading more about Leo Kubin's early years, in *The Forger and the Thief...*

Thank you
Kirsten McKenzie x

BOOK CLUB DISCUSSION QUESTIONS

1. What was your favourite part of *Painted*?
2. Did you race to the end, or was it more of a slow burn?
3. What are you like as an artist?
4. Would you want to read another book by this author?
5. What surprised you most about *Painted*?
6. How did your opinion of the book change as you read it?
7. What would you ask the author about the story?
8. Are there lingering questions from the book that you're still thinking about?
9. Which characters did you like best? Who did you like least? And why?
10. If you had to trade places with one character, who would it be and why?
11. What do you think happens after the official ending?
12. How did the setting impact the story?

ACKNOWLEDGMENTS

You wouldn't be reading this book if it weren't for the support I received from the incredible people in my life.

Firstly, thank you to Fletcher, Sasha and Jetta - my family; for allowing me to travel on this bookish journey. Your support means everything.

To Emma Oakey, my editor, my friend. Thank you from the bottom of my heart. I wish we still lived in the same country.

Andrene Low, an exceptional author in her own right, answered all my queries and questions at the drop of a hat, or at the many, many, pings of the Facebook messenger app.

Linda Surles. Everyone needs an American eye, and Linda gave me two of hers!

Many grateful thanks also to Vicky Adin for her continuity prowess, and to Kate Sluka for her enviable proofreading skills. Thanks also to Jillian McKenzie for advising me on the art side of things. And thank you to Geraldine Brettell for slapping away the comma's, among the many other extraneous words.

If I've confused anyone with my Antipodean terminology, or spelling, or random words, it is entirely my fault. Linda, Emma, Andrene, Vicky, Jillian, Geraldine and Kate did their best with what they had to work with.

Thank you to Bárbara Borba for doing the wonderful Portuguese translation of Painted. Or as it is known in Portugal - *Retratados*.

I still think my best typo was writing cellophane instead of cellphone. We should all spend more time creating with cellophane instead of playing on our cellphones xxx

ABOUT THE AUTHOR

Kirsten McKenzie fought international crime for fourteen years as a Customs Officer in both England and New Zealand, before leaving to work in the family antique store. Now a full time author, she lives in New Zealand with her family and alternates between writing time travel trilogies and polishing her next thriller. Her spare time is spent organising author events and appearing on literary panels at various festivals around the world.

Her historical time travel trilogy, *The Old Curiosity Shop* series, has been described as *"Time Travellers Wife meets Far Pavilions"* and *"Antiques Roadshow gone viral"*. Audio books for the series are available through Audible.

Kirsten has also written the bestselling gothic thriller *Painted*, and the medical thriller, *Doctor Perry*. Her last thriller, *The Forger and the Thief*, is a historical thriller set in 1966 Florence, Italy, with some ghostly links to *Painted...*

She is working on her second time travel trilogy, which begins with *Ithaca Bound*, and features many of your favourite characters from the *Old Curiosity Shop* series.

Kirsten lives in New Zealand with her husband, her daughters, and one rescue cat. She can usually be found procrastinating online.

You can sign up for her newsletter at:
www.kirstenmckenzie.com/newsletter/

Printed in Great Britain
by Amazon